REDEMPTION

MEGHAN

NEW YORK TIMES BESTSELLING AUTHOR

MARCH

Visit my fabulous website at www.meghanmarch.com
Cover Designer: Murphy Rae, www.murphyrae.com
Editor: Jovana Shirley, Unforeseen Editing,
www.unforeseenediting.com

ISBN-13: 978-1-943796-64-9

REDEMPTION

A MOUNT SAGA NOVEL

THE ANTI-HEROES COLLECTION
BOOK NINE

MEGHAN MARCH

MEGHAN MARCH

CONTENTS

ABOUT REDEMPTION

My daughter was kidnapped.
My sanctuary violated.
My best friend murdered.
My empire is crumbling before my very eyes.
There's no retirement plan for the boogeyman.
I never cared about that before.
Now that I have a family, everything is different.
I can never put my daughter at risk again.
I don't want this life for her.
But I can't undo the things that I've done.
I can't bring back the lives I've taken.
Everyone knows Lachlan Mount doesn't deserve a second chance.
But maybe—just maybe—a man like me can still find redemption.

For my beloved readers. Thank you for helping to make my dreams come true. I love you all.

CHAPTER ONE

MOUNT

Six feet. Three feet. Almost there. Doorknob.

I yank it open, and the familiar scents of leather, tobacco, and musty books fill my nostrils as I cross the threshold of the library and close the door as carefully and silently behind me as I can with these shaking hands.

I drop to my knees, the rug cushioning the weight of my body as I collapse onto my forearms, forehead resting on my clenched fists.

What have I done? What have I done?

Agony tears through me, immobilizing me until the tremors begin.

God, what have I done?

Tears I gave no permission to shed course down my face as the image of Keira wrapping our precious daughter in her arms, pressing kisses to her face, flashes through my mind. Anguish follows, blotting out the picture.

What have I done?

What have I become?

What will become of them?

I've ruined everything. The purity of my daughter. Her unblemished soul. The sanctity of her innocence. She was never supposed to know violence or danger. She was never supposed to know anything but love and safety.

I failed her.

I failed both of them.

A tortured sound rips through the room—the sound of a dying animal howling in pain. Locked in the prison I created myself, it takes me a moment to realize the torment came from my own open lips.

I can't hold the agony in. I can't hold any of it in anymore. I just can't ...

I press my lips to the carpet as a broken roar wrenches from the depths of my soul.

Helplessness. Fear. Terror. Gut-wrenching horror unlike anything I've ever felt. All the blood. V's body. I'd almost lost my baby girl forever.

The suppressed emotions pour out of me, along with torrents of salty tears as my legendary control shatters. My joints give way as my muscles go weak, and I sag onto the wool.

Inhuman noises vibrate through the floor, surrounding me in the suffocating haze of my own misery.

I did this. No one else. There's no one to blame.

I did this. Me. If I wasn't who I am, none of this would have ever happened.

But it did.

Because I am who I am.

Cracks in my once-impenetrable armor become rents and tears, until I fear I won't survive the emotional onslaught shredding what's left of my sanity with razor-sharp claws.

"*God, help me*," I whisper, uncertain I'll survive to draw in my next breath. "*What have I done? What have I done?*"

My fists clench, and my nails dig into my palms. I lean into the cutting pain. It's the only thing I understand right now. It's the only thing that makes sense and keeps me anchored to this moment.

The weight of my sins and the empire of darkness I've built crashes down upon me as my muffled sobs escape. The helplessness of my baby girl in that psychopath's hands slashes at my soul.

I almost lost her. I almost killed her. It wasn't him. It was me.

This is all because of me. I did this. All of this.

The magnitude of the nightmare I've created seeps into every fiber of my being. The bullet in his brain didn't fix anything. Nothing can fix this.

Nothing.

I did this. I brought death and darkness to the ones I love the most. The ones I would die to protect.

But I didn't protect them. Not even the purest innocence I've ever seen—conceived from my own essence.

I failed her. I failed all of them.

The Devil incarnate didn't come for me. He came for my soul. He came for my heart. And he ripped it out of my chest and showed me just how powerless I truly was.

All the bullets, all the blood, all the leverage, all the money, all the men—none of it could protect my daughter from being kidnapped or save the life of my best friend.

Tears of grief soak the rug for V. He died a hero.

It should have been me.

"And then I had to send my wife in to get her," I whisper into the carpet as disgust and helpless rage mix with the tears, becoming an amalgam of my failure, suffering, and horror.

What kind of man am I? Not worth the name or the breath it takes to speak the word.

God should strike me dead, but the pain keeps coming. *He won't let me escape so easily.* I wouldn't either. I deserve this. I created this. This is my nightmare. My living hell. My monster.

It can't be escaped—only slayed.

I failed.

I failed everyone.

My fingers dig into the pile of the rug, gripping the strands like they might hold me together as everything I am—everything I once believed—slips away like a ghost from my grip.

My strength. My confidence. My certainty.

My very identity.

And there I lie, prostrate with grief and the knowledge that Lachlan Mount must die.

CHAPTER TWO

KEIRA

"Lachlan? I thought you were in the library?" I stride into the courtyard with Aurora snuggled in my arms. I still haven't been able to put her down. I keep breathing in her scent like it's the most precious perfume in the universe. And it is.

My baby.

Our scare rocked me to my core. The horror of seeing the blood and V's body ...

An involuntary shudder ripples through me.

The weight of the world feels like a crushing mink stole around my shoulders. I have no idea what we're going to do next or what this means for our future. But Lachlan will have a plan. He *always* has a plan.

But he doesn't answer or turn to face me.

"Lachlan? Are you ..." I stop myself before asking if he's okay. I *know* he's not okay. None of us are okay—except the sweet-smelling princess asleep in my arms.

I pause a few feet away and reach for his broad, suit-covered shoulder with my free hand. Before my fingertips make contact, he spins around. I freeze as I take in his face.

"Who the hell are you?" The words come out like a hiss as I stumble backward. "You're not Lachlan. Who the hell are you?"

He extends a hand to steady me before I fall, but I find my balance and dart around the table, putting a solid hunk of metal between me, my daughter, and …

"Who are you?" My voice roughens and hardens.

He looks like Lachlan. The dark hair. The face. The height. The build. The suit. *Everything.*

"You're not my husband." My breathing turns shallow, and I can't control the short, sharp breaths that compete with my hammering heart.

Instantly sensing the change, Aurora stirs. Meanwhile, I'm still frozen, staring at his face. A face I know better than any other face on the planet. A face I've studied. A face I've fallen in love with despite all my best intentions.

He stares back at us, as if mesmerized. His gaze rivets on Aurora's dark hair before his nearly black eyes lock on mine.

"She's beautiful, Keira."

"Who the hell are you?" My tone is sharpened by fear, anger, and confusion as I back toward the door, needing to put as much distance between this stranger and us as I possibly can. My body feels like it's going haywire. All my senses feel like they're betraying me.

I know what I see—a man who looks *exactly* like my husband—*but it's not him.*

Aurora lifts her head, turning toward the man who's not her father.

Any move he intended to make is arrested completely

when he sees Aurora's face. The change that comes over his countenance makes him look less like Lachlan—softer, gentler, and more wistful.

"She looks just like a portrait of my father when he was a child. It hangs in the gallery of our family's estate."

"*Who are you?* Answer me, or I'm going to scream this entire house down, and you'll never get to say a word before they kill you."

It's the only reason I haven't screamed yet. Something tells me I'll never get answers if they kill him where he stands. And I have to know.

Who is this man standing in my house, who looks like my husband but isn't? Who is he talking about? His father? What family estate? What in the hell is happening? Am I going crazy?

That makes as much sense as anything right now.

"I'm losing my mind. This isn't happening," I whisper to myself as I back farther away, ready to run and hide rather than face whatever life is throwing at me next.

I'm not ready. It's too much.

"It's okay, Keira. I won't hurt you or Aurora or Lachlan. I'm not here for that. I'm here to help. Please, be at ease. I know this is a shock. I know it doesn't make sense."

"You stole his face!" My hushed yell upsets Aurora, and a small cry escapes her lips. I wrap my hand around her head, pressing it against my neck, whispering soothing sounds. "It's okay, baby. You're okay. Everything's okay. Mommy's fine. It's okay."

But my trembling hand belies my words. *It's not okay. I'm not okay. Nothing is okay.* The life I thought I knew and understood started crumbling days ago, and now, it's accelerating.

"I didn't steal his face," the man replies with a calm, reassuring tone that's completely lost on me. "He shares mine. I'm your brother-in-law. Aurora is my niece. Her grandmother insisted I come as soon as we learned what happened. You're all in grave danger. We need to get you out of here."

I shake my head, bouncing Aurora as she quiets down. I can't process what he's saying. It doesn't make sense.

A brother? A mother? What the hell?

Impossible.

Words spill from my lips without me even realizing I'm speaking. "You're lying. I don't believe you. Lachlan doesn't have a brother. He's—"

"An orphan who doesn't know his family exists, but that doesn't make us any less real."

My first instinct is to scream down the house, just like I threatened to do moments ago, but I can't force myself to do it.

Instead, I bite out, "Prove it. Prove it, or they'll kill you. They won't think twice. Not this week."

He nods slowly, as though he understands that I'm a woman on the edge and about to lose control. "I'm going to reach inside my breast pocket and pull out a piece of paper. It's a copy of a DNA match between your husband's results and my own. We truly are identical twins."

"What?" The word rips from my lungs with shock as he pulls the paper free and holds it out. I make no move to take it from him. "No. That's not possible."

I shake my head as he continues, "My mother and brother were kidnapped when he and I were both four months old. My mother was ransomed back to my father. He believed he was getting both of them. When she came back alone, without my brother, it destroyed our family. Please, Keira. I have no reason to lie to you. Look at my face. You can see the truth with your own eyes."

"Plastic surgery could do that too. I don't believe you. And no piece of paper is going to make me believe it either." Even as I say the words, I know I'm lying to myself.

"Look at me, Keira." He points at his face. "Plastic surgery can't do this."

"A clone then. Some high-tech trick to bring us down."

He smiles, and it takes my breath away. It's the same smile I've seen countless times before on my husband's face.

"Really? I mean, I believe they can clone people, but I promise I'm not one. My father and mother had identical twins. It's well documented, as is the kidnapping. I can show you the newspaper clippings. I can take you to my mother and father. They'll tell you the truth."

My knees lose their strength, and I tip backward to rest against the brick wall of the courtyard.

"This is not happening right now. This isn't real. I'm dreaming." I shake my head back and forth, as though to clear the overwhelm from my mind but I can't.

"Ma'am, are you okay?" Sal, one of the housekeeping staff, steps into the courtyard. As soon as she sees the man twenty feet away from me, she instantly apologizes. "I'm so sorry to interrupt. I didn't mean to bother you. Sir"—she nods to the man who isn't my husband—"please forgive me."

I reach out and grab Sal's arm. "Go to the library and knock on the door. Get Mount. Now. Right now."

Sal's head jerks from me to the man in the courtyard. "But—"

"Go do it—right now. And tell him he'd better be strapped."

"Ma'am?" The single word is drenched in confusion.

"Now." My implacable tone leaves no room for further questioning, and she scurries away.

"Are you going to let him shoot me?" he asks from across the cobblestone expanse separating us.

I bite down on my lip, body still shaking with every breath. "I don't know yet."

He smiles again, his perfectly even white teeth flashing. "This must be where they get the saying, *No good deed goes unpunished.*"

"I don't know who you are, but you came here for a reason, and clearly, that reason involves my husband, so you're going to get Lachlan Mount in his full glory, whether you wanted to or not."

The stranger's smile morphs into a grin. "The family reunion is going to be exciting then, isn't it?"

CHAPTER THREE

MOUNT

"Go away!" The pounding on the door of the library doesn't stop. I bury my face into the carpet. "Go away!" I roar.

"Sir, Mrs. Mount needs you right now in the courtyard. Your twin is there. She says you'd better be strapped. You need to come now!"

Instantly, the self-pity and self-destruction I was intent upon evaporate like raindrops on a hot New Orleans sidewalk.

"What the fuck did you say?" I'm on my feet, gun in hand, racing toward the door before I can even think about moving. Muscle memory controls my every move as I rip open the door and plow by the petite housekeeper.

"He looks like your twin, sir!" she calls from behind me as I break into a run down the hallway.

My toes dig into the carpet as I sprint toward the courtyard, cold metal in hand, ready to kill anyone who threatens my wife or child.

Never. Again.

I burst through the open double doors and skid to a halt.

"What the hell is this?"

"I'm right here." Keira's voice comes from behind me, but my gaze is locked on what could be my mirror image.

My arm shoots out to the side as I instinctively put my body between my wife and a man who shouldn't be in my inner sanctum.

"Who the fuck are you?" The question comes out like a rumble of thunder. "Where the fuck did you come from, and why are you here?"

Keira's smooth fingers grip the hand I have out to my side, and I register her body heat moving behind me.

"We're okay. But I don't know what's happening right now, and I don't know what to do."

Without looking behind me, I tell her, "Get Rory out of here. Go to the safe room, lock yourself in, and don't come out until I come for you."

"But—"

"Go!"

"He says he's your brother. Your twin. He says you and your mother were kidnapped, and she was ransomed back and not you. He says Rory looks like the picture of your father in their family estate. Who is he, Lachlan? *Who is he?*"

I stare at the man three strides away from me as her words float in my mind, attempting to process what she said.

"Keira doesn't have to leave. She doesn't need protection from me, and neither does Aurora. I'm not a threat. I'm only here to help you. We want to offer you protection. Your daughter is the only heir to our family's empire. Her safety and heritage are the reasons I'm here. Her grandparents want to make sure she's never at risk again."

More words to process, but my mind jumps on them immediately. Living on the streets as a kid teaches you a lot of things, and one of those things is to determine truth from lies very quickly. It's the only thing that's kept me alive all these years.

My body tells me instantly he's not lying. Some or all of what he's saying is the truth.

Holy fuck. Did not see this coming.

"Who *exactly* are you?" I ask without moving.

"Marco Giordano, the grandson of Comte Alessandro Marconi Giordano. The son of Alessandro Giordano and Francesca Comesetti Giordano. I'm your brother. Older than you by seventeen minutes. We're identical twins."

His words and the details that Keira gave filter together in my mind.

It's preposterous. Ridiculous. Utterly inconceivable. And yet … something indisputable within me says it's all true.

"You're the grandson of a Comte—at least, before the abolition of Italian nobility. Your daughter is the heir to our family fortune that is perhaps vaster than your own. Your empire is collapsing, brother. We're here to offer you a way out. Mother and I very much want all of you to be safe."

"My mother left me in filth on the steps of a church in the French Quarter."

The dark hair and face that make me feel like I'm looking at my own reflection shake, as if to say I'm wrong.

"No, brother. Our mother would never have left you.

You were taken from her, and she has not yet forgiven herself for it. She awaits you on the tarmac. All of you. I did not know what kind of reception I would receive, and I could not risk our mother's safety by allowing her to come here, as I'm sure you understand. If you wish to meet her, you can do so today. She has waited a very long time to see you again. It is her very greatest wish to see you and meet your family. She is the reason I'm here right now, at this very moment. If I had not come, she would have stormed your castle herself."

Staring at the man who claims to be my brother, I finally lower the gun. "How did you know where to find us?"

I don't bother to ask how he got inside, because anyone in this house would assume he was me. He's my doppelgänger. Identical twins indeed.

"For over forty years, our mother refused to believe you were dead. For years, I've been monitoring every DNA bank, newspaper, internet source, and more avenues than you can even imagine. When your DNA hit as a match to mine, I started looking for you in earnest."

He holds out a piece of paper. "But James Jones of PO Box 9979, Tuscaloosa, Alabama, was a dead end."

I hear Keira's sharp intake of breath. She and I both remember the moment she told me what she'd done—on that trip to Greece and Sicily in search of my lost heritage.

"Then, how? How did you find us?"

"Someone tried to kill me a week ago. Before he fell to his death, he called me by the name Lachlan Mount. I had never heard this name before, but it was the lead I had been waiting for all my life. To find my brother. To repair my mother's broken heart and relieve her of her guilt for what she could not prevent." He smiles, and it's like seeing another side of myself I didn't know existed. "You might have been a difficult man to find, brother, but it's not that difficult anymore. The newspapers are talking about you now. You are no longer safe in New Orleans. The man who tried to kill me was intent on killing you."

"I've never been safe." The truth comes easily from my lips.

He nods, as if apologetic. "But now, the safety of your wife and daughter is at risk. You would not be much of a man or a brother I would like to claim if you didn't care about that now."

Keira's fingers curl into my suit jacket. "You don't believe him, do you, Lachlan? He could be anyone—"

I reach behind me to wrap my arm around her and bring her body and Aurora's into mine. "He's not lying. And if he wanted to hurt me, he would've killed you both the second he saw you. I know the truth when I hear it. I've always known there were people out there who knew who I really was. I just never thought I'd meet one of them."

"Lachlan, you can't take him at face value. You—"

"I'm staring at myself, and my body knows the truth— I can feel it."

"But surgery—or a clone—"

For the first time since I entered the courtyard, I take my eyes off the man in front of me and look down at my wife. "He's not lying. He'd already be dead if he were."

I meet my brother's gaze once more. "I want to meet my mother."

CHAPTER FOUR

KEIRA

I stand, dumbfounded, next to my husband as he stares at the man who, in mere moments, has changed our lives irrevocably. Too many irrevocable changes in such a short time have my world spinning on its axis. I cling to my daughter like she's my anchor and lifeline to sanity. She's the only thing that makes sense right now, because nothing else does.

My husband believes this stranger of a man—who could be anyone—is his brother.

"How am I the only one acting like a Mount here?" The words escape my lips, and Lachlan and *whoever that man is* break their stare and look at me.

A smile curls the lips of the man who looks like my husband but isn't. I want to call him an imposter, but he's not even pretending to be that.

"I know this is hard to believe, but it's the truth." He looks from me to Lachlan. "You can meet her right now. I'll take you to her."

"No, Lachlan—"

My husband's arm tightens around me. "Keira, it's okay. I'm not leaving with him."

This time, it's my gaze bouncing between the two identical faces. "Okay ... then ..." I can't finish a single sentence. My brain is overwhelmed from everything I'm attempting to process.

"You're not?" The stranger replies with a furrowed brow.

I know he said his name, but I honestly can't remember what it was. *Marco?* Not important right now. Right now, the only thing that matters is figuring out *what the hell is going on here*.

"No. As you can see, I have things to attend to at present, but I will meet you both. Which airport tarmac?"

"Lakefront Airport. Hangar six."

The conversation happening between Lachlan and his doppelgänger seems like it's taking place in a completely different reality. One that I can't even believe is real.

This isn't happening. This is my mind breaking after everything we've been through. I'm losing it. This is how it starts. I'm going crazy.

"Thank you for coming," Lachlan says to him with a nod, like he could be speaking to any guest in our home, not an identical twin, who appeared out of thin air. "As you clearly made your way into our home without issue, I'm assuming you can show yourself out just as effectively."

A squeak escapes my lips. "You're not just going to let him ..."

The other man chuckles as my words trail off. "I had no idea what to expect, but I like you already, brother.

Thank you for hearing me out. I look forward to spending more time together."

He looks at me, and I can't get over the similarities between them. The hair. The eyes. *Everything.*

"My apologies for the shock, madam. I know this can't be easy. I swear we have no ill intentions toward you or your family. We are simply a brother and a mother who have waited decades for this moment. We come in peace, truly offering you sanctuary, protection, and the love of a family you never knew existed."

Lachlan's hand flexes involuntarily in mine, as though he's shocked by the man's words. That's at least something that makes sense—*finally.* My husband has never had that in his life. The love of a family is one thing he's never known beyond me and Aurora.

My heart stutters in my chest as a deep well of emotion I can't pinpoint with a name grips me. For the first time since I walked into the courtyard, I let myself think about the insane possibility that this man might be telling the truth.

What if Lachlan really does have a family? What if this really is his brother? What if his mother really is waiting on a plane to meet him?

Tears gather at the corners of my eyes. My emotions are all too chaotic and close to the surface after the week we've had. I truly don't know how much more I can take.

In that moment, I make a vow: *I will kill this man myself if he's lying and hurts my husband.* No one *gets to play with Lachlan Mount this way and cause him pain.* No one.

The intensity of the protectiveness coursing through my veins should shock me, but it doesn't. I'm Keira Mount now, and I am a force with which you do not fuck—especially when it comes to my husband and child. There's *nothing* I won't do to protect them from harm. *Nothing.*

This last week has forged me into a different kind of woman. I'm beyond a mama bear. I'm a Mount through and through. I will do whatever I have to do to protect my family.

The man nods and outstretches his hand to offer it to Lachlan. "We will wait for you. As long as it takes. There's no way our mother will let that jet take off until she meets you."

Lachlan pauses before reaching out to shake his twin's hand, as if he's not sure he's ready for physical contact. As if in slow motion, he extends his hand, closing the distance between their skin. I stare at their hands, freezing when I realize they look nearly identical too. Both have long, straight, tanned fingers and neatly clipped nails. Lachlan's heavy diamond pinkie ring is at odds with the understated gold signet ring on the finger of his doppelgänger.

My breath catches when their skin touches and their hands clasp. It's like time stops. The only one of the four of us breathing normally is Aurora as she snuggles against me.

The other man lets out a rough sound as his face lowers. "You have no idea how long I've waited to find you, brother." When he lifts his eyes, they're glassy with unshed tears. "This is truly a miracle." He sucks in a ragged breath, as if steadying himself through an onslaught of emotion. "We will await you at the hangar. Thank you. *Thank you, God.*" The last part he whispers, and his Adam's apple bobs as he swallows.

Lachlan nods, holding himself, as he always does—with pride, dignity, and undisguised power. "Until then."

Their fingers disengage, and we both watch as the man turns and walks out of our courtyard, looking exactly like my husband from behind. The same height. The same build. The same hair. *It's uncanny.* I stand, dumbfounded, as he disappears into our home, walking out of our sight—and out of our lives, which will never be the same.

Neither Lachlan nor I say anything for long moments. We both stare at the doorway the man exited.

Aurora shifts in my arms, and I hold her tighter.

"Did that just actually happen, or am I losing my damn mind?" I whisper into the electric air that surrounds us.

With a shaky hand, Lachlan reaches out to the nearest chair and yanks it away from the table before collapsing into it. His forehead drops into his hands as he sucks in ragged breath after ragged breath.

"*I have a brother. A brother and a mother. And a father.*"

Never before have I seen my husband lose his ironclad control over his emotions, but he's on the verge right now. His body shakes and heaves, and the only thing I know to do is to be his strength if he needs it.

Shifting our baby in my arms, I crouch down beside him, pressing my head against his suit-jacketed shoulder.

"It's okay. We're going to figure this out. Whoever he is, whoever *they* are, we'll figure it out."

"I have a brother." Lachlan lifts his face from his hands as tears stream down his cheeks. "He looks just like me."

It's like I've entered an alternate reality. *Lachlan is crying?* I give myself a mental shake. *Of course he is,*

Keira. You have no idea what this feels like. You've always known you had a family. He never has.

But still, my protective instincts rally. "How do you know he's telling the truth? How can you believe him so easily?"

My husband laughs brokenly through his tears. "There are some things you just know. *I have a brother.*" A sob breaks through the laughter, and my husband reaches for me and Aurora and drags us up into his lap. "*I have a family. I have a family. I have a family.*"

As I sit in his arms, tears slide down my face, dripping into Aurora's hair as her chubby fingers extend toward her daddy.

He reaches for her, burying his face in her sweet-smelling curls.

I hear him whisper, nearly inaudible, "*I've always had a family. I knew it. I always knew it.*"

CHAPTER FIVE

MOUNT

My entire body shakes like a junkie needing a fix as I hold my wife and daughter, absorbing the enormity of what just happened.

I have a brother. A brother I just let walk out of my home, unescorted, without worrying he's going to come back and try to kill me.

No wonder my wife thinks I'm insane. I would never normally do such a thing. But the sixth sense that has kept me alive all these years tells me the absolute truth: he's not a threat. He wasn't lying when he said he had no ill intentions. I know what those feel like. I've felt those all my life. But from him ... no. All I felt from him was ... *love.*

Love.

It's an emotion I didn't understand or have any familiarity with until Keira came into my life and then gave me a daughter. Waves of emotion wash over me as I hold my beautiful, brave wife and innocent baby girl.

Love.

That's the emotion swamping me right now. If I wasn't sitting, it would be more than enough to bring me to my knees for the second time today.

Only minutes before, I was in agony in the library, feeling like I was being torn apart and my soul was being ripped from my body. And now … laughter bubbles up from the depths of my being. *How is this even possible?*

"God certainly does have a sense of humor," I say through broken laughter and sneaky tears. I don't even recognize myself right now or how I'm behaving, but I don't care.

I have a brother and a mother and a father.

I have a family.

Salty droplets continue to slip down my face, unchecked, and for the first time in my life, I don't care. I don't care that I'm crying. I don't care.

I felt his love.

I have a brother. I shook his hand. He was real.

A sense of belonging I didn't know I was missing fills in a hole in my heart that I didn't realize was there.

How could I have known?

"How are you not freaking out right now and running a background check on him to make sure he is who he says he is?" Keira asks quietly as her searching gaze meets mine. Confusion lines her features.

"I don't know. I don't know how I know what I know, but I know *I have a brother.* I believe him."

"Marco Giordano. That's what he said his name was," Keira says, as if a light bulb just went off above her head. "He said you're the grandson of an Italian Comte. How can any of this be real? We have to check into him. I don't want you to get your hopes up—"

I silence her with a kiss to her beautiful lips. *My wife, trying to protect me when I'm the protector.* When I pull back, I take in the wild gamut of emotions running rampant across her stunning face.

"I know what I know. I can't tell you how I know, but I *know.* He's not lying. This isn't some elaborate scheme. I might not know exactly what his motives are, but I know what I felt in my gut. It's never led me wrong. It's kept me alive through more than you can understand. I trust it above all things. That man has no ill will or dark intentions toward us. I know *exactly* what those feel like. I've known my whole life how to spot those. That's the only reason I'm alive. But this ... this is different. This is something else entirely. This is ... *real.*"

Aurora fusses, and Keira rises from my lap to bounce her. I rise and reach out to take our daughter. She snuggles into me, her chubby little hand grasping the lapel of my suit before she settles down with her head against my chest.

This is what love feels like. And I have a brother who I felt it from too.

It's almost too unbelievable to comprehend.

"So, what now? You're ... you're just going to go ... to some hangar? Without any backup? Without ..." She stops herself short, but I know exactly what she wanted to say.

Without V. My best friend, my eminently trustworthy second-in-command, and the man who died, protecting my daughter. The reminder of his loss sobers me instantly.

I grip Keira's hand and squeeze. "V is gone, Keira. I miss him like a lost limb. He died a hero, and for what he did, I owe him everything. But I can't stop living because I don't have him at my back. He was like a brother to me, but now ... now, I might actually have a real brother. How can I not go?"

"I know, but—"

"Listen to me, Hellion. *I have to go. I have to.* You have no idea how many sleepless nights I spent wondering where I came from. Wondering why they didn't want me. Wondering if they were out there somewhere. *I have to go.*"

All further protest dies on her lips. "You're right. I'm sorry. Of course, we have to go. You're right. I'm just ... this is a lot, Lachlan. This week ... and now this ... it's a lot."

I release her hand to wrap an arm around her, pulling her into me, keeping Aurora tucked between us.

"I know. And you're holding up beautifully, darling. You are a queen among women. There is no one like you. You can handle this too. It's going to be okay. But first, I need to take you both somewhere safe so I can go meet them. Somewhere no one could possibly find you."

Keira jerks back, but I tighten my arm around her. "What? What are you talking about? I'm going with you, or I'm going nowhere."

"You're not going with me. I'm not taking you and Rory anywhere near a hangar with a jet until I know without a shadow of a doubt that it's safe. I will never risk either of you. But you can't stay here either."

"This is my home. If I can't go with you, then this is where I'm safest." Her jaw locks, like she's ready to fight, but even as she says the words, we both know she doesn't believe them.

"You haven't slept in days. We both know it. You don't

feel safe here anymore either." I know with certainty that it's part of the reason she's so on edge right now. Our home was violated. The peace of our sanctuary has been shattered. Replacing the bloodstained carpet changed nothing. I know when she walks down the hall, she still sees V's body where he fell.

"But—"

"Do you trust me, Keira?" It's a question I don't even have to ask.

"With my life. You know that." She sucks in a breath and lets it out, and I know she's grasping for control. "But you're not leaving me somewhere to go meet these strangers in a hangar."

"And you're insane if you think I'm bringing you with me to meet some strangers in a hangar." My tone is resolute. "I have to do this, but you're not coming with me. Not this time, Hellion."

"But—"

"There is literally nothing you could say to make me change my mind. Grab your purse and Rory's bag. We need to leave."

My beautiful wife—the strongest woman I've ever known—still has no poker face, and for that, I am eternally grateful. I watch in awe as she struggles with her emotions and pulls herself together like a general preparing to lead troops into battle.

"I'm telling you right now, I do not like this. I don't like this at all."

"I know. But it's what's happening. Get your things. I've waited a lifetime to meet my mother. I'm not going to keep her waiting long."

CHAPTER SIX

KEIRA

Every time I think I've found the limits of my strength, God gives me something else to overcome and get stronger.

It's a good thing, I suppose, because as the wife of Lachlan Mount, I have no room for weakness. I couldn't survive a day in his world if I were anything less than strength embodied.

My life is never going to be the same. I have been on a roller coaster of a ride since that day I walked into my office in the basement of Seven Sinners—my family's whiskey distillery—and found a man sitting in the darkness, telling me I owed him a debt.

Why would it be any different now that we're married? Of course, the roller coaster would continue.

But the first thing I do when I reach our master suite and find my purse is pull out my phone and open a web browser. I type in the name Marco Giordano and hit search.

If he's lying, I'm going to find him, and he will wish he

never set foot in New Orleans. A short huff of laughter escapes me as I realize that I'm the only one acting like a typical Mount right now. My husband has already decided to believe a stranger completely without confirming *anything.*

I get that his gut has kept him alive, but I have a duty as a wife and a mother not to let him walk into an ambush. I would never forgive myself if I didn't dig up everything I could find first.

"Whoa." The word pops out of my mouth as the search results load on my screen. "Oh my God."

I look at the photos of Marco Giordano that are at the top. I tap the screen. There are more pictures of Marco than I've ever seen of my husband.

Because he hasn't been hiding his entire existence from the regular world, like Lachlan has as king of a criminal empire.

"Holy shit." My head jerks back of its own accord as I see it—Marco standing next to a man who looks just like him, but older with silver hair. It's like seeing my husband in thirty years.

Oh my God. He was telling the truth.

I can't ignore the facts staring me in the face. *That's Lachlan's father. It has to be.*

I click on the link, and it takes me to an article about the Giordano family. I scan it quickly, feeling like I'm an archaeologist discovering the truth about an ancient civilization.

I gasp when I read a line in the middle. *The family became even more well known when one of the twin sons was kidnapped over forty years ago. He has been presumed dead for years, but rumors claim that the family has never given up hope of locating him. The Italian authorities were never able to identify a suspect in the disappearance.*

Instantly, my fingers fly across the screen, typing in a new search. *Alessandro Giordano son's kidnapping.*

Article after article appears. I click on the first one and almost drop my phone at the shock of the photo on the screen.

"It's Rory. Oh my God. He looks just like Rory."

"What did you say?"

I spin around, and my phone falls from my suddenly nerveless fingertips. It lands on the carpet as I stare at my husband.

My lungs heave as I point at the floor. "It looks like a picture of Rory. The picture of their son who was kidnapped. *It was you.* He wasn't lying, was he?"

Lachlan comes toward me, Aurora still in his arms.

My whole body trembles as he crouches down to pick up my phone. His gaze locks on the screen, eyes darting back and forth as he reads it. A tremor rips through him as he digests it.

"No, he wasn't lying," my husband whispers.

I rush forward to take Aurora from him before his knees go weak, and he takes a stumbling step toward the bed, sliding down to the carpet beside it.

"That's me. I was that kidnapped baby." A tortured breath leaves his lips as he drops the phone and jams both hands into his hair. "They didn't abandon me. I was kidnapped. They didn't leave me. *They wanted me.*"

Tears—the kind I've never seen before from him—pour down his face.

It's like watching a scene from a movie, because it surely doesn't seem real.

"*They didn't leave me. They wanted me.*" His body sags as years of pent-up grief and longing erupt into sobs from the strongest and most dangerous man I've ever met. "*I have a family.*"

Lachlan's sobs trigger Aurora to fuss and cry.

"No, baby, it's okay," I say to calm her. "Daddy's fine. He's okay."

As if struck by lightning, Lachlan jolts to his feet, shaking off the emotion that just weakened his knees. "Daddy's fine, baby girl. Don't cry. There's nothing to cry about. These are happy tears, sweetheart."

Together, the three of us drop onto the coverlet of the bed.

I let out a long breath. "So, he was telling the truth. Someone had taken you, just like that man took Rory." I shake my head in disbelief. "It's like it's all coming full circle. How is this even real?"

Aurora snuggles into her daddy's arms, and long moments pass before either of us speaks.

In a hushed whisper, I say, "We should go. You need to meet your mother."

Lachlan lifts his gaze to mine. "I need to go meet my mother. Because I have a family." He shakes his head with disbelief. "I have a family, and they've never stopped looking for me. Who would've ever fucking believed that?"

CHAPTER SEVEN

LACHLAN

With one last kiss pressed to Aurora's forehead and then Keira's lips, I leave them inside a safe house that no one but me and V knew about. It's the safest hideaway I have available. No one will ever find them there, especially with the circuitous route I took on the drive.

As soon as I close the door behind me, my mind is on what's to come.

My mother.

I have a mother. And she loves me. She never stopped looking for me.

It's like something out of a fairy tale, which is one thing my life has never been. It's hard to believe that it could turn into such a thing now, but I can't argue with the reality of what's unfolding today.

I have a brother. A twin brother.

During the drive over, Keira told me what she read online, and it took everything I had to keep the car on the road.

I wasn't unwanted. My mother didn't leave me on the steps of a church. Someone took me from her.

It's the kind of story I've always wished were true, in the darkest hours of the night, when I lay, unable to sleep out of fear or hunger. The fact that the fantasy I never told anyone about might actually be true is beyond mind-blowing. It's ... unbelievable.

"Get yourself together, Mount. Get yourself together." I slow my breathing, taking one deep breath at a time.

And then it hits me—*I might actually find out my real name.* It's one thing that Keira didn't tell me on the way over. It wasn't in the articles she had pulled up. I was always referred to as "the missing twin" or "the son of Alessandro Giordano."

I force my attention to the road ahead of me and focus on driving to the airport. It seems like it takes a year to get there even though it's less than a half an hour away.

What if she doesn't—

I cut off the thought. My mind wants to go a million different ways, trying to run with scenario after scenario of how this could play out, but I shut it down every time.

I don't want to think about it or imagine it. I want to experience the reality of it. I want to see her reaction to me. I want to see the expression on my mother's face. I want to know ... *if she loves me.*

One thing I would never let anyone know is how deeply it affected me not to have a mother, a father, or a family. Instead, I became strong and ruthless, taking the city of New Orleans as my own. But inside, in the darkest depths of my soul, part of me has always been a little boy who wondered if a mother could love him.

A snorting breath escapes my nostrils. "What would my enemies think if they knew that? They'd crucify me."

The thought helps center me and bring me back into my body. I grip the steering wheel harder with my fingers before relaxing them one at a time, as if the focus will help me not to fall apart again today. I've never allowed myself such a weakness before, but now ... it seems that all bets are off.

When the airport comes into view, I have to remind myself that I could be driving into an ambush.

My brother might mean me no harm, but what if he's working for someone? What if he's the perfect bait for an elaborate trap?

For the first time in my life, I don't really care. If it is a trap, then it's an excellent one, and I'll undoubtedly be caught in its snare. I never would have thought that I'd be willing to take such a risk—to risk leaving this world and my wife and daughter behind—but I have spent my whole life needing answers to these questions. *Where did I come from? Who am I?*

If there's a single chance that this is for real and he's telling the truth, then I can't miss the best opportunity life has ever given me to shine light on the darkness of my past. I'm highly conscious of the fact that this chance might only come once in my lifetime. I have no choice but to seize the moment. Something more than logic or curiosity drives me. I couldn't stop myself from going even if I wanted to. *I need answers. I have to know.*

Thankfully, I'm very familiar with the airport, as my own jet is hangared here. Hangar six is for transients, so at least that lines up with my brother's story.

My brother.

The reality of the thought is almost too unbelievable to be real. But I saw him. *His face. My face.* I felt him. I shook his hand. He was real. It was all real.

And my mother is inside that hangar.

But I can't abandon my self-preservation instincts completely even if I wanted to. Old habits die hard after all. I block the opening of the hangar with my Bentley. The plane won't be able to leave until I'm ready for it to do so. I'm strapped with forty rounds of armor-piercing bullets in shoulder holsters, another seven rounds at my ankle, and eighteen at the small of my back.

If this turns into a war, then I'm ready. But my instincts say it won't come to that. Not a single shot will be fired. I'd bet my empire on it.

Ironically, a war would be easier for me to handle. It's what I know. All I've known for years. But a family reunion? That I don't know how to handle. I'm completely out of my depth here.

I climb out of the car, letting the heavy door slam loud enough so that anyone in the hangar will know I'm here. There's no sneaking around. Still feeling like a lamb possibly being led to slaughter, I walk around the long front end, keeping the engine block between me and the stairs of the plane.

"I'm here," I call out, wanting to see who appears so I know exactly what I'm getting into—sooner rather than later. If I'm wrong and it's an ambush, I still have a chance of getting out of here alive.

My twin's head emerges from the open door of the jet. He takes in where the car is parked and where I stand. A smile spreads over his lips—not a smile like the cruel ones of my enemies, but one that says all my precautions are unnecessary.

He steps out of the jet with his palms out. "I promise you have nothing to fear, brother. You have my word of honor. You're safe here. Perhaps safer than you've ever been in your entire life."

The truth and sincerity underlying the tone of his words are undeniable.

Does he even know how to lie? I wonder absently as I step around the front of the car and walk toward the rolled-out red carpet leading to the lowered stairs.

But because I am who I am, I can't stop myself from warning him of the consequences of lying to me. "If you betray me, hell would be a welcome respite from what would happen to you."

His smile grows wider, and it's like looking at a happier version of myself—one that I wouldn't recognize, except for the joy that Keira and Aurora have brought into my life.

"I understand you mean that, and yet there is no reason for concern. I have spoken truth to you only. I will continue to do so. That is my promise to you, brother."

For the first time, I register his Italian-accented English. *How did I miss that before?*

Perhaps it's to be expected. My brain couldn't possibly process everything I was taking in when I rushed into the courtyard, prepared to kill to defend my wife. Staring at what could be a literal copy of myself was more overwhelming that I would've ever believed. It's still hard to process now, while he's standing ahead of me. There is no argument. He is my identical twin.

"Come, brother. Our mother awaits. There is no one

else on the jet right now, not even the pilot. He is inside the airport lounge. I wanted complete and total privacy for this moment for us. For the Giordano family."

For the Giordano family.

His words echo in my mind as I attempt to comprehend them. *The Giordano family.* My family. *Holy Christ.* I never expected …

"Has he arrived?" I hear a woman's voice carry from behind him. "Is it my baby boy? Is he here yet?"

My heart slams into my chest as adrenaline dumps into my bloodstream at the sound of her voice. It's like my body knows it and already recognizes it. Everything around me comes into sharp focus as I walk toward the red carpet one step at a time.

"Yes, Mama," my double says as his head turns toward the interior of the jet. "He's coming. I told you he would come."

Any thought of an ambush has been completely eradicated from my mind. I have to see the face that belongs to that voice.

The moment couldn't get any more surreal. I'm already staring at my own mirror image. *My twin brother's face.* It's almost all too unbelievable, but it's very real all the same.

"Come. She is not the most patient woman right now, as perhaps you understand."

He steps back into the jet, and I brace myself.

I could be walking into a hail of bullets, but if there's a single chance that my mother is truly inside, it's a risk I'm willing to take.

My feet bounce up the stairs, and I duck into the jet. I

scan the interior first, out of self-preservation, and freeze the moment my gaze lands on her.

My God.

My lungs seize, as if I've forgotten how to breathe.

I reach up to the ceiling, barely aware that it's because I need to steady myself as I take in the sight before me.

My God.

Finally, my lungs begin to work again, and I release a breath and haul in another.

Her mouth falls open as she sees me.

Time stops.

"Ohhh." Unintelligible sounds escape her lips as her small, beringed hand slaps her chest. "My son!"

Tears immediately spill from dark brown eyes down the most beautiful face I've ever seen—besides my wife's and my daughter's. Her hair is pure silver, twisted up into an artful arrangement.

I have no words. I have no sounds. I have nothing but an enormity of emotion rushing over me like a rogue tidal wave.

"My son," she whispers again as her entire body shakes with tremors that match those ripping through me.

Sobs escape her lips, and she covers them with her hand before falling forward out of her seat onto her knees. I can't understand the words spilling out of her now, but they sound like a prayer.

"Mama." My brother rushes to her side and drops to his knees. "Mama, it's okay."

She clings to him as she reaches out a hand to me. "My son. My baby boy."

Like a metal filing drawn to a magnet, an invisible

force draws me to her. I'm on my knees before I realize what I'm doing.

"Mama." The word my brother spoke slips from my lips, totally foreign and yet completely perfect. "Are you really …"

She reaches a hand to my face, and I don't realize I'm crying until she wipes my tears away.

"You are beautiful, my son. Beautiful. My *son.*" Her hand trembles against my skin as I cover it with my own.

"I never gave up on you," she continues as tears pour, unchecked, from her dark eyes. "I knew I would see you again someday. My beautiful baby boy. I could not leave this earth until I saw you again. *My son,*" she whispers as she bows her head to mine.

No words are spoken for long moments as the three of us kneel in a silent cloud of emotion, stronger than anything I've ever felt in my entire life.

The love of a mother.

Finally.

The love of my *mother.*

Something inside me breaks free, and a rough sob shatters the silence.

"You're my mother."

"Yes. Yes, my son." Tears slip past the tender smile curving her perfect lips. "I am. And I have waited so long for this day. So long have I waited for this moment." Her fingertips thread through my hair as she pulls me closer to her. "Luca. My Luca. You are home. You are home. *I never stopped praying.* And now, I have everything. *Everything. God has granted us a miracle.* I have both of my sons now. *It's a miracle.*"

I rise slightly to pull her trembling body into mine as I

hug my mother for the very first time. I weep into her hair as her arms wrap around me and draw me closer and tighter.

Warmth and love bloom inside my being in a way that I didn't even know was possible. My heart feels like it's grown wings and may fly straight out of my chest.

"*Mama.*" It's a word I always wished I could speak as a little boy, but life denied me—until this very moment.

This moment that is worth *everything*.

"Luca. My baby boy. You are restored to me. It is a miracle."

"I promised I would find him for you," Marco whispers. "I would never have stopped. And now, he is with us. It is a miracle indeed."

She lifts her head from my arms, and warm, dark brown eyes filled with love meet my gaze. *A mother's love.*

"You must come home with us. I cannot lose you ever again, my son. We have many, many years to make up for in a much shorter time."

Her words are a balm to wounds in my soul that I didn't know existed. On my knees before her, I feel complete in a way I never knew I could. I don't need a DNA test to know that this woman is my mother and that her love brought us together against all odds. I can see the truth all over her face.

Waves of gratitude and peace wash over me.

Somehow, I know that this woman loves me, no matter what I've done or who I've been or how long we've been separated. Tears stream down my face anew as I realize that this is *unconditional love.*

Keira gave it to me first, then Aurora, and now … *my mother.*

How can a man such as I deserve so much goodness?

"I have a mother," I murmur. I'm rocked by the enormity of the realizations unfolding. *I have a mother who loves me. Who didn't abandon me. Who never stopped praying to find me.* How can a man such as I be worthy of so much?

"You do, my son. You have a mother who loves you very much. And a brother who has moved heaven and earth to find you for us. For your family."

Another thought hits me. "Is my father ... is he still ... alive?"

Keira's quick digging online didn't say whether he was alive or dead.

For the first time since I boarded the jet, my mother's face loses some of the joy emblazoned on it. Instantly, I assume that he has already passed and I will never know my sire. But in this moment, I don't care. A mother is more than I ever expected. And a brother. Not having a father is nothing new for me.

But instead of confirming my expectations, my brother speaks. "Our father is still alive. He does not know we're here. He does not know we never stopped searching for you. He ... he does not speak of you. It is ... it is too painful for him."

I have a father. I have a father and a mother and a brother. How is this even possible? I nearly choke on the breath I suck in.

Marco continues, "He will be overjoyed to know you are alive, although very surprised when he learns of it. He is in Italy. To this day, he works tirelessly, even though he should have long ago retired."

"He will work himself into a grave. That is all he knows," my mother says with a hint of ice in her tone.

Clearly, there are family dynamics to which I'm not yet privy, but I don't care.

I have a family. That's the part that matters. The dynamics can wait.

This is all more than I ever thought possible. I don't care if my family isn't perfect. I don't care that my father has tried to forget about his second son. How could I blame him when I tried so hard to forget that I might have parents —somewhere—who could have once cared about me?

"It doesn't matter," I tell them with a shake of my head. I reach out to wipe the tears from my mother's face with my thumb. "This is more than I ever imagined. *I have a family.* As you said, it is a miracle."

"You must come home with us. Marco told me of your beautiful wife and my precious granddaughter. You must get them and come home to Italy with us. We can keep you safe. You can live in peace with your family. It is all I have ever wanted." She grasps my wrist with her thin yet strong fingers. "Please say you will come with us. America is not where you belong. You are a son of Italy. You must come home. It is your heritage. There is much for you there. So much love to surround you. I will not take no for an answer. Your brother will tell you how stubborn I am. I never gave up hope that I would find you again, my son. My dear Luca. I prayed every morning, every night, and all day in between for your safety, wherever you were."

I inhale sharply, stunned at her words as their meaning filters into my mind. "They worked. I should've died six dozen times over, but every time, against all odds, something kept me safe—even when I didn't deserve it. Your prayers worked."

I shake my head, overwhelmed by the magnitude of the truth. *My mother prayed for me nonstop.* How else would a man like me survive all these years without succumbing to a bullet? It's the only explanation that makes perfect sense.

"Come, Mama. Sit now, and you and Luca can speak of all of this. But not on your knees any longer, Mama. He is here. He is home. Please." Marco lifts our mother to her feet, and we rise as one.

As one family. It's mind-blowing. Life-changing. Incredible.

Luca. The name they keep calling me doesn't feel nearly as foreign as it should. Perhaps it's because names have never meant much to me. I never knew what mine was for certain, so I never put much stock in it. Lachlan Mount became my identity, but it was never more than that. It was only something others could call me because I was always a lost little boy.

"Where am I from?" I ask as I take a seat, facing both of them. "Where was I born?"

"*Roma.* You were both born in *Roma*, even though I wanted to give birth at the estate. Alessandro wouldn't let me. He believed we needed the most modern doctors because you were twins. He always worried something would go wrong. He was wrong ... until later."

I was born in Rome, Italy, not New Orleans, Louisiana.

"How old was I when I was taken?"

"Four months old. It never should have happened. I'm so sorry, my son. I'm so sorry. It was all my fault. I didn't know anyone would ever try to hurt us. I didn't know. It was all my fault."

Her tears begin spilling again, and Marco wraps his arm around her. He pulls her against his side.

"Mama, you know it was not your fault. You must forgive yourself. It is time. Luca is home. He is here and whole. You must forgive yourself. *Please*."

I reach out to take her hands and cup them between mine. "Please. Don't cry. I'm fine. I'm here. I'm alive. You didn't do anything wrong. You didn't leave me on purpose. You didn't abandon me. That's the only thing that matters. *You wanted me.*"

My words arrest her crying spell. "Wanted you? I adored you. Both of you. My beautiful twin boys. My beloved sons. You have never been loved more than I have loved you. I would *never have left you. Never have abandoned you. Never.* They had to beat me unconscious to tear you from my arms. I would *never* have let you go. Not my son. *Never, my son.* When I woke, you were gone. It was as if a piece of my heart had been cut from my breast. *Never would I have let you go.* I have lived that moment over and over again, until I made myself sick. If only—"

"Shh. Mama, you will make yourself sick again," Marco says as he comforts our mother.

They beat her unconscious to take me from her.

The truth tears through me, shredding my heart with the pain of her memory. *My mother loves me. My mother fought for me. My mother prayed for my return every day.*

"It doesn't matter now. None of it matters now." I bow my head over her hands before lifting them to my lips. "All that matters is that you're here and you're real."

She presses a kiss to the top of my head as her tears soak through my hair. "Yes, my son. I am here, and I am real. And now, you come home with us, where you belong. It is time."

Slowly, I raise my head and meet her gaze. The last thing I would ever want to do is break my mother's heart, especially when I just met her.

"I can't leave right this moment. I have obligations. I have … I have much to attend to here before I can go."

"You have people trying to kill you, brother. Someone tried to kill me, believing I was you," my brother reminds me. "This place is not safe for you anymore. You cannot safely stay here for long now. It is time to go."

Unused to people telling me what I can and cannot do, I check my ego as it tries to rise. "I know why you say that, and you're undoubtedly right, but even if I wanted to leave right now, I have a wife, a daughter, businesses …" I trail off, thinking of what I have to do tomorrow—bury my best friend and the only brother I knew before now.

"But they will come with us," my mother says, her tone insistent. "Your family is our family. Your daughter is my granddaughter. She is the sole heir to the Giordano empire. Marco has no children and will not. We believed our family line would die with Marco, but your daughter gives us new hope. She has a fortune at her fingertips. Her future is assured in ways you cannot yet understand. Whatever you have, we have more, my son. God has blessed us abundantly, and it is for you and your family. Islands. The estate and farms. A mountain home. Yachts. A fleet of cars and planes and more. Gold. Jewels. The best of everything. We have it all. It is your daughter's legacy. She must not be denied her heritage."

The enormity of what she's saying isn't lost on me, but that doesn't change what I have to do tomorrow.

"We will come. I promise you, we will come. But not today. Tomorrow, I must lay to rest a man who gave his life while protecting my daughter. I have to honor his memory first. And then my wife. She has a business too. A family of her own. Our life isn't so simple to leave behind."

"But your empire is crumbling, brother. You know it, and I know it."

The truth in Marco's words brings me back to this morning, when I was falling apart on the rug in my library.

My brother isn't wrong. In fact, he's exactly right.

"Be that as it may, I can't just walk away. I have things I must do. Obligations to take care of. I can't just run. That's not who I am, and that's not the man I'll ever be."

"Then, when?" my mother asks. "When will you come? I will not take no for an answer. You may not know me well yet, my son, but I am certain there is much of me within you. You are my blood. And I never give up. *Never*."

My face stretches with a smile that I didn't expect to possess me. "I have no doubt you are a fearsome creature in your own right. After all, you're my mother, and I'm not a man like any other. But you have to let me do this my way. I have to speak to my wife. We're a team. She's my better half in every way she could possibly be. You'll love her. It's impossible not to."

My mother's face softens—perhaps she realizes she's won even if the victory is not immediate.

"You will not take long to settle your obligations. We have much time to make up for, and you have much waiting for you at home. More than you could ever dream. I will give you one week, my son. And then I will come to your home, no matter how dangerous Marco says it would be for me to do so."

Leave it to my mother to give me an ultimatum. I should have expected no less.

Perhaps a quick vacation to Italy is exactly what our family needs to recover from the shock and horror we've all experienced this week.

With a nod, I reach out and take her hand. Once more, I bring it to my lips, pressing a kiss to the back. "A week it is. After all, how could I disappoint my mother?"

CHAPTER EIGHT

KEIRA

"It's okay. It's just me."

I wake with a jerk of my head at the sound of Lachlan's voice. I blink my eyes, but my vision is still fuzzy.

"I wasn't going to fall asleep. I was waiting up," I murmur through a yawn as his hand cups the side of my head. I burrow into the familiar scent and touch instinctively, thankful beyond anything that my husband is beside me once more.

"You should've slept soundly, like Rory."

I track his gaze to our daughter as she snuggles between the pillow and my body.

"She needed it more than I did," I say through another yawn.

"Right. I buy that completely," my husband replies with a wry tone.

With another blink to clear my vision, I study the hard planes and sharp angles of his face that I love so dearly, gratitude settling in my soul at his safe return. It's the same feeling I have every time he comes back to me. It's something I never take for granted with his business—especially with how our life has been unfolding recently.

That's when it hits me. *Lachlan looks different.*

Something has changed about his face. It's softer. Fewer lines. More ... at peace. The remaining cobwebs of sleep clear instantly as I remember the all-important reason he left Aurora and me in this safe house.

"Did you ... did you ... was it ..." I whisper, trying to keep my voice low so I don't wake Aurora. I don't even know what to ask. The experience I find myself having is so far outside of our norm that I can't even piece together the right words for a question. After all, they aren't questions I ever thought I'd be asking. But such is life with Lachlan Mount.

Instead of replying, he stares intently at me and Aurora. His normally sharp features soften even further.

"I never knew what that was like before. I wondered my whole life what it must feel like." His mouth curls ever so slightly, as if he's remembering something beautiful.

My lips part to ask what he means, but Lachlan continues before I need to speak.

"I felt the love of my mother. It was indescribable. I truly never knew what that felt like until tonight."

My lungs spontaneously suck in a deep breath that pierces my chest, straight to my heart. My hand flies to my mouth as my lower lip trembles and tears gather in my eyes. "You really ..."

He nods, and his nearly black eyes glisten with emotion. "I did." The words come out roughened with emotion I've only heard once before—on the day of Aurora's birth.

"It was really her?" I ask on a whisper, as if afraid to shatter the moment.

"Yes," he replies, lowering to the edge of the bed to sit beside us. "She's ..." He swallows and pauses before speaking. "She's more than I ever dreamed she could be."

"Oh, Lachlan." My heart is full to bursting as I reach out to grasp his hand. His fingers curl around mine, gripping them like velvet over steel.

"She's beautiful. She's strong. She's ... soft and loving. Just like you. Everything a mother should be." A tear tips over his lower lid and tracks down his face. "I don't know how a man who has done what I've done could deserve such a gift. It doesn't seem possible. It seems ... like something out of a fairy tale."

Instantly, the protective instincts I've had to adopt as Keira Mount rise. *Are they playing him? Is this a scam or an elaborate scheme?* If it is, *I will end them for this cruelty.* No one plays with my husband's emotions like this and lives.

"Are you sure? Totally sure she's really who she says she is?"

His lips curve with another soft smile—one I'd love to see on his lips forever. "Yes, I'm sure."

"How do you know?"

He releases a breath. "There are some things you just know. Nothing about what I experienced tonight was a setup or a scam. I've been through plenty of those, Hellion. This was ... this was something you can't fake. Something so genuine, it brought me to my knees."

I grip his strong hand even harder. "Are you okay?"

His smile turns bemused. "I don't know what I am anymore, and clearly, I don't know who I am either."

"You're the most formidable man I've ever met. You're law unto yourself. You're—"

He interrupts me with his own reply. "A lost little boy who just met his mother for the first time. It rocked me, Keira. All the way to the core." He bows his head over our hands. "She never stopped looking for me. She never stopped praying for me. *She loves me like you love Rory.*"

His head shakes from side to side, like he can't believe what he's saying. A hot tear lands on our joined fingers.

He's crying. Lachlan Mount is crying.

If there's one thing that could rock me to my core, it's that. But this isn't about me.

I squeeze his fingers tighter. "Oh, Lachlan. Of course she does. How could she not? You're her son. Her baby. I know the pain of finding your child gone, but I can't imagine the agony of having to endure it for over forty years."

My heart breaks and reassembles in a single moment as I empathize with his mother's suffering.

"And then the joy of meeting you—a beautiful man, who not only survived against all odds, but thrived. Reunited with her baby …" Tears spill down my cheeks as I attempt to envision it.

Lachlan looks up and meets my gaze. Glistening tracks wet his cheeks, and I'm awed at the depth of emotion he's allowing to show. The vulnerability is unlike anything I've ever seen him express.

"It was the moment I'd waited for my entire life." His

chest shakes as he sucks in another breath. "It was worth the wait. Every second."

Lachlan releases my hand and pulls me onto his lap. My arms wrap around him as his encircle me.

With his head buried in my hair, his body trembles as he inhales a sharp breath. "It was worth everything. *Everything.* A dream come to life. *How could I deserve this? How is this happening to me?*"

His uncertainty shocks me more than his tears. "Of course you deserve this. She's your mother. She loves you. You deserve this more than anyone."

"How? After all that I've done, how could God give me such a gift? After you, after Rory ... how is it that I deserve so much good after everything I've done?"

It's a side of my husband I've never seen before. In that moment, the enormous weight of the burden of being the man called Lachlan Mount lands on me. I realize that even though I know him better than any living human, I don't know him as well as I thought I did. I don't live with his actions haunting me. I don't see or hear what goes on in his mind. I don't know what he's done that he's grappling with, but I can imagine a hint of the darkness in which he has lived. It's a darkness I've learned to accept. After all, our relationship didn't exactly start with him asking me out on a date.

No. He decided he wanted to own me, and he went about making that a reality. He didn't exactly consult me about what I wanted. It was only later that I fell in love with him—after I was allowed to see his heart.

That's when the truth dawns on me.

Unconditional love. That's the only reason I have what I have in my life. That's the only way I could forgive him and move forward after how things started between us. I no longer care about how we became us, because his actions gave me everything that matters most to me in this world.

That's what he experienced tonight. Unconditional love. The unconditional love of a mother.

It wouldn't matter what Aurora did or said—she could be a serial killer on death row, and I would still love her. That's the unconditional love of a mother. That's the only force strong enough to rock my husband to his core. The tears, trembling, and vulnerability from the strongest man I've ever met make perfect sense.

Only love could do this to Lachlan Mount.

"I'm so glad you went. I'm so glad you met her."

"Me too." He speaks into my hair with a shaky breath. "Me too."

I lose track of time as he holds me on the edge of the bed with Aurora curling and snuggling against us. Her little body is completely relaxed, as though she has never experienced a single moment of fear or terror, which is no longer the truth.

But she knows love, I remind myself. *That's all she'll ever know for the rest of her life. Nothing but love will ever touch her again.*

Like tumblers on a vault clicking into place, pieces of why my husband is the way he is snap into my mind. *He never knew love as a child. He was at the mercy of a merciless system. Of course he became who he became. He never had a chance to become anything else.*

A haunting question floats into my mind. *What would Aurora have become if we hadn't gotten her back so quickly?*

I can't bear to think about the answer, but I also can't stop my mind from forming parallels between her kidnapping and her father's. *Eerie,* to say the least.

"What are we going to do now?" The whispered question slips from my lips.

Lachlan's head lifts, and he meets my gaze from beneath his tousled black hair. "Tomorrow, I bury V."

The mention of losing V sends a dagger of grief ripping through my heart. "You mean, *we* bury him."

Lachlan's hand finds my face, and his thumb skates over my cheek. "Don't fight me on this, Hellion. I can't risk you and Rory. I need you to stay here. Where I know you're safe."

"How can you ask me to miss his funeral?" My objection comes instantly. "That's not fair. I—"

"I'm not asking. I'm telling you. I can't guarantee your safety. You're not going, Keira."

I open my mouth to protest further, but his thumb slides over my lips.

"You're not going. We can fight about it if you want, but it'll have to be tomorrow. I don't have it in me right now."

His quiet, honest reply silences anything else I planned to say on the matter. I release a breath and press my forehead against his shoulder.

"What is happening to our life? What is happening?"

His arms lock around me as a tremor rips through his body. "It's falling apart. Falling the fuck apart. I'm so sorry. I've failed you. I've failed on every level—as a husband, as a father, as a protector, as—"

I yank my head back and cover his lips with my fingers as I pierce him with my gaze. "Stop it. Stop it right now. You didn't fail. Life happened. And now …" I trail off.

"And now, what?" he asks through my fingers.

I don't know what to say, but when I open my mouth, words fall out of their own volition. "Maybe it's not falling apart. Maybe it's falling together."

CHAPTER NINE

LACHLAN

"*Maybe it's falling together.*" Keira's words are the only thing that keeps me from losing it as I park a good distance away and walk alone toward the mausoleum I had built for myself before she came into my life.

Now, it will be V's final resting place.

My loyal and faithful best friend. He was the closest thing I'd ever known to a brother—until yesterday. And because of me, he's gone from this world.

It should've been me whose life was ended, not his. V deserved better than that. *So much fucking better.* But I can't change what happened. All I can do is accept the consequences and live with them.

Clenching my fists at my sides, I fight through the sharp waves of grief to keep my footsteps even. I wish Keira were here so I could lean on her steely strength, because mine is in short supply as darkness wells up in my soul.

As I reach the ostentatious mausoleum, with its Roman

columns and marble statue of Lady Justice with her sword drawn, my heart feels like it's being shredded in my chest.

This could have been for Aurora. I could be burying my baby girl right now.

The reality of what I've created is almost more than I can bear.

I'm tired of death.

I'm tired of violence.

I'm tired of putting my family at risk.

I'm tired of this life I created.

I'm tired of being Lachlan Mount.

I think of the brother I met yesterday. The one who looks identical to me, but who could never be like me. We may share the same DNA, but life has forged us into completely different men.

How many of his friends has he buried? I can't help but wonder. *How many men has he killed?*

I'd be willing to bet my entire empire that the number is zero.

And good for him. To take a life is nothing of which to be proud. Nothing to celebrate. And as many as I have taken … *it fragments your soul.*

The more good people I lose, the more I value life. And to put my innocent daughter's life at risk … *what kind of man does that make me?*

What kind of woman would my daughter become if she were raised within my world of death, brutality, and violence?

I told myself it would never touch her. I told myself I could protect them both.

I lied.

To myself and to Keira.

I thought I could control everything the way I'd always done—with an iron will, a clever mind, and a willingness to do what no one else would dare.

But I couldn't.

I failed, even if my wife won't admit it.

I turn to walk through the marble columns, into this final resting place, where I should be the one the priest is praying over. Instead, he prays over the urn containing the final remains of my best friend.

As he notices me, I'm faced with the truth I can no longer evade: *I can't do this anymore. I can't be this man. I can't live this life any longer.* My soul is screaming at me to run away. *Far, far away.*

And what then? Who would I become?

I can never be my brother. I can never pretend I haven't been the boogeyman.

Where does that leave me? Where do I go from here? What the hell am I supposed to do now?

I don't recognize myself any longer. I don't feel like me. I don't know who I am anymore.

The inky-black depths of despair and grief are calling to me, inviting me in, urging me to give up and drown myself.

A small, quiet voice comes from within me. *"You aren't Lachlan Mount. You never were. It was an identity you assumed out of necessity for survival.* You survived. *You survived to meet your brother and your mother. You have a wife and a daughter and everything to live for. A new day is dawning, a new life—"*

I ruthlessly shut the voice down with more truth: *I don't deserve any of this goodness in my life.* No one else can possibly understand how much I don't deserve it. No one but me knows what I've done.

The voice gets louder. *"God knows, and still, he blesses you with his favor."*

"Why would He do such a thing?" I reply aloud.

The priest thinks I'm speaking to him. "Why would who do such a thing, my son?"

I take in the man before me, dressed for funeral rites in his black cassock and white collar, with his Bible in hand.

"Why wouldn't God strike me down instead?" I ask him, uncaring that I'm revealing weakness—something I rarely do.

Father Thomas performed my wedding and has known me longer than most, so he's not surprised by the question.

"Because the Almighty isn't done with you yet," he answers as though it's a simple matter, except it feels like anything but. The priest continues, "He still has a purpose for your life. That's the only reason you're still here. God uses us all in mysterious ways, just as He has used you."

I open my mouth, as if wishing to correct him that it was *my mother's prayers* that kept me alive this long, but my lips lock together once more. I'll share my mother's existence with no one but Keira. I would never endanger her life.

Instead, I reply along a different vein. "God used me to commit violence and take lives? That was the Almighty?" I can't stop my questions.

Father Thomas is a man of the cloth, who actually takes his vows seriously and doesn't diddle little kids or get drunk on the wine—the major reasons why I've continued to trust him all these years.

I may have no answers, but perhaps he does.

"Did you commit violence for fun? Take lives for pleasure?" The questions he throws back at me stop me cold. "Did it give you joy?"

"No," I reply with a sharp tone and shake of my head. "*Never.*"

"Were they innocent lives you took?"

In a moment, their faces flash before my eyes.

"*Never.*"

"God works in mysterious ways, my son. He also forgives all in an instant."

Confusion sets in. This is one part I've never understood. "How? How could He possibly?"

"Because that is His nature." The priest continues as if he discusses these matters every day, and maybe he does, "Do you repent? Will you change your ways? Will you eschew death and violence and choose to live another way?"

Fucking hell. This is not the conversation I wanted to be having this morning. But when has my life ever gone according to plan?

I drop my guard and tell him the truth. "I feel like I'm falling apart, Father. I feel like it's all slipping away." My voice sounds hoarse and not at all like me.

"This is why we're told not to build a house upon sand. This is why we're told to build it upon rock."

"What does that even mean?" I ask with a harsh laugh upon my lips.

"The foundation matters, my son. Upon sand, it crumbles. Upon rock, it stands firm."

"I asked you an honest question, and you speak in riddles, Priest."

A smile graces his face, completely at odds with the

darkness swelling inside me. "Many have said the same thing about the good book." He raises his Bible with a shake of his wrist. "And yet the answers are there for those who have eyes to see and ears to hear."

"Riddles do me no good!" My frustration boils over into a yell, but I force my voice to quiet. "I don't need riddles. I need answers. What do I do now? How do I change what I've done? How do I get my family out of this hell of a life I've created? How do I fix the damage I've done? How do I kill this monster I've unleashed? How do I undo what I've become?"

The smile fades from his face, and I can only imagine what I look like. Possibly like the tortured beast I am.

I stand at a crossroads, between my past and my future, but I have no idea how to leave one behind and walk down a new road. I have no idea how to change my ways. The world I've created would eat me alive.

"How do I stop being myself?" It takes more strength than I anticipated to utter the question.

"Become born again, my son. Ask for forgiveness. Change your ways. That's all it takes to become a new man. It's a promise made to us all—that we can do it at any moment we choose. God is always ready and willing to forgive us for anything. But it is we who must ask for forgiveness and choose anew."

I shake my head as his hopeful words land. "It can't be that easy. Not for me. Not after what I've done. That's impossible."

When he doesn't reply immediately, I glance up from the marble floor to see something on the priest's face that I've never seen before. A new softness. A gentle kindness.

"Even for you, my son. Even for men who have done

worse than you. There's always a new choice to be made. All you have to do is believe that you are forgiven, and it is so."

With disbelief, I jam my hands into my hair and grip the strands. "It can't be that easy. Nothing's that easy."

"But it is. You don't even need me to say the words. Sincerely ask for forgiveness, vow to change your ways, and then you go free. You're absolved of your sins the moment you can forgive yourself in truth and release all guilt. God withholds forgiveness from no one. All you have to do is ask for it and receive it."

Shivers rake over my body as the enormity of what he's saying crashes into my mind like a container ship ramming the pier. Threads of hope begin to grow, but I can't believe they're real.

"*How?*" My question comes out as a harsh whisper.

"How do you ask?"

That wasn't what I meant, but I nod anyway, swallowing the lump in my throat.

"The words don't matter, my son. It's the sincerity behind them. How you feel in your heart. You can do it right now."

A rough laugh spurts from my lips. Of course he'd want that. Another sheep for his flock. A black sheep, to be sure. But I haven't met his one requirement—*I don't know if I can forgive myself.* That could take a lifetime, not an instant.

"The sooner you do it, the sooner you go free, my son. Free yourself from your torment. Only you can do it. This is the only way."

"What if I can't?" I whisper the question, feeling once more like a complete stranger to myself. And perhaps I am. Maybe I'm already someone else. Lachlan Mount wouldn't have this conversation.

Maybe he died on the floor of the library. What is happening to my life?

"Try."

Like it's the very hand of God Himself, an unseen force drops me to my knees on the marble slab beneath us.

Why am I spending so much time on my knees?

"Because it's where you need to be," the small, quiet voice replies.

Shaken by the force and the voice, I bow my head and whisper to the rock beneath me, "Please forgive me, even if I can't forgive myself yet. Please spare my wife and daughter. Please spare my mother and my brother. If there is any mercy or justice in you, take me and spare them. Free me from this hell I've created." A sob is torn from my chest.

A hand touches my hair—the priest's hand. "You are forgiven, my son. You are forgiven. Your freedom is always in your own hands. Only you decide how you go forward from this day. Only you decide. No one else."

Pop-pop.

Instantly, I'm ripped from my penance as the sound of suppressed gunfire disrupts the silence of the moment. All of my senses slam into full alert.

"Get down!" I grab the priest by the arm and yank him to the stone floor, covering him with my body as I move him toward the rear marble mausoleum. "Stay down," I order as I pull two guns from my shoulder holsters.

It was small caliber. Pistol. He has to be close.

Pop-pop-pop-pop.

Marble chunks fly over my head as bullets riddle the marble monument.

Where is he? I use the front column as cover as I peek around the side.

Pop-pop.

Eight rounds. How many more does he have?

"God have mercy on our souls," the priest says from behind me.

"Don't worry, Father. I'll get you out of here. You're not meeting God today."

"I have no fear of death," he wheezes.

I glance behind me to see him clutching his chest. *Fuck. Don't have a heart attack on me, priest.* That's the last black mark I need on my soul.

"Maybe you don't fear death, but I'm not fucking ready," I tell him as I scan the otherwise peaceful grounds of the cemetery. *Where are you, motherfucker? I know you're close.*

I hear the roar of the engine next, and my attention shoots to the narrow road running between the aisles of expensive mausoleum and monuments spread out under the live oaks. A black Suburban hurtles toward us, tires squealing as the driver slams on the brakes.

Fuck, it's an ambush. How many of them are there?

Guns in hand, I step out from behind the marble pillar. With both barrels pointed toward the SUV, my fingers caress the triggers, ready to unload forty rounds.

Before I pull them, an Italian-accented voice calls to us, "Come! Come! We must go! Get in! You must run!"

The door slams as my brother rounds the hood. Instantly, I lower the barrels.

What the fuck?

Pop-pop-pop.

"Get back in the car! Fuck! Take cover!"

I turn and grab the priest by his cassock. "We have to go. Now."

I drag him toward the SUV, using my body to cover him as bullets fly toward us. *Tink-tink-tink.* They embed in the opposite side of the vehicle as I open the door and shove him inside.

"Stay down!"

Fuck, where is he?

I scan the cemetery and see a dark human-sized shadow. A man hunches behind the corner of a mausoleum two monuments over.

He's reloading.

Good.

I got you, motherfucker.

Gunfire erupts as I unload in his direction. A scream pierces the air.

I got you. I fucking got you.

"Get in!" my brother yells from the front seat of the SUV.

"Not yet. I'm on the shooter. Go. Get the priest out of here!"

I slam the door behind me and start running toward the gunman.

"What are you doing?" From the tone of my brother's question, he must think I'm insane, but I don't care right now.

"I need answers!" I yell, arms pumping with guns in hand as I run straight into danger.

I guess that rebirth didn't last long.

CHAPTER TEN

LACHLAN

Keira is going to be so pissed at me. It's the only thing I can think as I sprint toward the man stumbling away from the blood-smeared mausoleum.

She told me not to come without backup. I assured her that I wouldn't be at risk. No one knew the time or location of the funeral, except for me and the priest.

Someone followed the priest. Or someone followed me. I don't know which.

Ever since V was cut down, I don't know who to trust to take my back. Suddenly, everyone's loyalty is suspect.

But my wife told me not to come alone, and I didn't listen.

She'll never let me go out without security again, I think as I launch my entire body through the air like a high school football player making a tackle.

My shoulder collides with the running man first, and I wrap my arms around his waist.

You're not fucking getting away from me. Not after this.

We hit the grass with a bone-rattling *thud*.

"*Fuck, fuck.* Just kill me then! Fucking hell!" The man's voice is overcome with pain.

I must've hit him somewhere he didn't like. Too fucking bad. Actions have consequences. *Don't want to get shot? Don't shoot at me. Easy enough.*

"Who fucking hired you?" I say as I crawl up his body and flip him over onto his back. *Hell. It's a fucking kid. He can't be more than eighteen.*

Blood splatter is all over his face, and his black T-shirt is soaked with it. I can't tell where he's hit yet.

"Fuck you!"

"Where are you hit?"

"Fuck you!"

"*Idiot*," I murmur, looking for the hole. Shoulder. *Fuck.*

He's bleeding way more than he should be for a shoulder wound.

Fuck. Killing a kid was not my intention today.

"If you don't want to die, you're going to answer my questions."

"I ain't answering shit! Kill me now, or I'll kill you, motherfucker," he spits at me, clearly out of the idiocy of youth.

"You have no idea who you're fucking with, kid." Without a second thought, I whack him upside the head with the butt of my pistol to shut him up and shove one of my guns back into the holster. "Don't fucking move if you want to live longer than five minutes."

He groans in pain, no longer so quick with his tongue.

Good. Now, I won't be so tempted to kill you.

I can't help but be glad the priest is gone. I reach

between us and unbuckle my belt. I slide it out of the loops and wrap it over his shoulder and cinch it under his armpit, attempting to slow the bleeding as much as I can.

"The fuck?" His dazed voice sounds confused. "What are you doing?"

"You're going to live long enough to give me the answer to the first question I asked."

"Fuck you, motherfucker."

The roar of an engine comes from behind me. Digging a knee into his chest, I spin around to see what I really fucking hope is the same black Suburban my brother was driving.

The door slams, and my double comes rushing around the front.

"What are you doing? I told you to get out of here with the priest."

"I dropped him off at the welcome center at the entrance. It was his idea. He said you need saving more than he does."

With a harsh huff of a laugh, I shake my head. In a split second, I make a decision—no one is going to know I have a brother. Not in this fucking town. Not a chance.

Using my body to block the kid's view of him, I lift my knee off his chest and flip him over like he's already a dead body.

"Hey!" the kid shouts in pained protest, but I truly don't give a fuck. I'm the only reason he's not bleeding out right now.

I didn't ask for this shit. I just wanted to lay my best friend to rest in peace.

Fuck. V.

"The cremains—the father was going to bless them before we laid V to rest."

My brother nods, and it's too fucking surreal right now to be staring at myself. "We'll get them. Perhaps we should take this as a sign that he's not meant to stay here, but to come with you instead."

"I don't know what this is a sign of, but we need to get the hell out of here. I need answers from this little prick."

My brother glances at the body planted face down on the grass. "I'm not sure whether I should be impressed or concerned that you haven't killed him yet."

For some reason I can't explain, his words make me smile. "I need to know who paid him. I need to know who the fuck is trying to kill me."

"*Everyone*," the kid says with a twisted laugh. "Everyone's out to kill you now, Mount. You're not untouchable anymore. We all see your weakness. Your day is fucking over. There's a new king in town."

His emphatic statements land like grenades in my gut. They're not a surprise exactly, but the fact that they haven't exploded is.

I focus on the most important thing he said. *"There's a new king in town."*

"Too bad you're not a better shot. It's unlikely your employer will miss you." I rise, grabbing him by the back of his neck and lifting him to his feet with his face away from my brother. Looking over my shoulder at my double, I say, "Put on a hat and sunglasses if you have them. No one needs to see your face."

With instant recognition of what I'm saying, he nods. "Of course. Give me a moment, please. I'll help you load him up."

His Italian accent has disappeared now—something I'm pretty damn sure is intentional.

This brother of mine might be a lot savvier than I realize. The fact that he's not flipping out or reacting like a civilian tips my curiosity into overdrive.

Who is he, this brother of mine, that this situation doesn't faze him? A question to be satisfied another time, obviously.

Within moments, he's back, wearing a New Orleans Voodoo Kings hat and expensive, dark sunglasses.

"Do you happen to have duct tape as well?" I ask my brother.

"Yes, and I also have zip ties."

Why he has them, I have no fucking idea, but I can't help but grin. "Excellent. Those will work perfectly."

"Who the fuck is that guy?" The kid tries to jerk around to get a look, but my grip on the back of his neck keeps him facing the direction I choose.

"You don't get to ask questions. You're lucky to be alive. For now."

"Fucking kill me then. I don't care. I ain't telling you shit."

"You already did, kid. You're a terrible shot, by the way."

With a shove, I propel him toward the SUV. My brother is already popping the back hatch and returning with a pack of long, clear zip ties.

"Planning a kidnapping?" I ask as he pulls a few out and proceeds to slide them around the wrists of the shooter and then his ankles.

The familiar *zipping* sound is the only response I get at first.

Once the kid's wrists are secured, his reply is matter-of-fact. "Preparation is the key to success."

I give the zip ties another yank to drive them tighter against the kid's skin.

"I like you even more already."

"Who the fuck is this guy?" the shooter asks as he nearly cranes his neck, trying to get a better look at him.

"Get the duct tape. He doesn't need to see or hear."

"Wait!" The kid struggles against my hold and the zip ties when he realizes we're about to stuff him in the back of the SUV. "No! Just fucking kill me here! Leave me here!"

My brother returns with a roll of black duct tape, rips off several inches, and hands it to me.

I slap it over the kid's mouth as his eyes go wild.

"Don't try to kill the boogeyman and fail. That's when things get very scary for you."

I look at my brother. "Give me the roll."

With a nod, he tosses it to me. Fear fills the bright blue eyes of the kid who stares back at me.

"Trying to die before you're even old enough to shave?" I ask as I yank a strip free and slap the end over one ear before wrapping it around his head to the other, covering his eyes last.

Like we've worked as a team before, my brother grasps the boy's other arm, and we load him into the SUV. His body flails, but my brother pulls the kid's back against his chest as he wraps an arm under his throat. It happens so fast; all I can do is blink.

"Go to sleep," he says.

The kid's legs quit flailing as I stare, wide-eyed, at my brother.

"Did you just—"

My brother shakes his head. "Of course not. He's unconscious. He'll be fine when he comes to."

What the fuck is happening to my life? Who is this man who looks like me?

Suddenly, Keira's reservations and questions seem a hell of a lot more pertinent than they did yesterday.

"Where did you learn to—"

"We should go. Quickly. Get your friend's ashes. I'll get the kid's gun."

Stunned into silence, I follow another man's orders for the first time in decades as the familiar sound of wailing sirens greets my ears.

"Fuck." I bolt into the mausoleum, grab V's urn, and run to the SUV.

I slam the door as he shifts into drive, and at a sedate pace, we make our way out of the cemetery and turn onto the main road. As we blend into traffic, the black-and-whites light up the cemetery entrance with their red and blue bubbles as they block the road we just exited.

"Who the fuck are you?" I ask, jerking my gaze to the man beside me.

A smile curls his lips. "Your big brother. Glad I could finally be of service."

CHAPTER ELEVEN

KEIRA

My phone rings, and I lunge for it. *Lachlan.* I pick up immediately.

"Are you okay?"

"Yes, but there's been a change in plans." The tone of his voice is cryptic, and my heart leaps into a galloping beat.

"What kind of change in plans? I don't like changes in plans."

"There was an unexpected guest at the service who now requires my attention."

I force myself to take a slow, deep breath. This is not my first rodeo. *I will not freak out. I am Keira Mount. This is my life, and I can handle it.* "Please tell me that doesn't mean what I think it means."

"I didn't get hit."

Hell. It does mean what I think it means.

"I really, really, really hate when people try to kill you. I am not okay with this."

"Hellion—"

The argument we had this morning about Lachlan wearing a bulletproof vest to the funeral pops into my head. "And you didn't think you needed a vest today. Aren't you glad I made you wear it? This is *not okay*, Lachlan."

"You're brilliant as well as a goddess among women, my love. I'm okay. Everything's fine. Don't worry about me. Thankfully, he was a terrible shot. Really, an embarrassment to shooters everywhere. But that also means I won't be home as quickly as I promised you."

"Lachlan ..."

He sighs heavily over the phone. "I know I made you a promise, and I will keep the part where I said I will come home safely."

"I don't want to be a widow, and our daughter needs a father."

"I know that. I have help with me. I'm not alone. Everything's fine."

"Who?"

This was another part of our argument this morning. Lachlan going by himself. I couldn't believe it. He would never normally do such a thing, but nothing has been normal this week. *Nothing.*

"A familiar face," is all he says, and it finally clicks that the shooter who tried to kill him might be listening to our conversation as well.

I choose my words carefully, just in case.

"You're not serious. *He's* there? The guy from yesterday?"

I can't for one second imagine the man with the perfectly tailored Italian suit, who looks exactly like my husband, is helping with *whatever* Mount is about to do to the man who tried to kill him. Because this will be *Mount* doing whatever he's going to do. I can't think of him as Lachlan when I know blood will be spilled. Compartmentalization is something I've become highly skilled at since I entered his world. Healthy or not, it's how I handle this crazy life that I call mine.

"Yes, and he's been very helpful."

"I don't even want to think about what that means. Where are you going?"

There's a beat of silence.

"You know I can't say. I just called to keep you informed so you wouldn't worry about the change in timeline. You have everything you need for much longer than you'll be there. I'll be back as soon as I possibly can."

I release a long breath, my shoulders drooping as I drop onto the sofa. "Is this really necessary?"

"Would I leave you alone for longer than I planned if it wasn't?"

It's a rhetorical question, as I already know the answer.

"For the record, I don't like this. You're not taking precautions. Things are getting dangerous—even for you."

"I know, and I'm sorry, Hellion. So fucking sorry. This isn't the life I want for us anymore. Just … give me some time to handle business, and I'll be home."

I've never begrudged Mount his business. I've always known what I was getting with him. It's not like our relationship started out in any normal fashion. I know exactly who I fell in love with.

I grind my teeth together. "My patience is wearing thin, but I trust you. Do whatever you need to do and then *come home to me and our daughter.* Otherwise, I'll be the one you need to fear. Do you understand me?"

"My fierce, beautiful wife. What did I do to deserve you?"

"You blackmailed and extorted me."

He laughs. "Someday, I'll make that up to you."

"You already have. Go do what you need to do and then get your ass back here. We have a lot to talk about after this."

"I'll be there as soon as I can. I promise, Hellion. I love you. Give my baby girl a kiss from me."

"I will. I love you too." As soon as I finish whispering the words, the call ends.

I yank my knees up to my chest and wrap my arms around them. Slowly and carefully, I breathe in and out, focusing on the predictable, even movements of my lungs and nothing else for as long as I can manage.

What am I going to do with him? What is happening to our life?

"I'm so freaking tired of people trying to kill my husband," I say to the seafoam-green walls of the safe house before closing my eyes and dropping my forehead onto my knees. "What kind of life is this for Rory? How can we keep doing this?"

With another deep breath and long exhalation, I center myself. *You knew what you signed up for, Ke-ke,* I remind myself. But that doesn't change the fact that I don't like it at all right now. *Not at all.* Not one single little bit.

CHAPTER TWELVE

MOUNT

"A strong room?" My brother looks around the room, lit with only a single bare bulb hanging from the ceiling, as he nods at the chair in the center. "I don't want to know what you've used this for in the past, do I?"

I drop the kid's feet as my brother holds his struggling body upright.

"Don't think too hard about it. You might give yourself nightmares," I reply and then pause, remembering what he did at the cemetery. "Then again, maybe not. You're full of surprises, aren't you?"

He smiles like the Sphinx, but the dark sunglasses still block his eyes. I pat the kid down before we sit him in the chair. The bulge in his back pocket gives away just what an amateur he truly is.

I yank the wallet free, locate his cell phone in his front pocket, and help settle him on the chair. "What kind of assassin brings his wallet to a job? *Idiot.*"

With the roll of duct tape in hand, I stick the end to his lap and wrap it around and around until there's no way he's getting off this chair, bolted to the concrete, until he's dead or I'm ready—whichever comes first. I give his torso the same treatment before pulling a knife from my pocket. With a single press of a button on its side, the blade springs free, and I slice the zip ties from his wrists. Once each one is secured to a metal arm of the chair, I reach for the end of the duct tape covering his eyes.

"This is going to hurt," I tell him, mercy completely absent from my tone. He's getting all the mercy he deserves in the fact that I haven't killed him yet.

Are you going to kill him? A kid? Who clearly is terrible at his job? The questions float in my mind, but I ignore them. All I can do is flow with the situation, however it develops.

Before I tear the tape away, I glance at my brother. "You should go."

"I'm not leaving you alone to do this."

"You don't exist," I tell him, hoping he understands what I mean. *He can't be seen. No one can know there are two of us.* For reasons I can't articulate, I know it's vitally important we keep it that way.

"I understand, but I need to see the injury first. Let me look before you take off the tape. I have a field dressing kit in the Suburban."

The kid struggles against the tape, unintelligible sounds coming from his sealed mouth.

"Shut up and stop moving if you want to live longer than five more minutes."

He stills, belying his words at the cemetery. Also, it shows just how much he can hear despite the duct tape over his ears.

"Get the kit and do what you need to do. Then, I get

my answers."

My brother nods and leaves the room.

"Who the hell are you, kid?" I say to myself as I flip open his wallet.

The blue eyes from the cemetery stare back at me from his ID.

Dumbass. You never bring a real ID to a job.

Clearly, he's either a moron or a rookie—or both.

But it's the name that stops me cold.

Remy de Marchand.

"Fucking hell." I drop my head back and stare up at the metal ceiling. "The Marchands are trying to fucking take me out? After all these goddamn years? You've got to be fucking kidding me."

My brother returns in the midst of my tirade. "You know the boy?"

I shake my head. "No. But I know his family." I look down at the license again and do the math quickly. "And they sent a seventeen-year-old to kill me? What the fuck is that about? If Leo and his old man wanted me dead after all these years, why would they send a kid? That makes no fucking sense."

My brother sets a large olive-colored canvas cube on the floor. "Seventeen? That's much too young to be having gunfights before noon."

"No shit. See what you can do to patch up his shoulder. It doesn't feel right to let him bleed out."

I stand and turn away from the boy. Staring at the wall, I murmur, "I'm getting too old for this shit." I drop my forehead into my palm. With my thumb and middle finger, I squeeze my temples. "What the fuck am I supposed to do with him?"

The kid makes a sound that must come from the pain of whatever my brother is doing to him, and I turn to watch.

"Do I kill him? Why would the Marchands start a war with me now? Do they really think I'm that weak? *Fuck.* This doesn't make sense. There's never been bad blood between us. They run their business in a way that doesn't interfere with mine, and we've always had peace. *Always.*"

My brother looks over his shoulder at me. "Would you really kill a child? Look at him. He's not even a man yet."

"Then, why would they send him to kill me? Why wouldn't Leo, that fancy fucker, come do the job himself? Why send a kid?"

My brother turns back to the silent form taped to the chair and presses what I assume is a quick-clotting sponge to the still-bleeding wound at his shoulder.

"He'll live. The bullet went straight through. Once the bleeding has stopped, I'll look closer. I can sanitize it and sew him up, but it would be better if he were taken to a hospital. I don't know what other damage the bullet might have done to his shoulder."

"They won't take him to a hospital. They'll have their own doc stitch him up. That's how this shit works. But, fuck, *why Marchand? Why?*"

I no longer have any interest in talking to the kid. Based on how he shot his mouth off at the cemetery, whatever he says will only piss me off. It's Leo and Old Man Marchand who will have the answers I need.

Well, at least I know how to get them to talk to me. *I have something that belongs to them.*

And if they want him back alive, they'll do what I say. After all, New Orleans is still my city.

CHAPTER THIRTEEN

MOUNT

"I need you to leave the room," I tell my brother's back. "Tape the clotting sponge on. I need a minute alone with the kid."

He turns to look at me, and it makes me pause. It's uncanny to stare at my own reflection, even with the hat and dark glasses blocking half of his face. I don't know if I'll ever get used to it.

"He's a child."

I shake my head. "It's not for the reason you think. Just… give me some space."

Without questioning me further, he rises to his feet and nods. "I'll be waiting outside."

It's not the same as working with V. He and I could work together without speaking. We were on the same wavelength in ways that defied explanation. Perhaps all those years together had us thinking much the same. Plus, he rarely questioned me. Only a few pivotal times do I remember him forcing me to pause and reconsider what I was doing. It was always well timed though.

Fuck, I miss my best friend.

But as my brother leaves the room, closing the heavy metal door behind him, I can't help but realize that even though life took someone from me who I didn't think I'd ever have to live without, it gave me something so precious in return that I still can't believe it's real.

Palming the cell phone I pulled from Remy's front pocket, I thank the Almighty for the stupid advances in technology they've made that benefit men like me. *Gotta love Face ID.*

Crouching down in front of the kid, I grasp the corner of the duct tape. "Brace yourself."

I don't know why I bother to give him a warning. He didn't give me a fucking warning before he started shooting—putting a priest in the line of fire, no less.

I yank on the end, and as the tape pulls away, it brings bits of hair and skin with it. Muffled cries come from beneath the strip over his lips.

"Actions have consequences, kid. Don't fucking shoot at someone like me unless you're damn sure you're gonna kill the target. Life gets very uncomfortable if you don't."

Tears tip over the lids of his blue eyes and slide down his cheeks—more as an automatic reaction to the pain, I'm assuming. Or maybe he really is just a scared kid who's in way over his head.

I think of myself at seventeen. *He wouldn't be the first to get too deep into things he didn't truly understand.* But somehow, I managed to survive, and there's a decent chance Remy might live to see his eighteenth birthday. *Decent, not guaranteed.*

I grab the corner of the strip of tape covering his lips. "One more."

He squeezes his eyes shut as I rip it free.

"Fuck, that hurts!"

"Shut up. That's nothing compared to what I could do to you." I toss the tape aside. "Kids these days. Fucking soft. You'd never survive on the streets."

"You don't know shit about me—" He starts to run his mouth, but instead of paying attention to his words, I hold the phone up in front of his face.

Instantly, it unlocks. I look down at the screen to see a picture of him with his arm around an equally young girl.

"You're the worst fucking assassin I've ever seen. Who's the girl? You care about her?"

He shuts his mouth.

"That's what I thought. Do you have any idea how fucking easy it would be for me to have her picked up and brought here in less than an hour to watch you be tortured to death? What the fuck, kid? Why would you ever put someone you care about in danger? Thoughtless. Fucking thoughtless."

Fear, the likes of which I haven't yet seen on his face, causes his entire body to still.

Reality checks aren't fun, but that's what makes them real.

I tap a few spots on the screen, and it brings me directly to his favorite contacts. "I bet that's Lily, isn't it?"

With a few more taps, I have her address.

I turn the phone to face him. "You see this? This is how you get people killed. You're a fucking idiot, Marchand. I would've thought Leo or the Old Man would've taught you better before they used you to start a war."

"They didn't! Don't touch her. I'll fucking kill you."

He wrestles against the tape, but there's nothing he can do to get free.

"You feel pretty fucking helpless right now, don't you? You made some very poor decisions today, kid. Decisions are what plot the map of your life. Life is like a game of Chutes and Ladders. One bad decision can have you sliding all the way down into a pile of your own entrails, where someone you love dies with you. Do you get what I'm saying, Remy? It was a *bad fucking decision* to try to kill me."

His jaw tenses, and I have to give him at least a little credit. He's not shooting his mouth off anymore. And he hasn't pissed himself, which is admirable. Plenty of grown men would've by now if they were in his shoes.

"She didn't do anything." His tone is a lot rougher and less cocky now.

I smile as I tap around some more on the screen of his phone. "Your whole life is in here, kid. Rule number one of being an assassin: don't bring anything to a job that can identify you or get people you love killed. I can't believe they didn't at least tell you that."

"I'm not an assassin. No one sent me."

I huff out a laugh as I find what I'm looking for—*Uncle Leo*'s contact information. "I believe you about the first—you're a piss-poor shot, and you made every rookie mistake in the book. The second … I'm not so sure about yet. But I bet Uncle Leo is going to tell me the truth." I glance at the kid's face, watching it go pale. "At least if he wants to see you alive again."

He swallows, and his Adam's apple bobs in his throat.

"You can't be more scared of Leo Marchand than you are of me."

The kid looks down and to the side.

Well, that could help.

I pull a burner phone from my pocket and punch in Leo's number. It's one I could have easily gotten another way, but this was more fun. The kid has plenty of lessons yet to learn.

Before I initiate the call, I walk to the toolbox against the wall. Inside it are things no human ever wants to see while they're duct-taped to a chair beneath a single bare light bulb. But instruments of death aren't what I'm looking for.

Ahh, there we go. A pin. Using it, I pop the side slide on the kid's phone and remove the SIM card. We don't need Uncle Leo tracking him to my exact location.

I drop both the cell phone and the SIM card into a Faraday cage as a precaution, then turn back around to face Remy de Marchand.

"Smile," I say as I snap a pic of him with my burner phone.

He looks a bit rougher than he did at the cemetery while shooting at me, but he's alive, which makes today his lucky day.

I send the picture to Leo's number first.

"Let's hope your uncle keeps his phone on him."

I have to give the kid some credit. He doesn't say a word. I look at the clock mounted to the wall behind his head. The second hand ticks fifteen times before my burner phone rings.

"You're going to regret this until your last breath, which won't be long in coming," a cultured voice says as soon as I answer the call.

"Why did you send your nephew to kill me?" I ask in response.

"*What?*" The shocked reply tells me everything I needed to know, even before he continues, "I'd never fucking send him to—*who the fuck is this?*"

"Ahh, Leo, I thought you'd never ask. You're speaking to Lachlan Mount."

"*Merde,*" he says in a hushed tone. "*Mon Dieu.* Fucking hell. No fucking way. I didn't send him. Why the fuck would I do something so stupid? He's a kid, Mount. A stupid fucking kid. Please, whatever he's done—"

I cut him off. "He unloaded an entire mag at me in a cemetery when I was trying to lay my best friend to rest. He nearly killed a priest as well."

"Fucking hell!" He sputters something in French that I don't catch. "I'm going to fucking kill him!"

"You're going to have to get in line, Leo. I'm not real happy with the kid myself right now."

I hear him pounding on something, and I can only imagine what's going through his mind.

"If you didn't send him to kill me, then why did he unload on me in a cemetery and almost kill me and a priest?"

"Because he eavesdrops and his French is shit."

I pause, no longer having quite so much fun at the Frenchman's expense. "So, you are trying to kill me. Now, after all these years of peace, you think starting a war is a wise idea?"

"No! That's not what I said! He eavesdropped on a conversation between me and my father."

"Old Man Marchand wants me dead?"

"No! Fucking stop saying that, Mount. That's not what we were talking about. We don't want war. Not with you. Not with anyone. We just want to run our business in peace. You understand? *In peace.* Fuck, he's my late sister's only kid. I promised her I'd protect him. Please, whatever you want, it's yours if you spare his life. You want a Van Gogh? Picasso? Renoir? A Degas ballerina? Anything."

"Your black-market art doesn't interest me nearly as much as what he overheard with his shit French."

Leo goes quiet. "I can't have this conversation over the phone. It's not safe. Please, Mount. Spare his life. He's a stupid kid. Still in high school. He plays football. He's not a killer."

"And yet his actions say otherwise, especially the suppressed handgun."

"Fucking hell, *Remy!*"

"I saw the opportunity, and I took it!" the kid yells.

"Shut up," Leo and I bark out at the same time.

"Fuck," Leo continues. "You're well within your rights to kill him. Clearly. But I am begging you, *show mercy.* Please. He's just a kid. A *stupid* kid."

I run my tongue over the fronts of my top teeth as I consider his request. I already didn't feel right about killing the kid, but still … I need answers.

"He said there's a new king in town. Who is it?"

"I can't talk about this on the phone. Please, Mount. Bring him to me. I will give you all the information you need. It will save your life—and your family. But if you kill him, I won't tell you shit, and your family will pay the price as well."

Cold chills—the likes of which I only get when things are about to get super fucking serious—skitter over my skin, and the hairs on the back of my neck and arms stand tall.

"If you're lying to me …"

"I'm not an idiot, like my nephew. You know that."

"You'll get him back after I get my information. You understand? You tell me *everything* in person, and then I'll decide if it's enough to let him go without teaching him a lesson he'll never forget."

"How can I trust that you'll let him go?"

"I guess we'll both just have to take this one on faith, Leo."

He spits something in French, but switches to English. "Fine. But we talk here. Every place you have is compromised, and I'm not getting involved with the nightmare that's about to explode in your face."

"You don't get to make the rules, Leo. I'm calling the shots here."

"And I'm trying to do this smart. Leave the kid where he is, if he's not going to die before you return him to me. You can give the word to let him go after you hear what I have to say. I promise, it'll be worth it to you."

"You'd better fucking hope so," I say into the phone. "You'd both better fucking hope so."

I pause and add, "If you double-cross me—"

But Leo doesn't let me finish. "I didn't get this rich or stay alive this long in my business by being stupid. I respect you, Mount. I always have. The house of Marchand does not want any part of this. I want Remy home safe. That's it. I have no reason to want you dead. I like the balance of power in New Orleans just as it is. As far as I'm concerned, I wish I'd never heard what I have to tell you."

The chills I felt return with a vengeance. My gut tells me I need the information he has. Something big is going down.

"Consider my curiosity piqued. I'll text you the details for the meet. Don't start doing anything stupid now. The kid's life depends on it."

CHAPTER FOURTEEN

MOUNT

"You're going to let me go?" the kid asks as I reach for another roll of duct tape out of the toolbox.

"Don't ask questions, kid. You're so far out on a limb here, it's a miracle you're still alive. Any other day but today …" I trail off as I rip a strip from the roll and turn to face him.

His eyes widen at the duct tape. "Come on, man. Not again. That shit sucks coming off."

I can't help but laugh. Only a stupid seventeen-year-old would think he gets any say in what happens when he's duct-taped to a chair in a room where many lives have ended.

"I don't trust you, kid. You're a wild card. Your uncle is lucky he and his old man have always been helpful and never fucked me over before."

I slap the tape over his lips before he can reply. I crouch in front of him and meet his hardened blue gaze.

"If you're fortunate enough to be alive when someone rips this tape off your lips again, take that pain as a reminder that children shouldn't be playing men's games. Go back to school—back to *Lily*—play football, and then do something fucking useful with your life that doesn't involve trying to kill grown men who would normally tear you apart limb from limb simply for the insult. Do you understand me, kid? You will never be hard enough for this life. *Never.* And trust me, you don't fucking want to be."

He narrows his eyes, and I can't tell if I've gotten through to him, but at this point, I don't care.

I rise and brush my hands off on my suit pants—reminding me that I'll need to shower and change before I go home to my wife.

I turn around and cross the room to grab a black hood from beside the tool chest. "Now that the after-school-special part of this is over, it's time to get back to work," I murmur as I drop it over his head.

With three strides, I reach the heavy metal door and haul it open. My brother waits outside, leaning against the wall, as I shut it and throw the heavy metal bar to bolt the kid inside.

"Ready?"

He nods. "Of course. Whatever you need me to do."

"That's exactly what I hoped you'd say. We have a meet to set up. And I can't do this without someone I trust, and today, that just happens to be you."

His lips curve into an instant smile as he pulls the sunglasses down. "You've never had someone at your back that you could trust more, brother."

"I'm starting to believe that. Let's see how you handle what's coming next."

~

"A boat? Really? Is that safe?" Marco asks as I drive us in a nondescript Toyota Camry along the river while explaining where I plan to meet Leo.

"You're going to make sure I'm safe. How are you at long-range high-caliber target shooting?"

"You want me to be your sniper?"

As I brake for a red light, I glance over at him. "Can you do that? If not, tell me now, and I'll find someone else."

"No, no. I can do it. Our father loves target shooting. He trained me himself in the Dolomites."

Our father. I have a father. The reality of the statement nearly causes me to miss the gas pedal as the light turns green.

As much as I want to ask what our father is like, I can't think about that right now. "Good. Then, you'll be fine. I have a sniper's perch for you and a few different options for rifles."

"You've used this spot before?"

"Yes. And no shots have ever had to be fired, so I consider it a lucky one."

"Good, because while I will do whatever I must do to protect you, brother, I will be very honest with you. Taking a life is not on my agenda for today."

"I wonder what that's like," I can't help but whisper under my breath.

Marco overhears my quiet statement. "It's quite wonderful not to deal in death, brother," he replies.

"That's a privilege I didn't get, growing up on the streets. Only the strong and smart survive. The more ruthless you are, the less people will try to fuck you over, take what's yours, or think you're an easy target to kill."

"You don't have to justify who you are to me. I understand that though we may be blood, our environments forged us into very different men." He reaches out a hand to squeeze my shoulder. "I am just happy that you survived."

"I'll be happy when I survive today," I tell him. "I don't ever take that for granted."

I pull into a parking lot and guide the car into a spot. As I shift the Camry into park, I turn in my seat to face him. "This is what we're going to do …"

CHAPTER FIFTEEN

MOUNT

The outboard motor on the johnboat sputters predictably as I maneuver it into a shadow not far from the coordinates I sent Leo.

Having a conversation in the middle of the Mighty Mississippi might not be the norm for others, but I use every resource I have at my disposal. My creativity has kept me alive in more complicated situations than this. But I know better than anyone that I can never let my guard down. There is no easy, safe meet with anyone. Not when you're Lachlan Mount.

I've spent my whole life looking over my shoulder. Staying alive has always been my top priority—at least until Keira and then Aurora came into my life. Now, they are my world. And keeping them safe and alive matters more than anything, including my own personal safety. I would throw myself into a hail of bullets without a single thought if it meant that Aurora and Keira could live free from fear of being kidnapped—or worse.

There's nothing I wouldn't do to protect my wife and daughter. Nothing.

Whatever information Leo has, it had better be as important as he says. The last thing I want to do today is shower off more of his nephew's blood. I just want to go home to my wife, kiss my daughter's sweet face, and forget this day ever happened. With that last thought of them, I put them out of my mind.

I can't chance being distracted for even a single second of this meeting. Leo Marchand is no fool. He was right when he said he wouldn't have gotten this rich or stayed alive this long in his business if he was stupid.

But still, I can't imagine what the kid overheard to make him think that trying to kill me was a good idea. The chills from earlier haven't left my awareness. It feels like something big is coming, and it's not a welcome feeling.

At least now, I'll know.

Knowledge is power. That's always the damn truth. Even when it's things you wish you didn't have to know.

I glance down at the battered Rolex on my wrist. It's been through hell with me, and I refuse to lay it to rest. It's a reminder of all I've faced and survived against odds that were never in my favor. I remember telling Keira once that I wanted it to be buried with me. *That didn't go over well.* She doesn't like to talk about the possibility of me dying.

Stop thinking about her.

I have to force myself to return my attention to the water. At precisely 6:09 p.m., an old shrimping trawler chugs up the river and slows at the coordinates I sent Leo.

"At least the French bastard is punctual," I murmur to myself as I wait for him to drop anchor. As soon as the metal hits the water, I notice a white flag flying off the stern, where the boat would normally fly the flag it sails under.

A rough chuckle escapes my lips. "Surrender or parley, I wonder?"

With a hand on the outboard, I tug the longshoreman cap over my brow and putter up to the stern of the boat.

"Permission to come aboard for parley?" I call out, hoping against all hope that Leo followed my instructions to the letter and came alone.

"Permission granted. You're welcome aboard with no reservations. The rules of parley are in effect aboard this vessel."

Glancing up at the tower where my brother sits as my sniper, I grab the coiled line at my side and toss it up to where that fancy fucker Leo stands.

"A three-piece suit aboard a shrimp boat? That's gotta be a first."

"My father always taught me to dress for the job I wanted, not the job I had," he replies with a trace of his French accent. "Shrimp boat or luxury yacht, a pocket watch always seems like an appropriate accessory."

"Only you, Marchand. Only you."

He ties off the line on the cleat at the starboard end of the stern. "I trust you can make your own way up the ladder."

With one last thought thanking no one in particular that my brother has my back, I reach for the metal rungs screwed into the wooden transom of the boat. "I got it. Just don't make me fucking kill you when I get up there."

"I'm French and the son of a merchant marine, Mount. I take parley seriously. I wouldn't endanger my nephew's life to kill you. I have no reason to want you dead. I like you perfectly well alive."

His words wash over me as I climb the rungs and swing a leg over the stern with my senses and instincts on high alert.

First, I scan the boat. "Are you alone?" I see no signs of life, but I can't be sure about what's down below.

"Of course. I would not double-cross you. I told you, I value the life of my nephew much more than you do."

My gaze travels over every inch of the boat that I see. "No one below?"

"No. I give you my word of honor. Would you like to see for yourself?"

My gaze locks on Leo. A lion's mane of golden hair, tanned skin, blue eyes, like his nephew. The collar of his white shirt is unbuttoned beneath his open navy pin-striped suit jacket with a white-and-gold pocket square. The gold chain of his pocket watch is clipped on his vest.

"Do I need to go see for myself?" I ask.

"No. I have no doubt that if I had henchmen below and they killed you, I'd receive my nephew back in pieces. Am I right?"

My chest rises and falls with a sharp laugh. "I doubt it'd even be that pretty. In shreds, more likely."

Leo pales beneath his tan. "I believe you. I came alone. I brought nothing with me but the information that I promised you."

A barge blows its horn as it comes up behind us, and I have to stop myself from drawing my pistol.

"And you didn't tell anyone where you'd be or who you'd be with?"

"Not even my father. He thinks Remy is with his girlfriend."

"Ah, yes, the young Lily. He makes for a shitty assassin, Marchand. Truly, the worst I've ever seen."

Leo's golden mane tumbles as he shakes his head. "He's not an assassin. He's a tight end on the football team. He's much better at that."

"Then, he should stick to football and leave the suppressed gunfire in broad daylight to the gangsters, like me and his uncle."

"I prefer my suppressed gunfire in the moonlight to daylight," Leo says, attempting a grin that looks forced.

"Enough small talk. Tell me why it happened, Marchand. Tell me everything."

"Come. Let us go inside. It's best if we're not seen together."

I point to his suit. "That's your fault. No one would recognize me in this." I gesture to my workingman's pants and stained shirt.

"Your wardrobe is your choice. Mine is a statement."

"Then, lead the way," I tell him.

"Of course. I have no fear of turning my back on you, Mount. You have no reason to kill me either. Consider it a sign of my trust."

"Consider it whatever you want, Marchand. I came for answers."

My hand hovers over the butt of one of my pistols as I follow him into the covered helm area. There's no one rushing up from below to kill me, so I take that as a sign of his trust as well.

Leo eases a hip onto the captain's chair and lifts his chin. "Feel free to sit."

"I don't need to sit. This shouldn't take long, I assume."

"No. The information I have is devastating, but it won't take long to deliver. I'll start with what my nephew overheard." He jams a hand into his hair. "I still can't believe he tried to kill you."

"Believe it."

With a tug at his golden locks, he begins, "There is a new player in town. His name is Kostegov. I don't know exactly which Eastern European hellhole he climbed out of, but he's a piece of work. He's declared himself the new King of New Orleans."

Instantly, I catalog the name. It doesn't ring any bells. *Fuck. How do I not know it? Am I that out of touch with the threats against me?*

"That's awfully bold for someone new to town," is all I say in reply.

"I'd never heard of him before. It was the Russians who told me. They have a taste for fine art. We were sharing a bottle of vodka, nearing the end of it, when his name came up. I thought it was bold as well—at least until they told me who is backing him. A name I know you've heard before. A palm I would guess you've greased before as well."

"And who's dumb enough to bite the hand who feeds him?" My mind shifts into high gear.

I've greased a lot of palms in my day. Criminals, civilians, dirty law enforcement, politicians, and officials at every level. His description doesn't narrow it down for me.

"John Pierre DuFort."

The chills I felt earlier skate across every inch of my skin. "The Fed or the father?"

"Both, as I understand it."

It takes everything I have to control my emotions and my expression so that I show no reaction to Leo. But inside, I'm screaming, *Fuck, not them.*

"*Fuck*," I let the curse slip out.

"Yes, that is why I said your places in this city are no longer safe for you or your family. They won't just take out you; they're coming for your—"

"Stop right there." I bite out the order. "Don't even say it."

Leo raises both hands in front of himself. "*Mea culpa.* But the threat is real. They know all about your fortress being breached, your daughter being kidnapped, and V being shot down. You're exposed. They smell blood in the water. The Russians say they're moving in any day. They won't miss this opportunity. Time is of the essence. They'll strike hard and fast to take you out—from both sides of the law. You were not supposed to see it coming."

For the first time in my life, I'm thankful someone tried to kill me. If Remy Marchand hadn't started shooting this morning, I wouldn't have known that a dirty Fed and his father, one of the joint chiefs of staff, were coming to take my head.

I might have been able to take on the cartels ... but this is different. This family ... they're not fucking right. I've heard the rumors. I've seen pictures. People might think I'm the devil, but the DuForts *actually* worship Satan.

It has taken every bit of my resources to keep as many of the kids of New Orleans safe from their fucked-up perversions ...

"You have a lot to process, my friend. I understand this is unwelcome news."

I can't help but laugh humorlessly as I stare up at the rotting roof of the trawler cabin. What the hell else am I supposed to do? "It's just another day in the life of Lachlan Mount."

"I do not envy you this life, Mount. I do not envy you at all. But as they say, with great power comes great responsibility."

I jerk my chin down to pierce him with my gaze. "What else do you know?"

"Nothing really. The Russians work with John Pierre, the younger, although the connection was made by the father. They are not happy that he's moving in this crazy Kostegov. According to the Russians, he's not stable. He's a savage and a loose cannon."

"Coming from the Russians …" I trail off.

Leo finishes the thought for me. "That's saying something, I know." He crosses his arms and leans back. "You see why I was not displeased you called me today, except for the circumstances. I like the balance of power in New Orleans exactly as it is. I don't want a savage loose cannon in charge of my city. With you, I know what to expect. With change, no one knows."

When I don't reply immediately, he prompts, "What will you do?"

I tilt my head to study him. "You know I wouldn't tell you even if I had a plan right this very fucking moment."

Leo smiles, looking more like a lion than ever. "Fair enough. Now, is that enough to free my nephew without further harm? I love the kid, even if he's a pain in my ass."

"You're not lying?" I know I don't have to ask, but I

can't be too careful. Not with this information that feels like someone handed me a ticking time bomb.

"Of course not. I wouldn't lie about this. You see why I couldn't tell you over the phone. I can't trust that the Feds aren't listening to my every word at this point. None of us are safe now. Not a single fucking one of us, which makes me very unhappy. I like my life. I don't want it to change. But it seems, change is the one constant over which none of us has control."

With a nod, I assure him, "Your nephew will be fine. Call your doc and have someone pick him up on the corner of Canal and Bourbon at 7:05. He'll be getting out of a black Sprinter van, wearing a jester hat, like the idiot he was this morning."

"Fair enough. We'll patch him up. Thank you for showing mercy."

"That wasn't mercy. That was me not being into killing kids. Which is more than I can say for those sick fucks coming after me. Have a good life, Leo. I appreciate the information."

As I turn and stride out of the cabin, Leo calls after me, "America is no longer safe for you, my friend. The DuFort tentacles have a long reach, and they will not show mercy."

I salute him before I climb over the side. "Thank you, Captain. Parley is concluded."

As I make my way down the metal rungs, my mind races.

Fuck, things just got serious.

CHAPTER SIXTEEN

LACHLAN

The Camry is already running when I make it back to the parking lot. I'm still in my rough clothes and longshoreman cap, but I don't care. Normally, I wouldn't think of returning to Keira without showering and changing into a fresh shirt and suit, but today is different. Today, nothing is normal.

I let myself inside and shut the door.

"Did you find out everything you needed to know?" my brother asks in a conversational tone, like I didn't just ask him to potentially snipe someone.

For some reason, his ability to roll with whatever life throws at me is comforting.

"Yes," I reply as I grip the steering wheel with both hands.

It's tempting to slam my head against the center, but that would be a show of weakness, and there's no time for that.

"Is it as serious as he alluded to on the phone?"

I filled my brother in on what Leo had said before I

went out on the boat. I figured, if things went south, *someone* had to know who to kill and why.

"Yes." I shift the Toyota into drive to begin a long, circuitous route back to the safe house. "Shit. I have another call to make. Grab my phone, will you?"

With my mind on the mess that's been unleashed in my life, I almost forgot about the kid. *Get it together, Mount. Now's not the time to get sloppy.*

Marco offers me the phone, and I put the car back in park for a second as I dial a number I know by heart. My cleaner picks up on the third ring, as per usual.

"Joyful Cleaning Services, Joy speaking."

"I need a recycling run made from the metal plant."

"A trash run?" Joy—a three-hundred-pound man who loves money, fried food, his mother, and me for saving her life—replies.

"No trash. Recycling only. Mardi Gras–style. Pick up at the metal plant at your earliest convenience. Drop-off on the corner of Canal and Bourbon at 7:05 p.m. Don't be late. Make sure the drop goes smoothly. Treat it like a care package."

"Got it," Joy replies, tone more serious, which calms any concerns I could possibly have. "We have one care package, Mardi Gras–style, for recycling. Metal shop pickup. Corner of Canal and Bourbon at 7:05 p.m. sharp for drop-off."

"Perfect. Thank you, Joy."

"Have a blessed day. Thank you for using Joyful Cleaning Services, where your business is always appreciated."

I hang up the call, hand the phone back to my brother,

and shift the Camry into drive. We're on the move again before he speaks.

"The boy goes free?"

I turn left at the first light and nod. "That was the deal. Marchand made good on his end, which means I live up to my word."

Out of my peripheral vision, I catch a glimpse of Marco crossing himself. Glancing over at him, I ask, "Did you think I wouldn't?"

"I'm learning a lot about you very quickly, brother. What I understand so far is that you are a man who lives by his own rules, which I respect very much. I respect even more that the boy gets to live. Well done."

His approval isn't something I needed or asked for, but it feels good all the same.

"Another thing I've learned is that you don't say much about very big things. Things that sound very serious."

I check my blind spot before I change lanes. "Habit. I've never had someone I could share everything in my life with."

"What about your wife?"

With a shake of my head, I catch Marco's gaze. "Would you want to bring home news of death and blood to your wife? I would never burden her with everything I do and have done. It's not hers to bear. There are a lot of things that she will never know, and that's exactly the way it needs to be—for her and for me."

A few beats of silence pass before he replies, "What do we do now?"

My mind has been wrestling with that very question since I climbed off the trawler and back into the johnboat.

"Do you still have a jet on standby?" I ask as I take

another turn that will lead us in the opposite direction of the safe house.

"Of course. I didn't know what to expect, so I came prepared for anything."

Without looking at him, I say, "Call your pilot. Ask how long it will take to be ready to fly."

"We're leaving?" Surprise colors his question.

Stopping at another red light, I turn my head far enough to meet his gaze. "I have to get my wife and daughter somewhere untouchable as soon as humanly possible."

The energy in the car shifts, and I know the seriousness of my tone is not lost on him.

"It was that bad?"

"It is what it is. A goddamn nightmare come to life, to be honest. But it doesn't matter. The only thing that matters is keeping Keira and Rory safe. They can't be touched by this."

Another few beats of silence pass.

"What about you? Are you staying or going? I will remind you, our mother will return, as she said, regardless of any potential danger, if you do not go see her when promised."

Running from a problem isn't something I've ever done. My whole life has been a series of challenges taken head-on. But this … this is different. This is … I don't even know exactly what I'm dealing with yet. And what's worse, the only people I can trust are those who share my blood or a bond of marriage.

No wonder I don't feel like I can trust my people. I have no idea if DuFort has already gotten to any of them. Anything is possible when Satan's spawn comes to play.

The possibility of staying behind and sending Keira and Aurora off with my brother without me enters my mind anyway. *What if tonight is the last time I ever see either of them alive? What if I never see my mother again? What if this is the only opportunity I have for this kind of happiness? How can I waste it?*

Sharp pain rips through my gut at the prospect, and that's all the answer I need.

"I made a promise to our mother." I pause, feeling the surreal nature of the words deep in the depths of my tattered soul. "And I'm going to keep it. We all go together. Call it a family reunion."

CHAPTER SEVENTEEN

KEIRA

The sounds I've waited for all day finally come as darkness falls. Still, out of habit, I pull a gun when I hear the garage door. Instead of one set of footsteps, my senses heighten, and my heart thumps harder as I hear two.

Thankful that Aurora is fast asleep in the baby's room, I move in front of her door, pistol in hand. "Honey? Is that you?"

"Yes, with a welcome guest." Lachlan's voice comes from around the corner.

"Thank God," I whisper as I come away from the door and set the pistol on the table behind the sofa.

As soon as he walks into the room, I catalog every feature of my husband's face.

Drawn. Tired. Yet still sharp and alert as ever. *Because he never gets to let his guard down.* We all need a vacation after the events of the past week. I don't know how much more we can take. My nerves feel a hairbreadth away from being totally shot at the strain of it all. And yet we persevere, because that's who we are.

It takes me a second to realize that Mount isn't the one wearing the suit. He's wearing a long-sleeved black shirt and black pants.

Having two of them is making this even crazier. My mind reels as I take them both in.

"Are you okay?" I walk toward my husband as he opens his arms to me.

Only once they're wrapped around me, squeezing me hard, do I feel like my world is something I recognize once more.

"I'm fine. We're all fine. That's what matters most."

I know there are a million things he's not telling me, and that's par for the course with Mount. Because he was Mount today, not Lachlan.

"What happened at the funeral?"

"It was interrupted, thankfully," he says against my hair.

I jerk back to meet his gaze. "Thankfully?"

Lachlan's expression is grave as he nods. Instinctively, I swallow the lump that swells in my throat.

"How bad is it?"

"I'll tell you everything after we eat something. We're starving. Where is Rory?"

I point to the closed door. "Sleeping, but that doesn't matter. Go see her. She needs her daddy."

Lachlan presses a kiss to my lips. "I love you more than life itself," he whispers as his forehead rests against mine. "Thank you for being so strong. I swear that I will spend the rest of my life making this up to you."

I bury my fingers in his silver-threaded black hair. "Whatever it is, we'll handle it. That's what we do."

As he pulls away, he presses a kiss to my forehead. "I

don't deserve you, but you're mine forever, Hellion." His words are barely above a whisper.

"Always. No matter what," I say, concern rising as I take in the serious set of his features.

Something happened. Something bad.

I don't know how I know, but *I know*. That can wait until they're not starving though.

"Go see Rory. I'll heat up what I thawed from the freezer earlier. It's not haute cuisine," I say, glancing at Marco, "but you won't be starving anymore."

"Anything is perfect," Marco replies. "I could eat a hoof at this point."

I smile at him, still in borderline shock from just staring at him. *They look nearly identical.* Down to the silver at the temples. It's just … uncanny.

That's when I recognize one key difference—Marco's face has different creases. Like he's spent much more of his life smiling than Lachlan, whose creases tell of a life spent deep in thought, which is exactly what it has taken to keep him alive and out of prison.

I want Lachlan to spend the rest of his life smiling. My heart grows wings at the fanciful thought. Right now, he can't even tell me what happened today because it undoubtedly included bullets and blood. *A constant in our life.* Even if I don't see it directly, I'm well aware of who my husband is and what his business entails.

I push all of that out of my mind and busy myself with reheating the pot of jambalaya on the stove for them both. Thank goodness it smells amazing.

Come what may, at least I can feed hungry men.

I have my husband, his brother, and my daughter with me under the same roof, I remind myself, focusing on what's right in front of me. *And that's something to be very grateful for.*

～

With Marco in the restroom, freshening up before dinner, Lachlan finds me in the kitchen, and we finally have a moment of privacy.

He leans against the counter, watching me stir the pot on the stove. I try to keep the words back, but I can't do it any longer.

"I know you said later, but I need to know what to expect."

My husband's nearly black gaze locks on mine. As is his nature, he doesn't waste any time or any words. "We have to leave. It's not safe for us here any longer."

"Leave the safe house?" I ask, searching for clarification as the spicy scent of jambalaya wafts around us. Something in the seriousness of his posture tells me that's not what he means.

He crosses his arms over his chest. "Leave the country."

I inhale a sharp breath. "For how long?"

Lachlan takes a step closer to me, grasping my hand to pull me away from the stove. "I don't know. But we have to go. Tonight."

"What about the distillery? Our home? Our employees? My family? Our life?"

He glances up at the ceiling before meeting my eyes once more. "If we don't leave tonight, none of that will matter."

Heat rises in my chest as my heart thumps faster

against my rib cage. For the first time, I know I can't settle for euphemisms and half-truths.

"Tell me *everything*, Lachlan. What's going on? I need to know. If I'm leaving everything and everyone behind, I deserve that much."

He presses his lips together, and I know he's calculating every word he's going to speak. Lachlan Mount does nothing without measuring the effects of it before it happens.

"You deserve everything. *Everything.*" He pauses and takes a slow, deep breath and lets it out before continuing, "If we stay here, there's a man and his father who don't just want my head; they will arrest you, throw you in prison, take our daughter. And the things they will do to her will break her body, shatter her mind, and destroy her soul—in that order."

Fear—*icy-cold fear*—the likes of which I've been feeling all too often lately, settles deep in my bones. *I will not let it overtake me.* I fight hard to maintain my composure and not give myself over to it. "What are you talking about?"

"The truth. The cold, hard fucking truth." He shakes his head. "These aren't gangsters coming for us. They're coming out of the darkness, but with the might of the United States government behind them. That's not something I can fight in the way I always have. Do you understand?"

"The Feds?" I ask as I realize my worst nightmares are manifesting as we speak.

"And worse. Which is why we have to go. You have to be untouchable. They can never get their hands on you or Rory. *Never.*"

"Lachlan—" I start to speak, but he interrupts me.

"I can only protect you until my dying breath. That's the one thing that haunts me. After I'm gone, I have no control over what happens to you. I need to know that you're both protected—for the rest of your lives. I can never rest in peace without knowing that."

"Lachlan—" I start again, voice shaking.

"Keira, listen to me. We're leaving tonight. I don't know if you're ever coming back. You will never know how sorry I am that it has to be this way, but this is the hand life dealt us. We have no choice but to respond. And my response is to protect my family at all costs. I don't care if my empire crumbles. It means *nothing* compared to you and Rory." He grips my upper arms, and I stare directly into his dark eyes as he continues, "I don't care what happens to your distillery. I don't care what happens to our home. I don't care about anything but your safety and happiness and that of our daughter. Do you understand me? Whatever it takes to ensure that, that is what I will do. Don't ask me to change my mind or my plans. This is how it has to be."

Tears fight to tip over my lids, but I blink them back. *I am Keira Mount. I signed up for this life. I know who I married. I knew what my choices could mean.*

The piper always shows up to be paid one day, and it's never the day you expect.

"I understand," I say, lifting my chin as I breathe through my nose. My entire body leans toward him, as though drawn like a magnet. "I'll pack our things. We'll be ready quickly."

My husband yanks me against his chest, and his arms

lock around me. "My brave, fierce wife. I didn't know it was possible to love anyone as much as I love you."

I snake my arms around him and squeeze him as tightly as I can. I know he won't break. Not my husband. He's strength personified.

"Whatever happens next, we go together. That's all I ask. *We go together*. Don't send me and Rory away from you."

His arms tighten their grip around my body as he whispers into my hair, "We go together, Hellion. We go together. That much I can promise you right now."

CHAPTER EIGHTEEN

MOUNT

I release Keira reluctantly when I hear the door to the bathroom open. With another kiss to her forehead, I inhale her scent and pray that I haven't sentenced her to hell with me.

She doesn't deserve this. She deserves so much better.

A husband who doesn't have to rush his family out of the country on less than an hour's notice. One without enemies who do unspeakable things …

But she got me, and I'm not giving her up, regardless of what that makes me.

Marco's voice interrupts my thoughts. "The plane is ready whenever we are. I would suggest we hurry though, as the pilot mentioned an airport official who has been asking him probing questions."

I lock eyes with Marco and catalog the concern I see there. *Fuck. I don't like that.* "Then, we go." I look over at Keira. "Forget the food. Pack fast. We're getting out of here."

Instead of breaking down in hysterics, like many

people would, whether male or female, Keira's steel-hardened spine stiffens as she flips the stove knob to off. "It can go down the disposal," she says without a second thought. "I'll hurry. It won't take but a few minutes. We'll be ready." She moves around me, heading for the baby's room.

My wife is fucking amazing. I only have a second to marvel before I call out, "Don't mind the sounds you hear next. I have to—"

She holds up a hand without turning back. "Do whatever you need to do. Let's get the hell out of here."

My brother watches me as I smile at my wife's back.

God, I love her.

I wipe the smile off my face as quick as it came and point to the sofa. "Help me move this?"

"Of course."

We each take a position at the end of the sofa and squat down. It's still uncanny, watching him move like me. My questions about the nature versus nurture debate are mounting by the hour.

"We need to move it away from the wall."

He nods, and we easily lift the sofa and move it toward the kitchen. I return to the wall, remove the Lake Pontchartrain landscape that decorates it, and hand it to Marco.

He doesn't ask questions, which is just one more thing I like about my brother.

My brother ...

The words hang in my head comfortingly as I step back a couple of feet. Thankful for the heavy boots I have on, I kick a hole through the drywall two feet above the floor on the right side of the stud V hung the picture on.

Then another lower. And another to the left. And another below that.

When I'm done, Marco is beside me, hands helping me to pull the drywall away from the studs.

"Holy shit," he says as I pull out black duffel bag after black duffel bag. "It's like a movie."

"Where do you think they get their ideas?" I ask with a laugh as I set them carefully on the floor.

There are four bags in total. Everything my family needs to walk away and never look back.

The shock on my brother's face is mirrored in his eyes as he meets my gaze. "You planned for a moment like this."

"I plan for everything. One thing I've found always to be true: cash, extra passports, gold, and guns are useful every damn time."

"And the wall?"

"Once we put the couch back, the hole won't be visible. Besides, no one living knows about this safe house except us. No one has a reason to come inside. However, if it ever becomes a liability, the house could be gone in seconds."

He blinks in confusion. "What do you mean?"

"The house is wired to blow."

"But the neighbors—"

"They're far enough away that a blast wouldn't affect them. That was a main concern when we picked it. Plus, the fire department is three minutes out and well equipped. A blaze wouldn't spread. It would look like a gas leak. V thought of everything. That was his job."

My brother shakes his head like he can't believe what I'm saying. It's a lot to comprehend for anyone, especially after the day he's been through. *A day in my life.* We might be twins, but we're not the same—that's for sure.

"I'm strangely impressed. You do think of everything."

"It's how we stay alive. But fireworks are unnecessary right now. No one has any reason to be looking here, and even if they did, they wouldn't find anything but holes in the wall behind the couch." I replace the picture on the wall before grabbing the handles of two of the duffels. "Grab the others. We're taking the minivan in the garage. It has a car seat for Rory. I'll come back to dump the food."

As soon as the words are out of my mouth, my wife steps through the doorway of the baby's bedroom with a pink bag on her shoulder and a fussy Aurora in her arms.

"She's ready. I kept most everything packed. I just need to grab my bag. It's on the bed."

"My princess," I say, walking over to press a kiss on my baby girl's face. "There's no reason to fuss. Mommy and Daddy are taking you to a new kingdom. One without monsters."

Instantly, she calms down, like she always does when I'm near.

I never knew I could be good with a baby. It was as shocking to me as it was to Keira. But then again, I never knew an innocent, precious princess could come from a man like me.

And she'll never be threatened again. Ever. No matter what I have to do or who I have to become, my daughter will never again be touched by this. She will never know anything but love for the rest of her life. I've sworn it over and over, and there's nothing I've ever meant more in my life. I will make it reality, whatever it takes.

"Thank you," Keira whispers as Aurora snuggles more comfortably in her arms.

I lift the strap of the bag from her shoulder. "You get her in the car seat. Marco and I will load everything up and deal with the food."

Keira's gaze darts to the drywall-dust-covered duffel bags before returning to my face. "I love you so fucking much. Thank God you are who you are."

A gorgeous smile, under the most unlikely of circumstances, gives my wife's entire countenance a radiant glow. To Aurora, she whispers, "See, there's nothing to worry about, baby girl. Daddy's got everything covered, because that's what Daddy does."

My lips curve in response to my wife's beautiful smile and confident words, but I won't breathe easy until we reach cruising altitude.

I glance down at the watch on my wrist. *Less than an hour, and we're out of this fucking country.*

CHAPTER NINETEEN

KEIRA

A small part of me wondered if our departure from the airport would include a shoot-out, but when the jet lifts off the runway and Lachlan is safely belted into the plush leather seat beside me with Aurora on his lap, I thank every power in the universe for getting us out of New Orleans safely.

Thank goodness we're safe. Thank God we're together. The words repeat over and over again in my mind as we climb and turn in the direction of our future.

Lachlan's words from earlier have stayed with me. *"I don't know if you're ever coming back."*

The enormity of what that could mean hasn't really hit me yet, but there's one thing I've had to learn since I entered the world of Lachlan Mount: to flow with whatever happens and make the best of it.

They don't teach you the skills I've needed to survive the last few years of my life in any school or college. Instead, this has been my front row seat in the university of real life. Fixed goals, plans, and opinions? Out the window.

Learning to adapt, overcome any challenge, and thrive, no matter what life throws at you? Those abilities have become invaluable. I've had to learn to trust more than I ever knew was possible. I've had to learn to bend beyond my limits—without breaking. And most shockingly of all, I've learned intense lessons about the depths of my faith within the darkness of my husband's world.

Being Lachlan Mount's wife has been nothing like I expected. I've been loved better and more deeply than I ever knew was possible for a person to be loved. And in return, I've loved harder and more fiercely than I ever was capable of before. My soul feels complete in a way I've never experienced. I have my soulmate beside me, and he holds my heart in his hands. Our daughter has brought us even closer together than I ever thought possible and forged new bonds between us. Aurora has given us both purpose and brought out new sides of Lachlan that I never knew could exist.

That first day in my office, he was a dark, shadowy figure, sitting at my desk—the boogeyman come to life to drag me into the underworld. He destroyed the tiny little existence I had been grasping and clinging to, and in exchange, he gave me an entire new world.

I could never have anticipated where life was going to take me as a result of the debt he said I owed him. I thought my life was ending, but in truth, it was just beginning.

I wouldn't trade any of it to go back to who I was or the life I used to live.

Every single thing that I value most came out of what seemed like the worst thing to ever happen to me.

It's a fact that's never far from my mind. It's the reason I live life differently now. It's the reason I didn't lose my mind when I had to walk away from everything tonight with almost no notice.

I trust that life is leading us where we need to go. It hasn't let me down yet, even during those moments when all hope seemed lost.

I reach out and grasp Lachlan's hand, giving it a squeeze as I gaze at the beautiful face of our daughter.

We got her back safely, against all odds. She's still totally and completely perfect.

If that didn't give me unshakable faith in life, I don't know what would.

Before tears can well in my eyes, I look up and blink a few times. And right in my line of vision is another reason to trust that everything is going to be okay. *Lachlan has a twin brother. And he came into our lives at exactly the right moment.*

I pull myself together, because I want to laugh and cry at the same time. It's the overwhelm of the insanity of the last week, combined with the soul-deep gratitude I have for the feeling of safety and security now wrapping around me from all sides.

We might not know exactly what awaits us on the other end of this flight, but it's not the bullets and blood we're leaving behind. My research into Lachlan's family while I waited at the safe house, alone with Aurora, gives me that certainty. What little I could find on the living members showed me that they don't live a life anything like the one we're leaving behind.

And the life they'll be able to provide for their

granddaughter … the possibility was unthinkable only forty-eight hours ago.

It makes me think of something I read years ago—that our destiny is granted with compassion. That we only know what we need to know when we need to know it. We're kept in the dark about our futures often because it's the kindest thing for us. I've never felt that it was truer than right at this moment.

Everything is going to be okay.

Lachlan squeezes my hand in return. "Are you okay?"

Blinking back the emotions engulfing me, I nod. "I'm good."

His dark, searching gaze caresses my face. "Sleep, Hellion. You need it. We're all safe now. Everything's going to be fine."

My features soften as I let go of any worry about the future. *Everything's going to be fine.* The tension leaks out of my frame as our fingers tangle together.

"I know. I've got you and Rory and a family we didn't know existed." A full-body yawn escapes me. "I love you. I'm going to rest for a little while," I say through the yawn as I wipe the moisture from my eyes and settle deeper into the thick cushions of the reclining leather seat.

"I love you too. Sleep. I'll be right here when you wake up."

CHAPTER TWENTY

MOUNT

Keira's breathing shifts in less than a minute. With a glance, I know she's asleep. Over the last few years, I've made a study of my wife. She's the most interesting subject I've ever devoted myself to, and I have no doubt she will be for the rest of my life. *However long that might be.*

As if taking a cue from her mother, Aurora releases a sigh and settles against my shoulder. Her chubby fingers ball into a fist that she drools on as she descends into sleep.

The silence of the cabin is permeated by the sounds of the jet engines and the four of us breathing.

"Your family is beautiful," my brother says quietly. He's no doubt keeping his voice low so as not to wake them.

I lift my gaze from Aurora's perfect little fingers and meet his. "It's more than I deserve. More than I ever knew was possible to have."

His lashes lower as he takes in my sleeping daughter.

"You're a lucky man. I'm glad you realize how lucky you are."

I nod as Aurora's tiny breaths heat a small patch of my skin beneath my shirt.

"The luckiest there ever has been." I lift my head to meet my brother's gaze once more. "We'll see how long that luck lasts."

My brother shakes his head ever so slightly. "Don't think about it like that. It does no one any good."

It takes me a moment to process that I'm being told what to do. A man in my position isn't ordered around very often. Until my wife, no one dared. The corner of my mouth curls when I realize I'm about to have more people in my life who believe they can be free with their opinions on how I should live and be. Instead of bristling against the potentiality, I let my smile free.

"You're my older brother by how many minutes?" I ask jokingly.

His grin comes much quicker than I have ever known how to smile. "Enough minutes to feel I can give you advice. I apologize if I sound bossy. I suppose I'm making up for lost time. I've waited many, many years to have my younger brother back. Forgive me."

"No forgiveness required. It's a new experience for me. Other than Keira, most people never tell me what they truly think. It's part of who I am. My presence doesn't exactly invite good-natured suggestions."

His grin grows until the smile lights up his entire face. He glances down at his watch for a beat and says, "Just give it twelve hours. You're about to be in a different world, brother."

Marco's comment reminds me of the question I've

been holding since before takeoff when I heard him speaking on his cell phone in Italian. More than ever, I wish I spoke the language.

"Did you tell her we're coming? Our ... mother?" The word comes out as though it were also of a foreign tongue. It's not a word I've had much cause to speak during my life, especially in reference to myself.

I have a mother.

It's still surreal to think about.

"Of course," Marco replies. "I wouldn't have lived it down if I hadn't. But that also means I need to prepare you for what you're about to experience."

"Prepare me?" I ask, wondering for a fraction of a moment if I've somehow gotten us into a situation I finally won't know how to handle.

"Given what I've learned about you today, I assume you're the kind of man who prefers to know exactly what's coming if you possibly can."

"Undoubtedly."

His smile widens, tugging at his cheeks in a way I don't think my identical face has ever been tested. It's odd to see the expression in the mirror sitting across from me. Something tingles within me, but I don't have time to figure out what it is before he continues speaking.

"Borderline spectacle."

The back of my head hits the pillowed headrest of the seat as I draw back in surprise. "What?"

Marco laughs quietly. "I know you have no frame of reference for this, so I'll try to explain the best I can." He pauses, as if searching for the words in English. "Our mother has waited over forty years for this day. She has dreamed of your homecoming for over *four decades.* You must understand that she is a very creative woman. *Exceptionally creative.* And combine that with the most closely held dream of her life coming true in your arrival, you must brace yourself because she will not be able to hold back from the pomp and circumstance."

I raise a brow. "Pomp and circumstance? I don't understand."

Marco's smile gives the indication of an inside joke, but it doesn't feel like it's at my expense.

"We're meeting Mother on her island."

"Her island?"

"Yes, it's been in the family for nearly five centuries. She doesn't leave it very often."

"She's a recluse?"

The beautiful woman I met in the hangar didn't seem reclusive to me.

Marco tilts his head from side to side, still smiling so widely that his eyes are creased at the corners. "Ehhh ... more or less. She's an eccentric. She has no reason to want to leave often. It's a beautiful place. Like Eden. She's not wrong to stay there either. Most of the outside world isn't nearly as beautiful as the world she inhabits daily."

My mother lives on an island that's been in the family for over five hundred years.

It's mind-blowing information, but Marco stated it like it's no big deal. I suppose for him ... it isn't. It's normal.

"How big is the island?"

His shoulders shrug. "Big enough. But not too big. She has a villa and terraced gardens. Her favorite place is the conservatory, where she paints."

"She's an artist?" I savor the knowledge like it's a

treasure. *My mother is an artist, an eccentric, and a recluse.* I like her more and more by the moment.

"Oh, yes, a very accomplished artist. Her paintings are famous. They grace galleries, private collections, and museums all over the world."

I'm taken aback by this admission. "Seriously?"

Marco's nod is proud. *Because he's a proud son, and I'm growing prouder by the moment.*

"Oh, yes. They're highly sought after by collectors. Extremely valuable. She's made the family exceptionally wealthy through her artwork. That's what has kept her sane these last four decades. Painting." He pauses, and I'm simply blown away.

I made my living in the darkness, and my mother's artwork is world-renowned.

"This is why you must expect a spectacle," he continues. "When I say that … I refer possibly even to pyrotechnics."

"What?" Aurora shifts against my chest as I blurt out the word on a half laugh.

Marco and I still, as though both making sure we don't wake the females sleeping on and beside me.

With his voice quieter, Marco continues, "Yes. As in fireworks. Those will wait until dark, most likely. But expect a red-carpet arrival. All the staff lined up to meet you on the terrace. And flowers. The flower arrangements will be massive. All cut from the gardens. It takes over twenty gardeners to tend to them all in a beautiful and orderly fashion."

The words he's speaking are coming at me, but my brain feels slow in processing them.

Fireworks?

Red carpet?

Terrace?

Flowers?

Twenty gardeners?

For the first time, perhaps ever, I'm dumbfounded. I have no idea what to say or think. *Can this even be real?* It doesn't seem possible, but there's no hint of duplicity in his words. He's completely sincere.

When I don't reply, Marco continues, "I know it sounds ... excessive, and likely, it will be. This is why I'm telling you now—to prepare you for what is coming." He pauses with another bemused smile. "I'm sure you're more accustomed to being welcomed by bullets than red carpets, but this is the life that is waiting for you. It is nothing like the life you have left behind. You are like a prince who is being returned to his kingdom. Our mother will spare no expense, and no detail will be overlooked. And the food ... I can only imagine what kind of banquet she'll have prepared for you."

"With guests?" The question comes out rougher, simply because my family's safety is my first priority and I can't expose them to people I don't know—at least not beyond those of my blood. Not yet anyway. I need the lay of the land first.

"No, no," Marco replies with a shake of his head. "Absolutely not. This is family only. This is simply our mother welcoming you home, along with the daughter she's always wanted and a grandchild she's dreamed of holding for more years than you know."

I note the one person he hasn't mentioned. "What about ..." I swallow before I speak more words that are foreign to my tongue. "Our father?"

Some of the lightness and joy dies out of Marco's dark, sparkling gaze. "No. Father will not be present. As we told you, he doesn't know you are alive."

My fingers itch to grip the arm of my seat, but I can't without disturbing Aurora. Instead, I hug her gently.

"He still doesn't know I'm alive? Why haven't you told him yet? Why hasn't she?"

Another shake of Marco's head gives me at least one answer before he speaks. "No. I suppose I should explain why." He releases a long breath before shifting in his chair and crossing an ankle over one knee. "Our mother and father are estranged. They've been estranged since Mother was recovered from the kidnappers … and you were not."

A few beats of silence pass before he continues, "From what I have been told and have experienced my whole life, losing you destroyed our family, our parents' happiness, and their marriage. They have been estranged my entire life. I've never seen them in the same place together. *Ever.*"

"Never?"

He shakes his head again. "No. Mother and Father do not see each other. They are never in each other's presence. They live completely separate lives, although they are still technically married. Neither one believes in divorce or dividing the family's assets."

The knowledge blows me away. *Losing me destroyed them. Their marriage. Their happiness.* My brother grew up with parents who wouldn't be in each other's presence because *they had lost me.*

How is this even possible?

I don't realize I spoke my last question aloud until Marco answers it. "They are both very stubborn people.

Perhaps that's where you get the determination to live your life, brother. Our parents are quite impressive in their stubbornness."

"I don't know what to say."

Marco's smile returns, but it's more sheepish than before. "It is a unique family—I will grant you that. But there is much love. Mother is overjoyed, awaiting your return, and when Father is told of your existence, he will …" Marco purses his lips for a beat before continuing, "He will be stunned and thank God. And he will be elated at the existence of your daughter. He will finally have an heir to his empire, which is something that has weighed on him heavily for many, many years. Now, he will be able to rest, knowing that the Giordano family line will continue after he is gone and his life's work and dedication to his heritage was not for nothing."

I assess my brother, trying to keep up with everything he's saying. One question stands out in my mind. "Why didn't you have a child to give him the heir he needed? Or are you … not so inclined?"

Another long sigh leaves Marco. "I would have if I could have, but I am unable to have children. There was a fever that swept the country estate where I was living with Father the summer I turned sixteen. We both took ill, along with dozens of others. Some didn't survive, but those who did all shared one fate in common—we were left sterile. No longer able to have children." A blazing warmth comes from him as he looks at me with Aurora nestled in my arms. "Undoubtedly, you would have faced the same fate, but God spared you. You can still create life. Perhaps that is why you were taken from us. So you would still be able to hold your perfect daughter in your arms."

Fate isn't something I spend much time thinking about, but with Marco's revelation, I'm nearly leveled by what might have been.

If I hadn't been kidnapped, I wouldn't have everything that matters most to me in my life. I inhale a sharp breath. My hand cups the dark curls crowning my daughter's head. Silently, as I fight the tears welling at the thought, the words *thank you* burst through my mind. *Thank you for making me a father. Thank you. Thank you. Thank you.*

As if he knows what I'm feeling, Marco says, "You see, all things work together for good. We might have missed much of your life, and you were removed from your heritage and those who loved you, but none of it matters now. All that matters is you coming home. Our parents will both be ecstatic. If you could only feel the joy that beats with every thump of my heart, you would understand. It is a feeling like no other. All will be beyond grateful for your presence and the happy family that comes with you. It is poetic, if you'll allow me such sentiment."

I blink back the tears that have gathered against my will. "I had no idea. About any of it. About you. About them. I could never have imagined."

"Of course not. How could you? I know it must be much to process, especially with how different your existence has been. But you have been loved every day from the day of your birth until now, whether you knew it or not. And this is why you must expect a spectacle from our mother. I would not be surprised if she found doves to release." With that comment, he chuckles, and a tear rolls freely down his cheek.

What must it be like not to care that another man sees you cry? The question ghosts through my mind before I feel a wet trail sneak down my cheek that I'm unable to brush away with my hands full with my sleeping baby.

I decide that I don't care either. In this moment, there's no one to call me weak. Not even myself. Because I don't know who I am anymore.

I don't feel like Lachlan Mount.

I don't know who Luca Giordano is yet.

But I don't care. I don't need a name to feel the joy rolling off my brother that's taking up residence in my own heart. A heart that I thought was dead and black until Keira woke it from its death-like slumber and Aurora's birth sent it bursting through my chest with a love I never knew I was capable of feeling. And now … an entire family. A mother, who anticipates my return with such excitement that she might find doves for the occasion …

A quiet laugh escapes me, joining the chuckles of my brother.

"What a life, man. What a life …"

My brother's smile nearly splits his face in half. "It's a good one, brother. A great one even. I cannot wait to introduce you to all you have missed. It will be my pleasure and my honor. You have no idea how long I've waited for these moments that are to come. It will be incredible to have our family reunited once more. If the beating wings of my heart could fly this plane, we'd be there in moments instead of hours."

CHAPTER TWENTY-ONE

MOUNT

As I try to comprehend just how massively my life is about to change, the woman who saw to our comfort as we boarded the jet pads silently up the aisle, stopping next to me and Marco. She takes note of the sleeping ladies and smiles.

"Can I get you gentlemen anything to eat or drink?" she asks in a whisper. Glancing at me, she says, "Mr. Giordano mentioned you would be hungry on the flight."

With her question, my stomach releases a grumble. I'm impressed that she isn't looking from me to him and back again, taking in our similarities. As we were boarding, Marco mentioned she'd been with the family for years and was eminently trustworthy.

"Food would be welcome. Thank you," I reply.

"What do we have for the flight, Margarite?" Marco asks.

"We have a lovely sautéed garlic chicken with steamed vegetables and whipped potatoes. We also have a spring mix salad and, of course, pasta with sauce made from the

Giordano family estate tomatoes." She glances at me. "And if you prefer something else, sir, I have more options."

"The chicken and vegetables would be great. And obviously, I have to try the pasta and sauce."

Marco smiles as I speak. "I hoped you would. It is better freshly made and eaten in the kitchen at our country estate, but at least, this way, you will taste part of your heritage sooner." He inclines his chin as his gaze shifts to Keira. "Should we wake her to eat?"

I look over at my wife, who is sleeping like she's dead to the world. "No. She needs the rest."

"Whenever she awakens," Margarite whispers, "I am happy to fix her a plate. There is no need to worry that she will go hungry if she does not eat now."

"Thank you," I reply. "And the baby ate before we took off, so she'll be fine for a while."

Margarite nods with a sunny smile. "Excellent, sir. And to drink?"

"Still water."

"Wonderful. And for you, Mr. Giordano?" she asks, turning her attention to Marco.

"I'll have one of everything you mentioned with sparkling water. Thank you for preparing it quietly so as not to awaken our guests."

"Of course, Mr. Giordano. I will be as silent as a mouse." She dips her chin before moving back toward the galley.

"Rory could sleep through a hurricane and not wake up. Keira and I were both stunned when Mardi Gras didn't even wake her."

Marco smiles at my sleeping daughter. "She's a

Giordano through and through then. Our father could sleep through the end of the world and miss all the festivities."

The mention of our father draws my immediate attention. I have so many questions, but I start with one. "What is he like?"

Marco's smile dims its wattage as he leans back in his chair. "You will meet him soon. He is ... he is hard to describe. As dark as you and me in coloring and occasionally in his mood as well. He has his own demons that he wrestles with, of which he does not speak. He can be a hard man, but he is a good father. Firm. Exacting. But loving in his own way. He took being a father very seriously. He wanted to make sure I became a man who could handle the responsibilities that would come upon my shoulders, and he is proud of who I have become ... although he does not approve of all of my decisions. He would have been happier if he could have made them all for me instead. But he is a good man. A strong, proud man. You will like him. He will like you very much. He will be amazed at who you have become and what you have accomplished without any of the resources that you should have had at your disposal."

Marco's description of our father leaves me wondering what I will think of the man who sired me. I understand having demons to wrestle with that you can't speak of with others. Perhaps he and I will have more in common than I would have guessed.

"I look forward to meeting him."

My brother's smile brightens once more. "It will be the shock of his lifetime. To see you—a copy of him at a younger age—and both of us together." Marco laughs, as if anticipating how our father will react in his mind, before continuing, "I don't know that he will believe his eyes at first. But once he touches you, he will know you are in fact real. I cannot imagine how that will change him to know that you are alive and safe and prosperous."

In that moment, it hits me that Marco might have grown up with extreme wealth, luxury, and parents, but every moment of his life was affected by my absence. While I knew nothing about my family, except for childish daydreams I would indulge in when reality became too hard to face, they all knew I existed and was stolen from them. From how he spoke of our stern father and eccentric and reclusive mother, my absence must have felt like a ghost haunting them all.

Not knowing what I was missing, I made the best life that I could out of the cards I had been dealt. The Giordano family instead lived a life that was forever altered by my disappearance.

Our conversation falls into a lull, overtaken by the drone of the jet engines for several minutes.

When Margarite reappears with place mats and cutlery, she pauses before setting them down on the table between us. "May I?"

"Of course," Marco replies with a wave of his hand. "Although I do not know how my brother will eat with a baby in his arms."

"It won't be the first time," I reply with a wry smile. "Fatherhood has taught me more lessons and tricks in a short time than I ever thought I would learn. Doing things one-handed or one-armed has become the norm. At least for now."

"Why do I get the sense that you wouldn't hand her off

to me for the world?" Margarite asks with her tone just above a whisper.

"Because you're a perceptive woman, clearly," I reply, looking up at her. "And this little one is my princess. She's safest in her father's arms and always will be."

Margarite presses one hand to her chest. "Oh, my heart. I believe it just melted. There's nothing like a father besotted with his daughter." With a genuine smile, she spreads out navy place mats and white cloth napkins before carefully setting out the cutlery piece by piece.

As she retreats once more, Marco meets my gaze. "Given the events of your day and what I gather about your life ... your sentiment about your daughter delights me but also surprises me. Although perhaps it shouldn't. Our gentle mother is fierce, like a lioness, when it comes to me—and now you. Our father, however, has never been quite as demonstrative in his affections."

I shift Aurora against my chest, where her heart beats against mine. "I never knew I could love anyone as much as I love her. Like our parents, I know what it's like to have her stolen from me." I shudder involuntarily at the memory as the remaining traces of the gut-wrenching, heartrending moment sweeps over me. "It was absolute horror. Like something out of a nightmare."

"I can't imagine," Marco says quietly. "I thank God with you that she was safely returned."

I nod, breathing in her sweet baby scent. "Before she was taken, I loved her and spoiled her. Now, it's hard for me to be away from her. I want her in my sight as much as possible. In my arms is even better. She's a treasure. The most precious gift I've ever been given. I want to shield her from everything dark in this world—because I know how much there is. That's the reason we're on this plane. If it were just me and Keira, it would be different. But not with my princess Aurora. She deserves far better than the life she was born into, even though it was a life of luxury. It was tainted. Hell, I'm tainted. But … she's my second chance. My chance to be the man I didn't know I could be. And I want to be that man for her. I want to give her the world. A perfect, beautiful world that's nothing like what I've known."

"That perfect, beautiful world is awaiting you, brother. Life is giving you exactly what you didn't know was always yours." His gaze dips to Aurora's dark curls of the same color. "And she will be the princess at the center of it. She will want for nothing. She will have the best of everything. And more than that, she will be safe. You all will be."

A niggling thought pushes its way into my mind. "I don't think you can guarantee that. Even you said someone tried to kill you, thinking you were me. Where? When?"

"I was in New York. It's not a city I enjoy. But do not worry about that. He cannot tell the tale. And on our family's properties, you will be completely safe. Italy knows nothing of Lachlan Mount. You might have been famous in other circles, but they do not extend there. Otherwise, we would have known of your existence much sooner. Someone would have said something about the similarities between us. Our worlds do not collide, brother. Have no fear of that."

His reasoning isn't exactly as sound as I'd like, but once I sort out the situation, I'll make sure Keira's and Aurora's safety is guaranteed. That's a job I take seriously every single day and will for the rest of my life. Now, it's my purpose in life, for as long as I get to live. And for the first time ever, instead of being haunted by the thought of what would happen to them after my own death, I feel something that approaches peace.

My brother will take care of them. And my father. And my mother.

They're words I've never thought before, but they fill me with hope for the future. A future I never knew could be possible.

CHAPTER TWENTY-TWO

MOUNT

W hen Margarite arrives with our meal, Keira doesn't even twitch at the scents.

She is exhausted, I remind myself. Where I was used to being nocturnal, she has always slept soundly. But not this week. She has barely slept at all. Like me, she didn't want Aurora out of her sight. It was too much for her.

Silently, I thank the powers that be for gifting me with such a woman. The only one who ever tempted me enough to face the risks of tying myself to her forever.

The night we were married, beneath the stained glass, is one of the best memories I've ever had. I will never forget Keira's beauty, bravery, and dignity in that moment when she agreed to become the wife of the most terrifying man she'd ever met. She truly is a queen among women.

Every day, I work to become worthy of her. Someday, perhaps I'll succeed. But I haven't *yet.*

My thoughts are interrupted by Marco's movements as he removes his suit jacket and folds back the cuffs of his shirt before he reaches for his silverware.

For the first time since I saw him, I see something that doesn't look like I'm staring into a mirror.

Bold black inked lines peek out, and I recognize cherry blossoms wrapping around both of his wrists. Taken aback by the discovery, I stare, open-mouthed, at my brother.

"If we were already in Italy, I would say you could catch flies that way, brother," he says good-naturedly at my reaction before I can suppress it.

"You're tattooed." I state the obvious.

He grins. "Quite."

No way. No fucking way.

His grin is contagious.

There's no way my proper, well-mannered brother, who was raised in the lap of luxury, has ...

My thought trails off as I remember him saying our father wished he could make his decisions for him.

No fucking way. You've got to be kidding.

Just like earlier today, I realize that my brother is full of surprises. And I like him all the better for it.

"I've seen those kinds of tattoos on men in suits before. But they were always Japanese gangsters," I say, unable to keep the amazement out of my tone.

Marco smiles, and I read a bit of enjoyment on his features. "Rest assured, I'm not Yakuza. But ... I do share their affinity for a beautiful body suit."

"No fucking way." Normally, I wouldn't curse with Aurora in my arms, but I'm too stunned at the moment to school my language.

His grin widens. "Does it make me sound American to say, *Yes way*?"

"How? Where? No wonder our father wanted to make

your life choices for you. How does he explain the heir to his empire having a body suit?"

"It is a long story, but we have a long flight ahead of us, so we have time, I suppose. The how is with great patience, although quite painfully at times. The where is Japan. I spent several years there during my wandering phase that commenced when I turned eighteen and left Italy and our parents behind. And our father doesn't address it. I wear a suit anywhere I go with him, although he has never asked me to do so. I do it out of respect."

My mind is running to keep up with his revelations. I want to know everything about this man who shares my face and my DNA.

"Tell me your story. I would love to hear it."

He turns pasta on his fork and savors a bite before he begins to speak. "I was raised in almost complete and total seclusion from the world. After our parents lost you, they were not willing to take a chance that they could lose me as well. I never saw the outside world. Only our family's properties and estate."

Thinking about how I felt after getting Aurora back, I reply, "I completely understand their reasoning."

He takes another bite and swallows before replying, "I'm sure you do, but although I didn't know it was unusual as a child—because it was all I knew—I began to chafe at the restrictions as a teenager."

"You wanted to see the world?" I ask, finally taking a bite of my own food. The tomato basil of the pasta sauce is the first delicious flavor I savor.

He nods, cutting into a piece of chicken. "I read so much about these places that my parents would not allow me to go." He glances up to meet my gaze. "I was spoiled with *Lago* Maggiore, the Dolomites, and the estate in Tuscany, but I wanted to see everywhere. Everything. I did not share my parents' fear or know the terror they must have felt. Something you clearly understand about them that I never could because I haven't had that experience."

"They were willing to do anything to keep you safe."

He dips his chin in agreement. "And they did. But it drove a wedge between us by the time I was eighteen. I didn't care that they didn't want me to go. On the day of my eighteenth birthday, I left. They couldn't keep me captive in a gilded cage any longer. I wanted freedom more than I wanted anything else." He pauses, turning his neck to stare out the window. "I'm astonished they didn't lock me up to keep me from going."

I think of Aurora leaving at the tender age of eighteen, knowing nothing about the world that could swallow her whole with a single bite, and empathy that I've never felt before surges through my chest.

"I'm surprised it didn't kill them."

Marco looks back to me. "Indeed. But it did not."

"Where did you go first? Japan?"

He shakes his head. "No, that was much later. First, I went to Kathmandu."

"Nepal?" The shock in my tone makes the question louder than I expected.

"Yes. I wanted to climb the Himalayas." He smiles wistfully. "I was an adventurous one."

"And did you?"

His nod is slow. "I did. For three years, I lived and climbed where most people could not survive. Sherpas, snow, and ice were my only company. I found God in the Himalayas. It was life-altering."

I try to picture my brother at eighteen, and instead, I can only see myself—a young gangster running the streets of New Orleans without a clue as to what he was doing, but doing it anyway because it felt like the only way to survive.

"That's incredible."

"It was incredible. My spiritual journey began, and it kept me away from Italy for over a decade."

"Where did you go next?"

"Thailand. After all the snow and cold, I wanted warmth and sun and beaches."

Stunned that my brother has lived many lives, I eat silently with one hand while waiting for him to continue.

"In Thailand, I fell in love with martial arts. I studied under a Muay Thai master who let me live in his home. With my long hair that I hadn't cut since I left home, I mopped and cleaned and became a warrior under his tutelage."

"Incredible," I whisper again.

"It was. He was a wonderful man. A bachelor who was married to martial arts. He taught me discipline, strength, and commitment to ideals greater than myself. It was the education of a lifetime."

My brother and I may look the same, I can't help but think, *but we are two completely different men.*

"That's how you put Remy de Marchand to sleep?"

"That was a choke hold from my training in Japan. My love of martial arts took me there later. I competed against warriors, earning a few belts even. I still have them, although our father did not approve when he learned of what I was doing."

"Who cares if he approved? That's incredible." I find

myself using the same word over and over because nothing else seems to fit this story of my brother's.

"They were good days of my life. Very good days."

"And the body suit?" I ask, glancing down at the ink encircling both wrists.

"I saw the Yakuza at many of the fights when I competed. I wanted to look like them—albeit Italian with long, braided hair and a short beard. I found a tattoo shop where it was rumored they had their work done, and I took a chance by going there. It ended up changing my life once again."

"The tattoos?" I ask, beyond curious.

"Those, too, but before that. I saved one of them from an assassination attempt. The shop would never have dared ink me with one of their body suits but for the Yakuza whose life I saved. He paid for all of it. He made sure his artist did his finest work, thankfully with modern machines instead of by hand, in as little time as it could take."

"I've always wondered how long they endure the pain for those suits."

"Over a hundred hours. And I felt every single stroke of those needles on my skin." He turns over his wrist, fork in hand, and looks down at the ink. "It was worth it." Glancing back up at me, he adds, "Even though our father was horrified when I finally came home and he saw me."

Feeling like I'm figuratively on the edge of my seat, I ask, "What did he say?"

"There was a lot of yelling and cursing. I was only able to quiet him when I told him I was home for good. That my wandering years were over."

I can't help but smile. "He didn't care after that, did he?"

Marco shakes his head with a matching grin. "No. He might have wanted to strangle me, but he wanted me home with him in Italy more. So, he forgave what he called my 'youthful indiscretion' and hugged me harder than he'd ever hugged me before."

I picture their reunion, even though I don't know what our father looks like. From Marco's comments earlier, I presume he looks like an older version of us, so that makes it easier.

"And our mother?"

"She appreciates art of all kinds. Even on her son."

My smile widens. "Really?"

"She told me to put on a Speedo so she could see more of it," he says with a broad grin and a quiet chuckle. "Of course, I started off with telling her I was home for good. That made it much easier than with Father."

"I like her more and more," I reply as my heart warms with his story.

"She is a wonderful mother. Although I'd never tell our father, it was harder to leave her than him. When I came home to visit, my heart broke to leave her again. That was when I finally realized that I was happiest in Italy, with my family. The world might hold many treasures and exotic places, but there is truly nowhere like our home."

"I can't wait to see it," I say, my voice thick with emotion that I didn't expect to feel. Everything about this last week has been unexpected, and the surprises just keep coming.

Marco eats a few more bites before pausing. "Are you sure you wish to eat with Aurora in your arms? I can finish quickly and hold her for you. I have never held a child before, but it would be my honor for the first one to be one of my blood."

As I stare at my own face, the words feel like they could have come from my own mouth, only a few years earlier. Instantly, I know that I can trust him with my most precious treasure. "I'd never held a baby before her either. If you don't mind, I don't think she would."

Marco's face lights up. "It would be my honor. Let me finish quickly, before your food grows cold. The tomato sauce is exceptionally good. But I'm biased about Giordano tomatoes. Wait until you pick them ripe off the vine in Tuscany and smell them as they cook down with our basil and secret blend of spices. It is heaven on earth, like you've never before experienced."

"I'm beginning to realize that there's a lot I've never experienced before."

Marco's grin comes easily, and it occurs to me that I love seeing him smile. It's not something I've seen often in my own reflection.

"Just wait, brother. There is a whole new life ahead of you now."

CHAPTER TWENTY-THREE

KEIRA

As the plane descends, I realize I have no idea where we are actually going. It should make me uneasy, but with Lachlan beside me and the nightmare we lived in New Orleans thousands of miles behind us, I feel more relaxed than I have felt in weeks.

The smile on Lachlan's face made that possible. If nothing else, I love his brother already for this new ease I've never seen in my husband before. Just like when we left New Orleans behind for Dublin and I was introduced to a brand-new Lachlan Mount, I feel like I'm once again being gifted with a new version of the man I love.

And this time, it's a version I never expected.

Lachlan has always been intense. Focused. Driven. Determined. Ironclad control exercised at every moment. But this man ... this man who has a brother is different still.

I've heard him laugh more times on this flight than I did for the entire first year I knew him. I've had to stop myself from reaching out and hugging Marco at least a dozen times.

The changes he has wrought, in such a short time, feel miraculous.

It's not often you hear a woman fleeing the country and leaving her whole life behind—possibly *forever*—as feeling peaceful, but that's exactly where I am.

With my daughter snuggled in my arms while my husband grins as Marco points to something out the window, for the first time since I entered the dark world of Lachlan Mount, I feel like I can let my guard down completely. Maybe that's not the smartest thing I've ever done, given the reason we're running, but I don't care. This moment is beyond beautiful, and I'm soaking up every second of the joy I possibly can. With my mind, I take mental snapshots of the two of them together. Identical, but not the same.

I keep catching peeks of ink on Marco's wrists as he gestures, and I've had to bite my tongue to keep from asking about the tattoos because I don't want to interrupt the brotherly bonding. It's like witnessing a miracle. One my husband has been waiting his whole life for without even knowing it.

A wave of gratitude crashes over me, and all I can do is hug Aurora tighter. Her chubby fingers tangle in my hair and tug, but I don't care. In this moment, my world is perfect.

"You see, there is the airport. There, we shall change planes and fly to the islands. It is a very short flight. Technically, we will be in Switzerland, but only for a moment."

"And our passports? They'll want to see them when we land?" Lachlan asks.

Marco shakes his head. "Possibly, but unlikely. The family is well respected here. We are treated … somewhat differently than others. Perhaps it is unfair, but I do not argue with good treatment ever."

The peace I've been feeling continues to grow. *Thank God for Marco. Thank God for the Giordano family. Thank God for all of it.*

"Privilege has its uses," Lachlan replies.

Marco's grin is practically ear to ear. "Indeed. Especially when returning with a long-lost member of the family."

"Have I mentioned yet that I'm really glad you showed up when you did?" Lachlan asks, swallowing as his gaze connects with his brother's.

"It was my pleasure and my honor. Long-awaited. Ahhh. Look there." Marco points out the window. "Do you see the balloon? I would bet my inheritance that it is for you."

My husband's face becomes unreadable as I peer beyond him out the window to see what Marco is pointing at.

"Oh my God." The words pop out of my mouth as we streak by a hot-air balloon with a giant red heart emblazoned on the side. "Really?"

"Yes, if I had to guess," Marco replies.

My gaze darts back to Lachlan to see him press a palm to the cabin window. His lower lip drops as he inhales sharply.

My heart feels like it might burst out of my chest with

the intensity of the emotion flowing through me. I can't begin to imagine what my husband is feeling.

I haven't met his mother yet, but I already love her too. Anyone who loves my husband enough to arrange for a heart hot-air balloon is already one of my favorite people in the entire world. I want to hug her for the softening expression on his face. The disbelief. The realization that he is … *loved.*

I shift Aurora and press a palm to my chest to help me handle my overflowing emotions. *Thank you. Thank you. Thank you.*

"Wow," he whispers before going silent.

"Spectacle. Remember, she has waited over four decades for this moment. She is a very demonstrative mother. Thank you for understanding how much this means to her."

The captain's voice comes over the intercom with the announcement that we will be landing imminently, and the cabin goes silent.

Without turning his head away from the balloon, Lachlan reaches for me. I clasp his hand with my free one, and he squeezes it—hard.

I feel that squeeze all the way to my heart. *My heart.* I don't know how much more it can take of this overwhelming feeling of love, but I'm willing to try to find the limit.

Lachlan doesn't let go of my hand until we are taxiing on the runway.

"You said we were changing planes?"

Marco nods. "And I shall be your captain for the next leg of our journey. I promise, I'm a very good pilot, especially with precious cargo."

"You fly too?" Lachlan sounds surprised and impressed, and I have to admit that I am as well.

"Helicopters and planes. I'm instrument-rated as well. For this short flight, we will be traveling aboard a seaplane we use to come and go from the islands."

"I've always wanted to fly on a seaplane," I say, and both men look toward me.

Marco's white teeth flash. "Then, today is your lucky day."

I have a feeling he's absolutely right—in many more ways than one.

CHAPTER TWENTY-FOUR

LACHLAN

A nod with a wave from airport employees is all the attention we get when we disembark from the jet in the family hangar. It wouldn't have been a problem to show our passports—they're excellent and real—but not to need them is even better.

Marco and I grab the bags and load them into a red seaplane that sits in the hangar. The more I allow myself to live in the moment, the more surreal it becomes.

My brother and I are loading luggage into the family seaplane. Because *I have a brother. Who has a family seaplane.*

I don't know when having a brother will feel normal, but it still fills me with emotions and feelings I haven't had time to fully process in the mad dash to get out of the country.

But first … *my mother.*

Seeing the hot-air balloon with a giant red heart on the side of the silk, floating amid the thermal currents of the sky, still seems the most surreal of it all.

My mother is welcoming me home. Tears prick my eyes at the very thought—an unusual sensation, to be sure. One I haven't felt many times in my life, but today, it seems all bets are off. Everything I thought I knew and understood about life and my place in the world has been replaced by a reality that has not yet become fully clear.

I picture the woman in the jet, with the dignified posture and beautiful silver hair, dropping to her knees and crying as she beheld me and clutched my hands.

The prick of tears turns to a sting, and I haul in a deep breath. *Hold it together, Mount. You're not going to start crying now. Keep it tight.*

Despite all the violent and dangerous moments that I've faced in my life, this one has me nearly coming apart at the seams. *This* is the one that has me nearly breaking—and all I'm doing is loading bags into a plane.

Get it together.

Like I have so many times in the past few years, I turn to Keira. My beautiful wife. My strength, even if she doesn't know it. Her shining red hair glints in the shaft of Italian sunlight cutting through the shadows of the hangar as our daughter rests peacefully on her shoulder.

"I love you," I tell her, and her gaze cuts to mine.

I can read the questions in her eyes at my sudden declaration, but I don't care if it seems out of place. It's the truth. She knows it. I know it. And I couldn't *not* say it right now.

Her lips curve into a sweet smile. "I love you too. Are you okay?"

I nod slowly. "I'm about to introduce my wife and daughter to my mother. I'm so far beyond okay that I couldn't possibly tell you what I am right now."

Marco overhears my statement, and his entire face softens. It's not a look I'm used to seeing in the mirror, but I love seeing it on the face we share regardless. It fills me with the hope that, someday, it might be a look that Keira sees on my face more often. Less harsh control over my environment and more peace.

Peace.

The one thing that's been lacking in my life for its entirety. Keira and Aurora taught me love, but peace has eluded me … until perhaps now, if I'm lucky. And the thumping of my heart in my chest makes me feel that I am indeed lucky. I know that I've lived this long only to experience this moment of homecoming. This moment of family. This moment of joy.

No one would say I deserved it.

They would all be right.

But I'm going to live it anyway, deserved or not. No one is taking this from me.

"Are you ready to board?" Marco asks as he shuts the door of the cargo hold.

I look to Keira and hold out a hand. "Ladies first."

As she takes a step toward me and grasps my hand with her free one, she squeezes hard. "I can't wait. Let's do this."

"I'll take Rory. Up you go." With a smooth handoff, I kiss my daughter's face and stabilize Keira as she climbs up the ladder, over the pontoon, and into the plane. As soon as she's settled, I climb up and strap in beside her.

Five minutes later, Marco is strapped into the cockpit. "Put on your headsets. One for Rory too. It will be loud."

After the three of us are situated with onboard ear protection, Marco performs all of his in-cockpit preflight checks, makes a notation on a clipboard, and turns around to give us a nod. "Can you hear me?"

"Yes," Keira and I both reply. "Loud and clear."

"Then, away we go."

With Aurora in my arms, the engine of the plane roars to life. We're rolling forward out of the hangar, and I'm grateful to see no one standing in our way, trying to prevent us from taking off.

Could it really be this easy? It seems incredible that everything has gone so smoothly and easily when so much of my life has been punctuated by unexpected difficulties and challenges. *But maybe ... maybe that can also change?*

An overwhelming sense of fate weaves through me and around me, and I feel—more so than ever before in my life—that I am exactly where I am meant to be and doing exactly what I am meant to be doing.

Marco speaks to the tower in what sounds like German, and within moments, we're taxiing to the runway and turning to face the long strip of pavement ahead of us.

"Prepare for takeoff," he says before he throttles the engine and the plane rolls forward.

I hope he knows what he's doing, I think as we hurtle down the runway and then gracefully lift into the air.

Marco continues speaking to the tower for a few moments and then switches over to English. "Everyone good? We are headed back into Italy."

"You speak German too?" I ask him.

"When you grow up on the border of Switzerland, it is an easy language to pick up. I speak Spanish, French, and Portuguese as well. My Russian is not very good though."

"Wow," Keira whispers into the headset. "And here, I just speak a bit of Gaelic and French. Clearly, Rory is going to need to spend some time with her uncle and become multilingual."

In that instant, a vision of my daughter growing up like a princess, speaking more languages than her mother and me combined, springs into my mind. "An excellent idea," I add to Keira's comment.

"It would be my pleasure," Marco replies before pointing at the shimmering lake. "We are not far from Maggiore. See it ahead of us?"

Keira and I both peer out the windows, taking in the beautiful blue water and all the buildings with red tiled roofs surrounding the end we're approaching.

"It is not a long flight. We shall be there before you know it. Ahh! You can see the balloon again just there." Marco gestures out the side window, and the hot-air balloon comes into view once more.

I can't believe this is happening. But it is. Warmth and heat fill my chest, and I cling to Aurora like she will keep my tears from escaping.

My daughter reaches up to tug my hair, as if to say, *It's real, Daddy; believe it.*

Marco's voice fills our ears again as he points out landmarks, but I'm too lost for words to reply. Thankfully, he and Keira converse easily, and neither realizes how overwhelmed I am by the moment.

Who would expect the infamous Lachlan Mount to be so close to the breaking point? No one. Never. That's not something anyone would expect from me, especially not now.

But I'm quickly learning something new about myself: bullets and blood don't faze me, but emotional reunions with my family—that is almost more than I can handle.

Get it together, Mount.

Even the name I call myself sounds surreal in my mind. *Everything* about this moment feels surreal. And through the fog dulling my hearing, when Marco says that we're approaching the islands, I can barely take it all in.

I hear Keira gasp as she sees the islands in the middle of the wide expanse of the lake, but I feel like I'm caught in a dream.

Is this even real? Am I in a coma? Can this really be happening? It almost seems easier to think I'm making all of this up, like it's some fantasy conjured by my mind instead of moments unfolding in my reality.

"Oh my God," I whisper as Marco circles the islands, allowing us to see their beauty from the air.

Trees. Gardens. Beautiful architecture.

How can this be real? How can this be my family? I was left in filth as a baby in front of a church, unwanted and unimportant. The system tried to eat me alive, but I fought it and ran and grew even stronger. I built my own world out of blood, sweat, daring, and necessity. *How can this fairy tale be happening in my life? How can this be possible?*

Everything I've done and been pushes at my mind, but as the pontoon touches down on the water, it all evaporates.

My past no longer matters.

This moment—right here, right now—is all that matters.

Everything that has come before has led me to this moment, and I'm going to grab on to it with both hands. No one is taking this happiness from me. *No one.*

As Marco guides the seaplane across the water toward

a stone boathouse and dock connected to a massive seawall, I spot giant arrangements of greenery and flowers dotting the red carpet lying across the platform that leads up to elegant stone steps. And that's where I see her. Hands clasped together over her chest, silver hair set off with a beautiful purple dress. She looks like a queen, waiting to welcome her long-awaited son home.

My mother.
Waiting for me.
And my family.
A dream come true.

CHAPTER TWENTY-FIVE

LACHLAN

Keira squeezes my hand as Marco shuts down the engine, and two men appear to help guide us into the dock and secure the plane.

"Are you ready?" Marco asks before removing his headset. "Brace yourself."

"More than ready," I reply as my daughter's tiny hands grasp my shirt and my hair. "Beyond ready."

"Then, we shall go and not keep Mother waiting another moment. Please be careful as you exit. The dock floats, so it might shift as you step onto it."

The door to the plane opens, and the Italian sunshine streams into the cabin. With one hand, I remove my headset and seat belt, shift Aurora, and rise from my seat, headed for a brand-new life I never anticipated having.

As soon as the dock shifts beneath my weight, I hear her gasp. My mother and I make eye contact in the next moment.

Beringed hands cover her mouth as she watches, with tears streaming down her face, as we walk toward her.

"Ahhh. My beautiful son. My beautiful granddaughter. Ahhh." Her tears glisten in the sunlight, taking nothing away from her own beauty.

My heart expands beyond any size and shape it's ever held. Like it's too large for my chest, I feel like it could explode any moment from the emotions rioting through my body. *Joy. Love. Awe. Wonder. Surprise. Amazement.*

She rushes toward us, arms splaying wide. "My son! My son is home!" The words come out between sobs of pure happiness, and I close the distance between us with my free arm open.

It's a moment I will never forget. As soon as her small frame collides with mine, I wrap my arm around her, pulling her against me.

Words I can't understand fall from her lips in Italian, punctuated by cries and sobs. Tears soak through my shirt as her body shakes and trembles while her arms grip me tighter than I knew was possible.

"This day has finally come," she says, switching to English, pulling away ever so slightly. One delicate hand rises to touch my cheek, and the other reaches out to Aurora. "My precious child. And your precious child. My heart. Oh, my heart."

"This is Aurora. We call her Rory. She's the most perfect, innocent child you could imagine."

Tears tip off her lids as she stares into my daughter's dark eyes.

"A princess. A princess who has come home to her kingdom." My mother's gaze, wet with tears, lifts to mine once more. "You have no idea how happy I am in this moment. It is almost more than I can bear."

My heart jerks in my chest, and I swallow. "I can

relate." I hear footsteps behind us, and I shift, taking in my stunning wife as she steps forward. "And this is the love of my life, the other half of my soul, my reason for being— Keira. Keira, this is my *mother*." The word comes out rough with emotion.

The tears shining in my wife's beautiful eyes threaten to tip over the lids. "I'm so happy to meet you."

My mother's hand presses to her chest while her gaze shoots to the heavens for a beat before coming back to Keira once more. "A daughter too. It is more than I could have ever asked for. A son, a daughter, and a granddaughter. God is good. So very good. Please," she says, opening her arms. "Please, may I hug you? I am called Francesca."

"Of course," Keira replies with a voice choked up by the glistening tears slipping down her cheeks.

She steps forward, and together, the three of us are enveloped by my mother's thin but strong arms.

For several moments, no one speaks. I'm soaking up these emotions that I've never felt before. *Fulfillment. Completion. Belonging.*

The three most important women in my entire world are wrapped in my arms, and for once in my life, there is nothing else I could possibly want.

The missing piece of my existence has clicked into place, leaving me overwhelmed with the perfection of this moment and the perfection of life itself.

I don't know how I could possibly deserve this gift. I have no idea how I could be so blessed after everything I've done and what I've been. But somehow ... somehow ... life intervened in the most unexpectedly perfect way I could never have imagined.

I tighten my arms around my world.

Nothing could stop me from soaking up all of it and enjoying every moment. How could I do anything else?

After several minutes, my mother pulls back a few inches. "I do not wish to let you go, but I must not keep you standing on the dock all day. You have been traveling for many, many hours. You will want food and drinks and rest. I have everything prepared for you. Everything is ready for you. This is a day I have planned a million times in my mind. Please, come. Let us go up. We must take care of your needs."

Marco and the two men who helped dock the plane walk toward us with all of our bags in hand. His wide smile threatens to split his face into two halves with its enthusiasm.

His free hand touches my shoulder. "Yes, let us go up and get you settled so you can enjoy the festivities Mother has planned," he says before his gaze locks on our mother's shining eyes. "I expect you had a banquet prepared at least."

"You shall not be disappointed, my son. A feast awaits. I hope I did not go too far. I wanted to go much further, but I held myself back." She glances at me with her eyes glistening with unshed tears. "You must forgive me if it is too much. I have so long waited for this moment. I wanted you to know exactly how much we have missed you and longed for your return. I knew this day would come. I am just so grateful it did not come later. I am so happy it is today and my wait is over."

"It could never be too much," Keira says quietly as she strokes a hand across my back. "Lachlan deserves everything you could possibly think of and more."

In that moment, I can see my mother fall head over heels in love with my wife—something I do repeatedly almost daily.

"You see him for who he truly is," my mother replies with love beaming from every fiber of her being.

"He is unlike any other man who has ever existed. Thank you so much for this beautiful welcome."

"It is my honor." My mother's gaze lifts to Marco and the men carrying the bags. "Then, we all go. Please, follow me."

Her hand slides into my free one, and like the dutiful son I never knew I could be, I squeeze it in mine, prepared to follow my mother wherever she leads.

My mother. It's surreal.

And yet I'm experiencing it.

With each step of her capable but slight frame, I feel more and more like a protective son—a role I've never played before. Aurora's fingers thread through my hair as mine grip my mother's hand to help her up each stair.

While she seemed so full of energy at the bottom, as we pass each stunning trimmed hedge and massive flower arrangement on the stone walkway, I can feel her energy flagging. *Perhaps the excitement of the day? Or perhaps she doesn't often climb these stairs any longer?*

But she doesn't pause. Step after step, she leads us higher into the most fanciful gardens I've ever seen in my life.

"It's like a fairyland," I say, my voice hushed, in awe of the bright-colored flowers and artfully shaped verdant foliage surrounding us on every side.

My mother finally slows and meets my gaze. "The world can be many things for many people. Mine is beautiful, because I have decided it should be so." A peaceful smile slips over her lips, and she shifts her gaze to Aurora and then back to me. "And now, to share it with you and the beautiful family I did not know I would be so blessed to welcome … it is a gift. Truly a gift beyond imagining. Thank you for coming."

"I wouldn't have missed this for anything," I reply with raw and honest emotion roughening my tone.

When we reach the lawn at the top of the walkway, I take in the silk tent, floral arches, tables laden with trays of food, and six-foot-tall ice sculptures, shaped like angels standing as sentinels over the entire affair. As if coming from a distance, the music of a string ensemble lilts over the scene. It's a regal and dignified lawn party to celebrate a momentous occasion.

And we are the momentous occasion.

"How beautiful," Keira whispers from behind me. "How elegant."

My mother bows her head in Keira's direction. "I hope you don't mind. It isn't often I have such a reason to celebrate." With a twist of her neck, she glances at Marco. "You told them I'd be festive, did you not?"

My brother's laughing grin stretches his face—yet another expression I've never seen while looking in a mirror. "I had to prepare them. I did not know if you would have doves flying or pony rides for Aurora."

They both chuckle. It's clear to me that my mother and brother have a very easy relationship, and a pang of something squeezes my heart. It's not jealousy or envy. I'm … *grateful* they have that. Perhaps that means my relationship with her will be much the same.

"You didn't need to do anything. Not a single thing. It

would still be the greatest homecoming of my life," I say as I squeeze her fingers and lift her hand to my lips to kiss. "Thank you so much. Truly, thank you."

The smile on her face is even more dazzling than the one stretching my brother's cheeks. She reaches out a hand to him. "Both of my sons," she says as tears gather along her lids. "My twin boys are home. It is almost more than I can bear. My heart has never been so full. It could burst, and I would die as the happiest woman in the world right here, in this moment. I have *everything. Everything.*"

Marco grasps her hand, and together, we stand there, speechless and motionless, as *our mother* stares at us, both with shining eyes and a heart full of joy.

Keira leans against my side, and for the first time in my entire life, I want nothing. I need nothing. I am complete. I am whole.

I am home.

CHAPTER TWENTY-SIX

KEIRA

Aurora fusses in her father's arms, and we make an easy handoff, like we're pros at this parenting thing instead of still learning. It takes me a moment to realize why she's wiggling so much.

An ornamental duck with brilliant feathers quacks and waddles along the perfectly trimmed lawn, as though well acquainted with the place—and I suppose he must be.

"Ma-ma," she says, pointing at the duck.

Not wanting to disturb the heartfelt moment, I bounce her, but Lachlan's mother notices immediately.

"If you put her down, she will not be able to catch him. Lorenzo is quite the escape artist. He and Donatella live here on the island, along with some wild ducks with whom they have made friends."

"She's quicker than she looks," I say with a smile, lowering Aurora to the grass.

"Then, Lorenzo must be even quicker."

As soon as Aurora's feet touch down on the lawn, she takes a wobbling step toward the duck while holding my hands. I know that her clothes will need changing before she hits her knees and begins crawling to try to catch up with him. But watching Lachlan's mother's face—Aurora's *grandmother*'s face—tells me that I would buy her a new change of clothes every single day if I could simply be in the presence of such awe and joy.

"Oh, look at her! What a beauty. And so smart. She's going the other way to try to catch him." Francesca claps her hands. "Brilliant strategy, Aurora. Such a smart girl. A true Giordano." She reaches out a hand and grips Lachlan's arm. "I spent all of these years praying for my son to return, but I had no idea I could be blessed with a granddaughter as well. When Marco told me what he had learned, it was like the angels were shining down on us and granting us a gift more precious than we could ever have imagined. An heiress to enjoy our family's treasures. It was a miracle. Totally unexpected. Your daughter will want for nothing in her entire life. She has every material thing she will ever need."

I already knew Aurora's future was secure. Lachlan had promised me that over and over again. He made provisions for both of us. We would want for nothing. But after the past week, everything solid and secure in my world was shaken and shattered. Life as I had known it was over the moment I saw V's blood on the carpet. And yet, somehow, we emerged from that nightmare into a new world where safety, peace, beauty, and love seem to be the bywords.

Part of me is afraid to trust this new reality just yet, but hearing Lachlan's mother speak about our daughter and her future releases untold tension I've been carrying since the day she was born.

As of this moment, Aurora isn't just the daughter of New Orleans's most notorious, infamous, and creative criminal kingpin. She's also the granddaughter of Italian nobility, and her family's greatest wish is that she be raised in luxury, wealth, and safety so that she can take her place at the head of the family's fortune one day.

As a mother, there is nothing I wouldn't do for my daughter. Literally nothing I wouldn't do to secure her future in the best, brightest, and most advantageous way.

A box of emotion I've kept compartmentalized for much too long breaks free, and I drop to my knees on the grass as Aurora comes scrambling toward me. As her chubby fingers reach for my arms, tears pour down my face as I realize I no longer have to worry about anything.

My daughter is safe. Her future is secure.

The relief of the moment completely levels me. I wrap my arms around her as I sob quietly and squeeze her tight.

I never have to wonder what will become of our daughter. Never again.

She's safe. We are all safe.

"Oh, my dear. You have all been through much." Lachlan's mother closes the distance between us and shocks me by kneeling down at my side. Her thin arms wrap around me and Aurora and hug us both tightly. "It is okay now. You are okay. There is nothing more to worry about now. Oh, my sweet child. I cannot imagine what love you have for this beautiful girl. My heart is near bursting with it, and I have only just met her."

"Thank you," I whisper through the tears. "Thank you. Thank you for coming for us. Thank you."

"Hellion, you gut me with your tears." My husband's voice is rough with emotion as he drops down to join us on the grass and wraps us all into his strong arms. "Everything's okay."

"I know. I know. I just … I'm so grateful to be here. Rory's safe—and I feel like I can finally let go."

My husband's grip tightens on me, as if he knows the burden I've been carrying and how heavily it weighed upon me.

"Your daughter is the safest she has ever been in her entire life," Marco says, joining us on the lawn. "She is a Giordano now. Lay down your fears when you are ready. You have no need of them any longer."

"No one will harm my family," says Francesca with finality. "Never again. You have my word, Keira. Here, Aurora is safe. Anywhere on our family's lands, she is safe. For four decades, we have made safety, security, and privacy our top priority. You are in a new world now, darling. I know words might not be enough to show you, but I hope you see it for yourself soon."

"I see it already," I say, lifting my head to meet Francesca's gaze. "And that is why I'm crying."

Lachlan yanks me tighter into his chest and whispers in my ear, "I will never fail you again, Keira. I swear on my life. I will never fail you again."

CHAPTER TWENTY-SEVEN

LACHLAN

Holding my wife's body in my arms, I'm beyond thankful that her trembling comes from relief instead of fear. There is nothing to make you feel like less of a man than failing to protect your family when they need you.

I still haven't forgiven myself, but someday … someday, when my wife no longer cries at the thought of safety and security, I may be able to do so.

"Well, we certainly look like a family, do we not?" Marco's question shifts the energy of the moment and causes each of us to survey the scene before our eyes.

All four of us, on the lawn—surrounded by ice sculptures, party tables, silk tents, and waddling ducks—is quite a sight to behold.

"The most beautiful vision I have ever seen on this island is unfolding right before me," my mother replies, tears finally drying.

"I'm so sorry I lost it," Keira says to me and my mother as Aurora buries her face in my neck.

"You have nothing to apologize for," I tell her. "It's I who owe you the greatest of apologies."

Keira shakes her head. "No, you're the one who has given me more than I could ever imagine. And without you, we wouldn't be here, safe and happy, surrounded by the love of a family we didn't even know existed."

"She does have a point," my brother interjects. He pauses briefly before adding, "And there's still one more member of the family for you to meet to make this reunion complete."

My mother sucks in a sharp breath before letting out a long sigh. "You must tell him, Marco. You must tell him now. Our staff is amazing, but even they will not be able to keep a secret of this magnitude for long. The news of our joy will spread quickly. You must go to him now."

"Before I even get to partake in this feast?"

"What do you think will take longer? The second course or the news of our family reunion to reach Milan?"

"Your point is taken, Mama. I shall go to him now. He deserves to know, especially now that they are truly here."

Keira and I make eye contact as they speak about my father.

My father. Another surreal thought.

It's almost more than I can assimilate right now. I have a brother, a mother … and a father who doesn't even know I'm alive.

It's more than I ever dreamed could be possible, and yet … my brother kisses my mother on the cheek, ruffles Aurora's hair, and meets my gaze.

"I hope you are ready to have a father as well. He will wish to meet you immediately." Marco looks to our mother. "He will come here if Luca is here. He will not be able to stay away. Is that acceptable to you, Mama?"

"I have never kept him away from his family's home. That choice was always his own. He is welcome to come and meet his son. Please tell him that I extended the invitation personally. This is a joy that must be shared with all who deserve it, and despite what he has become, I will not deprive him of such a wonderful event. Go, Marco. Go tell your father his long-lost son has returned home and brought his family. The Giordanos celebrate today. All Giordanos."

My brother and mother share a long stare that seems to communicate more than words could express. With solemnity, Marco dips his chin as he assents to our mother's wishes.

"Yes, Mama. I shall fly to Milan directly. This is a moment I've waited for my entire life. I shall not delay."

Part of me wants to rise and offer to go with him. To meet my father and tell him of my existence personally, but I remind myself that two identical twins spotted in public will cause many more questions and inquiries into the family, which is the last thing I want to incite. I'm so used to being the one who must leave to take care of business that it's totally unfamiliar to see someone else assume the role.

As Marco releases our mother, I meet his gaze and hold out a hand. When he clasps it, I rise, using his strength to help me to my feet. Relying on the strength and assistance of my brother is still a completely new experience.

Once standing, I grip his hand tighter. "Are you sure you want to go alone?"

He stares back at me thoughtfully. "I must go alone. This is my duty. I must tell him myself. I cannot take the chance that someone else will tell him that they saw me with my twin. It would not be right."

"I agree with that completely, but still, it feels wrong to get here for our family celebration and have you leave immediately."

Marco's face softens. "Our family celebration will continue every day for the rest of our lives, brother. It is not only this moment, although this moment is one I shall cherish always. Besides, I have had over forty years with our mother's sole attention focused on me. It is your turn to bask in her love and attention. She has much to give and has waited so long to share it with you."

Our mother's voice rises from behind me. "He is right, my son. Marco will be fine. This is his duty and honor. A day that will never be forgotten for as long as any of us live. He will fly safe and return home directly to continue the celebration of this day long into the night. Milan is not far by plane. Marco will return soon. Have no fear."

It's harder than I expected it would be to shake my brother's hand and let it go, knowing that there are things he must carry on and do without me. Somehow, our bond has already formed stronger and deeper than I realized possible. Perhaps it's the blood we share or the face. Either way, I don't like to see him leave, but I recognize that he must take this journey by himself.

"Fly safe, brother."

Marco nods. "I go with God and shall return with our father. Enjoy yourselves. I shall be back sooner than you realize."

I release his hand, and Marco bows ever so slightly. *A*

remnant from his martial arts training? I can't help but wonder.

There's still so much I want to know about him, but my questions must wait for another time.

Patience, I remind myself. All in good time.

But first, it's time for my father to be informed that I'm alive.

I can't imagine how such a shocking announcement is going to impact him. If it were me, nothing would stop me from meeting the son I believed was dead. *Nothing.*

Fleeting thoughts shoot through my mind. *Will he even care? Will I matter to him at all? What if he doesn't come?*

The thoughts surprise me, but I don't latch on to them or believe them. They're the leftover beliefs of an abandoned little boy who is abandoned no longer. *Of course he'll care. Of course I matter. Of course he will come.*

Because that's what fathers do.

I crouch down and open my arms to Aurora, who shoots toward me like she's been waiting for the opportunity her whole life.

With my arms wrapped around the most precious gift I've ever been given, I watch my brother take off at a jog toward the stone stairs that lead back down to the plane.

"I love you, Marco! Be safe!" our mother says, and I marvel at the entire scene unfolding before me.

I have a family. And soon, I will have a father.

"Wait! Marco!" she calls, and Marco pauses and spins back to face her.

"Yes, Mama?"

"A photograph. You must take a photograph. That stubborn man might not believe anything he cannot see. I shall take it—in the family gallery. In front of your grandfather's portrait. He will not be able to believe his eyes when he sees the three of you together."

I rise with Aurora in my arms, and my mother beams with a giant smile.

"And his granddaughter as well. That will get him here quickly, the way nothing else possibly could."

CHAPTER TWENTY-EIGHT

MARCO

Proof of life—that's what I carry in my pocket on the screen of my mobile phone. I only let myself look at it for a brief moment after Keira helped my mother take a few pictures for Father.

My first photos with my brother and my niece. It feels surreal. Even more surreal is that I'm flying on a direct course to Milan to tell him of our miracle.

My brother is alive.

Our family is complete.

The moment I have wished for my entire life has almost manifested in reality.

As a young boy, I did not understand why my life had to be the way it was. I was grateful for everything my parents gave me, but I did not understand why I couldn't go to school like the children with whom I played on our family's properties.

My father tried to tell me that it was because more was expected of me than could be taught to me at the schools they attended, but as a child, I only wanted to be what I perceived as "normal."

The Giordano family has never been *normal.*

The darkness that stole into our world, took my brother, shattered my parents' happiness, and altered the course of my life has pervaded every moment of my father's existence. There was no simple joy from spending time with his son. There was training. Preparation to be made so that I would not be so vulnerable to abduction. It was like a gray cloud hanging over our every interaction.

I was there. Alive. Present. Needing his love and affection and attention. But even though he saw me, he always saw what was lacking—Luca.

It was as though Luca's absence had captured his mind and stolen from him the ability to enjoy anything else in life.

My mother, a beauty full of love, became his enemy the moment she returned without Luca.

I was only an infant then, but from what Mama has said over the years, I know it was sudden and heart-wrenching when he sent her away from him for coming home without his other son.

The little boy who simply wanted both of his parents to be in the same place at the same time is still alive and well within me.

Carrying this photograph, I know I have exactly what I need to make a long-standing dream of mine come true.

However, after all these years, I have to wonder, what will their reunion do to my mother? She is all that is good and loving in this world. My only source of softness and affection. Do I truly want to expose her sweetness and gentleness to the harsh reality that is the man who my father has become?

She believes she knows him still, after all these years, but she doesn't know him like I do. I have seen him shut out his emotional side because, in truth, I believe he fears it will overtake him and crush him if he were to allow himself to feel anything.

He is proud of me though. That I know. He is proud of the man I have become—despite the alterations to my physical appearance. He sees me as a capable steward of the family's businesses and properties. But I know that every time he looks at me, he sees only half of the twin sons he had. He sees loss and pain and heartbreak.

Perhaps that is painful for him, but it has been even more difficult for me.

To know that every time you stand in your father's presence, he is reminded of the very worst thing that ever happened in his life is a very heavy burden to carry, and it has been my whole life.

It is for this reason that I could not stay and enjoy the family party for even another moment. I have to repair this breach in my family's joy and happiness. I have to heal the hole in my father's heart.

While my mother had faith and hope to cling to and found joy in loving me twice as much, my father has only had business, success, and money to attempt to cement over the missing piece of his life.

In truth, I do not know how he has survived this long. I feared the bitterness and regret would take him long ago. But he has survived this way, somehow, against all odds. *Perhaps for today.*

The entire flight feels like it is being flown by someone

else. I am present and attentive, but it is as though the controls are manned by a power far greater than my own. It's as if I'm being pushed to Milan as fast as possible.

My landing is smooth and effortless, and an airport employee is waiting at the hangar to welcome me. Speaking the fewest number of words possible, I thank them and climb into the Ferrari I keep for driving in Milan. The width of the car barely fits in the lane, but I don't care. It carries me as quickly as possible to the headquarters of the Giordano empire, based in the heart of Milan.

My father claims that city life suits him better at this age because of its conveniences, but I have a different outlook on the matter. I believe instead that the noise and constant activity of the city make it easier for him to forget and block out the memories that haunt him daily.

I try not to judge my father or his choices, for I have never walked in his shoes. I have never had my wife and son kidnapped. I have never experienced the loss that he has. While I try to understand him, I often fail because I have never been to the depths of grief and bitterness, where he has lived for many years.

As a child, I often thought that as he grew older, my father would change and soften. That, one day, he would realize he was lucky to have a son even if he no longer had two.

I was wrong. The hardness only sharpened until he and I could no longer work side by side.

For the past ten years, I have chosen to stay away from Milan the majority of the time and let Father direct all business that needs to happen in the city. It has been easier this way—to love him from a distance since he could not love me in close proximity.

It doesn't matter how many subjects I excelled in or how victorious I am in business or life. Nothing I do has been able to shatter the deep freeze he has locked himself into for decades.

But now—*now*—I have the panacea in my pocket.

Proof that his second son lives.

Proof that the empire he tends to so carefully shall not die with me.

Proof that there is a God and He blesses us with a new beginning for the Giordano family.

I have no idea what kind of reaction I will get from my father, but as I board the elevator to the top floor of the marble building that houses our family's offices and my father's city apartment, I know that life as I know it will never be the same after today. I know that my father will never be the same after today.

When the elevator chimes to announce my arrival on the top floor, I step out of the ornate mirrored car onto the white marble floor. My suit is wrinkled and rumpled from the flight from America, which my father will no doubt find distasteful, but the news I bring is more important than a freshly pressed suit.

There are no markings on any of the doors, but I choose the one that I know houses his secretary—a dragon of a woman who can withstand his sharp edges. In truth, I don't like to speak to her, but it always prepares me for what stands on the other side of the door—the real dragon.

As soon as I step inside the reception space with its white walls and molding trimmed in gold leaf, Rosalina rises. "You do not have an appointment today. Your father is not expecting you."

"Is he busy?" I ask her, my tone civil.

"Your father is a very important man. He is always busy."

"I would not have come without warning unless it was imperative I see him immediately."

"I shall see if he can accommodate your unscheduled request."

It takes a lifetime of practiced self-control not to retort with a sharp remark, but I have learned that fighting fire with fire only results in burning everything down.

"Thank you," I say instead, wondering for the hundredth time if she is protective of him due to his status or because she has some claim on him to which I am not privy.

Regardless, it matters not. Not today. Today is a day of celebration for the entire Giordano family.

After a hushed conversation over the telephone, Rosalina dips her chin in my direction. "*Signor* Giordano will see you now. Please keep in mind he has an appointment for dinner, for which he will not thank you for making him late if you take too much of his time."

With a smile, I release a pent-up breath, accompanied by an audible sigh. "I shall do my best not to upset anyone's plans, Rosalina, but I make no promises."

Her brows dive together, accentuating the two vertical lines between them. I have never seen her smile, but that is the least of my worries today.

I stride around her, and when my hand lands on the heavy brass handle, I pause and take a long, slow, deep breath.

Before she can chasten me for wasting time, I depress the door handle and step inside my father's inner sanctum.

The marble floor is covered by a priceless oriental

carpet, stood upon by antique furniture from Italian and French nobility. Heavy mahogany bookcases with thousands of rare books line all four walls.

As a child, I used to dream of working with my father in this room, but once I became an adult, I wanted to stay as far away from it as possible.

Joy did not live here.

This is where my father attempted to work himself into an early grave by long hours each day and night.

"I have asked again and again for you to give me notice before you interrupt my plans. Still, you struggle to give a simple phone call of warning to Rosalina—"

"He's alive," I say simply, cutting off my father's admonishment.

"Who's alive?" he asks, still looking annoyed that I arrived without warning.

"Your other son."

My father shoots to his feet and slams his hands down on the desk. "Impossible! Do not come here with your outlandish claims! Do not speak to me of him!" Rage rolls off his frozen, aged frame in frenetic waves.

Instantly, I'm grateful for what my mother remembered just before I left. Even after being banished from his presence for more than forty years, she knew what to expect better than I did. For some reason, I believed he would welcome the news, not look at me with murder in his gaze.

"I have met him and hugged him. He—"

"Is a charlatan. Someone has taken advantage of your gullibility. You are a brilliant man, Marco. How could you be so stupid as to believe such a fairy tale? He is dead! Long dead! How dare you interrupt my—"

"How dare you speak so hatefully to me when I bring you news of a miracle? Your son. Luca. He is alive and well. He has a family of his own."

"I do not believe a word you say. It is impossible. Leave now. I do not wish to speak of this for another moment. Go!"

"I should go." The words grate from my throat as I retrieve my mobile phone from my pocket and pull up the photo. "But first, I will show you the proof that Mother swore you would need before you believed a word from your own son. How she still knows you so well after all these years, I don't understand." With a shake of my head, I stride forward and toss the device on the desk in front of him.

The phone lands with a *thud* on the contracts upon the leather blotter.

"Look at that and tell me I am gullible. Look at that and tell me I am stupid. I dare you, Father. I dare you."

For long moments, he stares at me with eyes wide and angry.

"Look at the photo, or I will take it and leave you to wonder if what I said could possibly be true. And then you'll have to follow me, back to Mother's island, and beg for entrance so you can meet your son."

He sucks in a breath and stares at me with those wide, crazy eyes. "You brought him to her! How dare you disturb her with your nonsense!"

With anger flowing through me that I do not wish to feel, I swipe out a hand and grab the phone from his desk and hold it up to his face. "*Look at us. Look at us together.*"

My father finally breaks his wild stare and glances

down at the photo on the screen. I know his intent is to look away immediately, but he can't. Instead, he reaches out with gnarled fingers and grips the edges. His expression is unreadable for a moment, before something unbelievable happens.

His mouth falls open, his shoulders curl in, and his hands shake.

Void of the intensity and ferocity of moments ago, he whispers, "It is not possible. I tortured the man who had taken him. He said Luca was dead. He said he killed him. This cannot be ..." The words trail off as Father's curled fingers form a fist that he brings to his mouth. "How? How could I be seeing two of you? How is this possible?"

His knees give way, and he falls backward into his heavy leather chair while I'm stunned at the knowledge that my father tortured the man who had kidnapped my brother.

This explains so much. So much.

While epiphanies burst in my mind, Father shakes his head back and forth, his face pale, leaving a stark contrast between his skin and his nearly black eyes.

"Plastic surgery. Something," he whispers in a weak tone, as though he has seen a ghost. "That cannot truly be ..."

"Why do you wish to push away a miracle that has been given to our family?" I ask in an equally quiet tone. "I have spoken at length with him. Lachlan is the name he has been using. He has never known where he came from. He thought he was unwanted by his family because he was abandoned on the steps of a church in America. New Orleans."

"America." My father breathes the word. "He swore to

me he was dead. He said that was the purpose of the kidnapping—to visit vengeance on us for what we had printed in the paper. How could Luca have ended up in America?"

"When did he tell you he was dead, Father? When did this happen?"

"A lifetime ago. I believed all hope was lost." My father shakes his head. "He looks just like you. And my father." With one hand balled into a fist in front of his mouth, he cracks. Tears escape his eyes in shining streaks down his face. Bewildered and confused, he meets my gaze once more. "How could this be? How could this be?"

"It's a miracle, Father. A miracle."

With a harsh, broken sob, my father slumps against the high leather cushion of the chair, clutching the phone to his chest.

"How could this be? Is this a dream? A nightmare? Am I dead? What is happening?"

Waves of love flow out from me to encircle my father. I have never seen such emotion from him, and now, I'm finally beginning to understand that there was much that happened that I did not know. None of us—me nor Mother nor the staff—knew that my father had found the man who took Luca. None of us knew what he had done or what he had learned.

All I saw in him was bitterness and regret. I didn't know the burden or knowledge he carried. My heart breaks for what I did not know. For the judgments that I could not stop myself from making about his harsh behavior.

Please forgive me, Father.

My father leans forward in his chair, head shaking from side to side, as if completely bewildered.

"How?" he whispers as he stares at the photo, his gnarled fingertip reaching out to trace the faces.

My heart seizes at the first moments of tenderness I've seen from my father in my entire life.

"By the grace of God, Father. Luca is a strong man. One whom you will love to get to know, for he made his way in the world all by himself. He overcame odds that even you would have shied away from. He did what he had to do to survive."

"But how did you find him? How?" Tear-shining eyes lift to meet mine.

"I never stopped looking. Mother and I had been looking for decades. Every lead broke my heart. Every dead end. Every look-alike who wasn't him. We kept looking. Mother never stopped praying. We never lost hope. And then one day, we got the break we needed. It took longer still for us to find him. But we found him. I brought Mother to him."

His head jerks back at my admission. "You took her to America?"

I nod. "Yes. And it fulfilled her every dream to meet her son. And today, he arrived in Italy, with his family." I point to the phone still in his hand. "Do you see his daughter, who he holds in the photo? That is Aurora. She is your granddaughter. Mother met her today, along with your daughter-in-law, Keira. They are happy and healthy, and Luca wishes to meet you very much as well."

"Did you tell him we are rich? Is that why he came?" Suspicion snakes back into his tone.

"He is very rich as well, Father. It was not money that motivated his visit. It was love for his family. To protect them. He is … a different sort of man from you and me,

Father. He …" I trail off, not knowing how to describe my brother without prejudicing my father against him.

"He is what?" my father asks impatiently, his gaze riveted back on the screen.

"He is American. Through and through, despite his Italian blood. You will have to meet him for yourself to learn more. Mother has invited you personally to her island. She is having a welcome party for them as we speak. Your presence is requested so that it can be a true family gathering."

CHAPTER TWENTY-NINE

LACHLAN

"The Giordanos were Italian nobility, but not the useless kind. They were not much for being courtiers, but preferred instead to build a legacy for the future. And when the nobility was abolished, the Giordanos became rebels of a sort. Your great-great-grandfather started a newspaper anonymously and began to print the truth, even when it was not popular with the government. The people, however, ate it up like sweets. Italy has not always been an easy place to live. We have been through much hardship and change over the years. But the Giordanos have adapted and thrived."

In the family portrait gallery, my mother explains some of the Giordano family history and the men and women whose likenesses are captured in oil on canvas.

I, however, can barely concentrate.

Right now, my brother is telling my father that I am alive. That I have returned to the family.

If I could be anywhere right now, it would be a fly on

the wall of that conversation. I wish more than anything that I could see and hear his reactions firsthand.

Is he happy? Is he handling it well? Does he wish to come and meet me immediately? Or does he think I'm an imposter, even with the photo?

"I should have gone with him," I can't help but say as my mother moves down to another portrait.

"Oh, no, you should not have. Such a shock from seeing both of you in the flesh, without knowing in advance, would have likely killed him. From what I have been told by his very unkind secretary, he is not in good health. She lives in fear of finding him fallen over dead on his desk one day. Which is probably fair. The man has tried to work himself into a grave for more years than I can remember."

None of the comments about my father, despite his obvious success in business, have been flattering.

In that moment, I picture myself in my library in New Orleans before I became fascinated with Keira. *Would I have worked myself into an early grave because I had nothing else to live for?* Undoubtedly. Mistresses didn't keep my attention for long. And the grind of my business dealings was my only other focus for many years.

I hadn't felt joy … maybe ever.

I didn't know happiness beyond the next conquest.

I knew death.

I knew dominance.

I knew darkness.

Keira will never understand the fate worse than death from which her very existence saved me. A spark of light in the darkness. A flash of hope in a world of death and despair. She was the life ring, tossed into the depths of hell, that I used to find my way back into the world of the living.

I am not the same man I was before her. She changed *everything.* I don't even think the same way anymore. Love altered me at the very deepest levels of my soul.

Even if my father is a terrible, miserable old man, I know there is hope for him. Because I am his son, and there was hope for me, even when I didn't realize I needed it.

If I can change, anyone can change.

I look down at the perfect face of my daughter in my arms and the sparkle of innocence in her dark brown eyes. I know she can melt even the hardest of hearts.

Silently, I tell her, *Your grandfather will not be able to resist you, princess. Your very presence can convert a man instantly.*

CHAPTER THIRTY

MARCO

He fidgeted the entire flight. My father, the son of Comte Alessandro Marconi Giordano, *fidgeted* the entire flight back to *Lago* Maggiore.

I have never seen him less than absolutely composed. Ruthlessly composed even.

My father, who allowed for no weakness of any kind, *fidgeted*.

If I were a child still, I would be concerned. As a man, I understand why he cannot restrain himself.

Change is constant in life, but when you have as much money as my father has always had, you begin to believe that you can control the changes in your world. That, somehow, money trumps fate. But today, I believe my father is learning that he is not in control. He did not foresee this change coming. He did not allow for the possibility that Luca could still be alive because of the hidden knowledge and secrets he has kept to himself all these years.

I know he wants to ask to see the picture again on my

phone, but he doesn't. Instead, he restlessly sits in the copilot's seat, shifting constantly with fractured attention.

I can't imagine what's going through his mind right now. I do not envy my father his life. It is perhaps the reason I am so different from him, much to his great despair when I was younger.

The day I told him I was leaving Italy, perhaps for good, to follow my own path, I nearly broke him. One son had already been taken from him, and he was determined to make me into a son who could fill the emptiness left by my brother. Despite his constant molding of me, I could not be shaped into the image he sought.

Life doesn't work that way.

I was destined to become what I became—my own man. Thankfully, when I returned, he ceased trying to force me to be what he wanted. I don't know if it was the tattoos—the physical reminder that I made my own choices—or the sheer gratitude that I had come back and he would not have to live out the remainder of his life without either of his sons. I've often thought he finally learned to appreciate my differences after he was deprived of them.

And now, as I set the plane down on the water in a smooth landing, I can't help but wonder what he will make of a man who is even less malleable than I was. Alessandro Giordano has never met a man like Lachlan Mount. No longer the infant who was taken from my mother's arms, my brother is a formidable force of nature.

A smile tugs at my lips as I imagine what kind of result there will be when these two forces of nature collide. And that is before I consider the potential fireworks that could take place when my father and mother see each other after all these decades separating them.

My mother is also an unpredictable woman, who should never be overlooked or underestimated. I would do so only at my own peril.

"How long have you known?" My father asks his first question of the flight immediately after I shut the engine down and glide the plane toward the dock, using the momentum of the slowing propellers.

I look over to see the side of his face as he continues to stare directly ahead.

"How long have I known what?"

"That he was alive. How long have you known?" The *without telling me* hangs unsaid, but I hear it regardless.

"Over a year."

His head jerks toward me. "And you kept this from me intentionally?"

"Yes. I didn't know where he was. Just that he was alive. It was a DNA test result that led back to an untraceable post office box in America. There was nothing I could tell you, except that a person with my DNA was alive."

"You made the right choice. I wouldn't have believed you if you'd told me then," he says, admitting the truth with quiet humility.

I meet his gaze with kindness in mine. "It's why I didn't tell you. It would have been agony for you to know that it was possible he was alive and not to know more."

"And it was not agony for you and your mother?"

I let my smile fully unfurl. "No. It was cause for celebration. For hope. For more prayers. For believing that our dream would finally come true."

"I would have spoiled that for you both. You knew this. It was good that you did not tell me until you did." The honesty coming from my father is more shocking than anything I could have imagined being said today.

"To find him, the hope needed to be stronger than ever before. We did not keep it from you out of cruelty, but out of kindness. It was hard not to run to you to tell you the truth. I wanted to bring you concrete proof, and that I could not provide until I saw him with my own two eyes and determined for myself that he was truly my brother."

The pontoon bumps against the dock as Marvin, one of the gardeners, ties off the bowline to the cleat.

After a few moments of silence, Father stares at me with his chin bouncing ever so slightly in agreement. "You made the right choice. Thank you for not letting me prevent this day from happening. I cannot imagine how overjoyed your mother must be to have both her sons alive and well and on her island."

"You will see her joy for yourself, Father. Are you ready?" I ask as Marvin reaches for the door on the passenger side of the plane.

With a lift of his chin, he says, "I have never been readier for anything in my life. Please, let us go. I wish to see them both. It has been much, much too long."

I don't know what to expect as we make our way from the plane to the stone stairs. Mother would have seen the plane flying in. She must know we are on our way up. The electric potential of the moments to come grows with each step we take.

My father, who is not a young man anymore, strides up the stairs the same way he must have when he was four decades younger. There's a spring in his step I have not seen since I was a boy. The urgency of his gait as he rushes without running is more than I anticipated.

Because you have no idea what he's feeling right now, I remind myself. *Or what the last forty-plus years have been like for him.*

And if I'm being honest, I do not want to know the pain he has felt. I would not want to live with the agony he has endured, both self-inflicted and otherwise.

I don't think he notices a single leaf, petal, or sculpture on the trek up to the main gardens that lead to the villa. But the moment he sees Lachlan and our mother, his stride falters, and he falls back a half step and freezes.

For long moments, nobody but the child in Lachlan's arms moves. Finally, Father looks to me and then back to Lachlan. Without a word, he sinks to his knees on the grass, and his fists clutch at the blades.

As if in slow motion, Lachlan crouches down and lowers Aurora to her feet. Still holding each of her small hands, he walks slowly toward our father's kneeling form while she takes one wobbling step after another.

Finally, he speaks, breaking the silence that encapsulates us all. "This is your grandfather, Rory. Would you like to meet him?"

A rough breath escapes our father, and I am moved to tears as he opens his arms to the tiny little girl in welcome.

CHAPTER THIRTY-ONE

LACHLAN

Aurora stumbles into the older man's open arms, and I pray I haven't miscalculated. I pray that my father can't resist the sweetness of my little girl—because I'd hate to have to kill him right here and have a pool of blood spoil our perfect family moment.

When he closes his arms around her and tears pour down a face that looks like mine will look in a few decades, I know that I'm not going to have to kill anyone today.

"My granddaughter," he whispers through an onslaught of tears. "I have a granddaughter."

"It is a miracle," my mother says quietly from beside me.

I would hazard to guess that there's not a single dry eye on the entire island right now. Keira takes three steps forward and kneels in the grass.

"She might get your suit a little slobbery. I'm sorry about that. She's teething."

My father, a man who could no more deny I am his son

than I could deny he is my sire, looks at my wife for the first time.

"She is beautiful. You are beautiful." He looks up at me, eyes shining with tears. "And my son. My Luca. You have come back to us. This day ... this day ..." He switches to Italian, and whatever he says has my mother sobbing and my brother squatting down and reaching out to wrap an arm around the older man's shoulders.

We all draw nearer as he sobs into Aurora's dark curls. She squirms away, reaching for her mother, and he releases her gracefully.

"My son," he says as he stares longingly at me and then looks to Marco. "My sons."

He tips forward, his forehead touching the grass, and we all wait in silence while he has his moment. After all, we've each had ours already. But his emotional state draws forth a poignance from me that I've never before felt.

Tears roughen my throat, and I'm grateful I don't have to speak. I lower onto the grass beside Keira and reach for Aurora. She plops onto her rear in between us and yanks grass from the lawn.

"Ma-ma," she says as she sprinkles her treasures over her feet.

"Brilliant girl. A Giordano through and through," my mother says as she sinks beside me with a hand on my shoulder. "Beautiful and brilliant."

My father lifts his head from the grass and stares at each of us with bewilderment on his face.

"I did not know. I did not know. He told me you were dead. If I had known, I would never have stopped searching. I would never have given up hope. But he told me you were dead. He swore it on his life and his family's life. I believed him. He lied to me, and I believed him. I believed his lie, and it cost me everything."

I have no idea who my father is talking about, but the only person who makes sense is someone involved in the kidnapping all those years ago. Marco didn't mention they ever knew who did it, and the media that Keira searched hadn't reported any leads.

But the old man—my old man—clearly knew more than the papers.

Someone had told him I was dead. Someone had convinced him that it was the truth. *And it changed everything.*

I think of the foster homes that were my first memories and then the streets that became my world. *Cold and merciless.* The exact environment that it would take to make me the man I became. A man strong enough to survive anything. Strong enough to seize an empire. Strong enough to overcome every obstacle and challenge.

I cannot hate my past. Somehow, I know that serves no purpose. Instead, in this moment, where my father's grief and joy collide, I let the past go. Completely.

I reach out and wrap my arms around him, pulling his shoulders toward me. "It doesn't matter now. None of it matters now. What matters is right here. Right now. This moment. Our family. We're all here. Nothing that came before has any hold on us. Today is what matters. Right now is what matters."

My father's sobs grow louder as he clutches at my suit jacket, holding on to me as if I'm his anchor to this world.

I'm strong enough for both of us, old man, I think as he shakes. *Your son is not weak. Your son is a king of his own world.*

Keira's hand squeezes my thigh, and my mother's hand remains on my shoulder. I lift my head to see Marco with his hands together and head bowed, as if praying over us all.

"It's a miracle," my mother whispers.

My father holds on tighter and tighter until he finally releases me and pulls back six inches, shifting his grip from my back to my shoulders. His dark gaze burns into mine.

"My son. You are my son. My Luca. You are home. I thought God had cursed me and our family, but I was wrong. You are strong. You are well. And you are *home*."

"A miracle," my mother says once more.

My father breaks his stare to look at her. "And you are more beautiful than ever, Francesca. What a stupid, stupid man I have been. All this time I have wasted. I do not deserve such joy, but I cannot shut it out. I want to ask how or why, but I do not care. I do not care how or why today happened. All I care is that it is so."

CHAPTER THIRTY-TWO

KEIRA

I've never seen such a range of raw emotion on display. This family reunion is beyond description.

Grief.

Disbelief.

Regret.

Joy.

Relief.

Gratitude.

Devotion.

I don't feel like an outsider, because Lachlan is the other half of my soul, but I know that what he and his family are feeling truly has nothing to do with me.

Except that's not entirely true. But for me, this moment wouldn't be happening. I was the one who submitted that DNA test without his knowledge. Because I had seen the gaping hole Lachlan Mount's unknown origins had left in his heart and his life.

This was a man who believed that no one cared about him and that he mattered to no one. He'd grown into manhood on the cruel streets of New Orleans, believing that was the truth. It had shaped him into the hard and ruthless man who was waiting in my office to take my body in payment and claim me for his own.

I would never have believed that the Lachlan Mount I first met is the same man who now cries with his father, his mother, and his brother. I didn't know he had the ability and capacity to transform to this degree. I didn't know *anyone* had that ability or capacity.

But once more, Lachlan Mount has blown away every single one of my fixed beliefs and expectations. I shouldn't be surprised anymore. But I have to admit, I am constantly surprised by my husband. I had no idea he could become the man he has become.

His beginnings would make anyone believe otherwise. But now, to find out that everything he believed about himself was a lie … as his mother has said repeatedly, *it is a miracle.* None of it was true. He wasn't unwanted. He wasn't abandoned. He was taken. Stolen. And yet still loved beyond anything he could have ever imagined.

Watching this reunification unfold and being part of it, with my hand on his thigh, I am overwhelmed by the magic of life and the very grace by which we have been touched.

I didn't know that the urge that led me to submit that DNA test could result in this beautiful homecoming and reunion.

Looking down at the grass beneath me, I press my palm against the blades for support and whisper a mental prayer.

Thank you, God. I did not know this much happiness

was possible. Thank you for giving this moment to my husband and his family. Thank you.

With each beat of my heart, I wonder if it could explode from an overload of joy. I didn't know it was possible to be this happy for anyone. But experiencing this with Lachlan has shown me that my heart can handle so much more than I ever realized.

Others might think that a man who has done what Lachlan has done and been what he has been couldn't possibly deserve such a beautiful experience, but I know they'd be completely wrong. Lachlan Mount has done more good than anyone would believe. He's saved more lives than he has taken, many times over.

He might have been the ruthless king of the New Orleans criminal underworld, but only because that was the role life had cast him in. In his own way, he brought order to chaos, and safety and security to many of those who would have been devoured by the streets, like he would have been if he hadn't been so determined, strong, and resilient.

Lachlan Mount is a man unlike any other.

A force of nature.

Law unto himself.

But in this moment, he is transforming into something even more.

A loving son.

A devoted brother.

I knew it was possible, even if the whole world didn't believe it. I watched him go from being a controlling and demanding captor to a devoted husband and doting father. After witnessing such change in a man who others feared, I stopped judging what I believed was possible.

Lachlan Mount has shown me that *anything* is possible. He has proven to me over and over that he is beyond comprehension and categorization.

I've known from the beginning that I had absolutely no control over him. On the contrary, it seemed that I would never be in control of my own life ever again. But loving Lachlan Mount has been the education of a lifetime. It is my privilege to be a witness to this miracle, because no one deserves the sweetness and love of this homecoming more than he does.

His capacity to transform has been miraculous. It only seems right and fair that his life story should include miracles as well.

It wasn't only Aurora who could melt his heart. It was love, wherever and from whomever was brave enough to offer it to this formidable man.

"Ma-ma," Aurora says as she leans toward my face, making smacking noises with her lips.

I think of how long we've been on the island and realize that it's time for her to eat. I don't want to break this beautiful moment, but I have to feed my daughter.

Somehow, Lachlan knows immediately as well. I swear, his fatherhood gene expresses itself at every opportune moment.

"Aurora needs to eat," he says, meeting my gaze.

I nod, still not wanting to interrupt.

"Of course she does," Lachlan's mother says, lifting her head. "And we have plenty of food. Mountains of it. I didn't know what you would like. I chose picnic-style so we would not be rushed and nothing needed to be eaten immediately."

There's a moment of silence, and then she speaks to

her no-longer-estranged husband. "Would you like to join us for a meal, Alesso?"

At the sound of his name, Lachlan's father fastens his gaze on her. I can't imagine the roller coaster of emotions he's gone through today. From believing his son was dead, to learning he wasn't, to meeting him and his family, *and* seeing the wife he hasn't seen in over forty years? I'm grateful and thankful the older man's heart could handle it all.

"It would be my honor to share a meal with *my family*," he replies with a hushed tone, almost as if he cannot believe he is speaking the words.

"Excellent. Then, we shall eat. After that," she adds, "you must all rest. You will be exhausted from the travel and excitement."

Shockingly, my husband yawns. "As much as I wish I didn't need sleep, it has been many days since I've rested well. Food and sleep would both be welcome. Thank you, Mother."

She beams with unbridled joy as he calls her Mother, and her face, already stunningly beautiful, becomes serene and transcendent.

"Then, that is exactly what you shall have, my son. Please, come. Let us eat."

CHAPTER THIRTY-THREE

MARCO

For the first time in my life, I'm having a meal with my whole family.

I grew up with every material thing a child could possibly want, as well as plenty of love, but one thing I have never experienced is a true family meal.

Today, it isn't only my brother's, mother's, and father's lives that have changed irrevocably, but also mine. An entire life was denied to my brother through the winds of fate, but this simple pleasure of a family dinner was denied to me.

Seeing my mother and father in the same place at the same time ... I truly never knew if that would ever happen. And today, it has.

While it may seem that this homecoming and reunion are not about me, I am equally affected and blessed.

My mother has said it over and over again—*we have been blessed with a miracle*. I feel it acutely.

Watching my family take their seats at a table together —my father, mother, brother, sister-in-law, and niece—I am overwhelmed with the sight and the rush of emotions that crash through me like a rogue wave.

I am beyond blessed. I am touched by God's favor.

I feel no hunger as I watch the moment unfold before me like I'm watching a movie of someone else's life. It is so surreal; it feels like it's not even happening to me.

Something as simple as watching my mother offering my father a platter of cured meats and cheeses shouldn't feel like I'm seeing another miracle happen, but it does.

I thought I was prepared for this—for what this would mean to me and my family—but I was wrong. This is so much more than anything I could have imagined or for which I could have prepared myself.

The lack of awkwardness between my parents is a blessing I did not expect. One would think after over forty years apart, they would not know how to be around one another, but it feels like they've been together this entire time.

It makes absolutely no sense, but they've settled back into a pattern they must have created long ago.

My father lifts another platter to offer my mother her favorite grapes. *He never forgot her favorite grapes.* My heart clenches, and the realization nearly brings me to tears.

How do I deserve so much? How can my life be so blessed?

They are questions I've asked over and over throughout the years, and I've never received any answers. But I accept it for what it is. Somehow, I must deserve this. Somehow, I must be worthy of these great gifts that I have been given.

Nothing and no one could compare with the heart-expanding joy I feel that keeps tears perched on my lashes, ready to fall at any second.

My father seems to have softened and gentled in an instant. The hard, sharp edges that were his trademark seem to have disappeared. It's astonishing to witness his love-filled gaze as he watches his granddaughter's tiny hands artlessly smear strawberries on her sweet face.

It's like a completely new universe has opened up before me. A new world. A new life. And it is full of new possibilities and potentialities.

I knew that bringing my brother here would change everything, but even I, with what I believed was my expanded awareness, did not understand the magnitude of change I was helping to unleash.

Much-needed change.

If I am honest—and that is one thing I require of myself always—I did not realize how stagnant and subdued life had become before now.

My father's health has been on the forefront of my mind for years. I did not know if he would survive to see this day that I hoped would eventually come to fruition. And even if he did survive, I wasn't sure he would be able to accept it or feel joy after so many years spent drowning in bitterness and regret.

But in everything, I am a student. And today, I see that what I believed possible was only a small fraction of what life has shown to be the truth.

Words cannot describe what it is like to experience this. It is ineffable. I simply watch and witness the beauty taking place at the table before me. Keira cutting up small bites of food for Aurora. Lachlan—or Luca, as he shall always be to me—watching them solicitously, as if waiting for any opportunity to assist. Catching the glances of my mother and father across the table, as they sneak peeks at each other after all these years apart. For years, I have wondered how their reunion would go. I have imagined it so many different ways. Tempestuous, explosive, loud … but never this. I was totally and completely wrong.

I never expected this *peace*. This *love*. This … *completeness* of our family.

Now, more than ever, I am grateful my brother has sired an heir. Not for the future of the family line or to maintain our holdings, but because I believe her innocence has affected us all. My father was brought to his knees. My mother retained her intrinsic sweetness.

As Mama has said and will no doubt continue to say over and over, *it is a miracle*. And I, for one, simply count myself lucky to witness it.

And even luckier to watch the healing of my family begin.

CHAPTER THIRTY-FOUR

LACHLAN

None of us truly wants to sleep and allow this initial stage of our family reunion to end, but I know that I can't stay conscious for much longer.

I've been running on fumes for hours. It's a wonder that I didn't fall asleep on the flight, like Keira and Aurora. But then again, it's not. I had the first opportunity of my life to talk to my brother, and even more than that, I couldn't rest until my family was safe. My body wouldn't let me sleep.

Now though, it's as if a biological cue has been triggered and my body knows that it can release its typical hyperawareness and vigilance and take refuge in much-needed rest.

I barely managed to eat. It wasn't important. Feeding my daughter was. And the fact that it was happening during the first meal that my family had ever shared together ... *priceless*.

Not for all the riches and treasures in the world would I have missed this moment.

Even though my mother and father hadn't been in each other's company for many, many years, I could not tell. It seemed like they were together just yesterday. I can't imagine what this is like for my brother, for whom so much has changed so quickly. It seems change is in the air though.

Only days ago, I was in despair. On the floor of my library, I hit rock bottom. I felt myself break.

How is it that after giving myself over to such torment and accepting the reality of what I had done that life lifted me into a totally different dimension?

I will never understand the mysteries and perfection of my life, but I will not question them either.

I have been saved *over and over again*, when I did not deserve it. I used to wonder why. *Why me? What did I do to deserve this?*

But there were never any answers, so I quit asking.

When Keira came into my life, I didn't hesitate. Something deep in my soul knew that she was important to my continued existence. I couldn't take a chance that she wouldn't understand, so I took her instead.

Only through a miracle could she have fallen in love with me—another gift I didn't question because I was afraid questioning it would make it disappear.

But her love never disappeared. It only grew. And then with Aurora, a completely different world opened to us, and it changed *everything* for me.

I tried to continue being the same man I'd been before, but I couldn't. I feared I was growing soft. But even then, I couldn't make the same decisions anymore. I couldn't treat life so callously. Her birth changed me at the most basic biological level. It was something I had no control over.

Something I thought I could escape, unchanged. But I was wrong. I felt myself losing my grip on my empire. I couldn't rule with an iron fist the way I used to. I couldn't crush people and problems the same way.

It felt like the end of me. The end of life as I knew it.

I understand now—there are no endings. Only new beginnings.

I've been gifted with a precious new life that I will not squander. For myself, for my family, for my future, I will cherish this gift and nurture it into all it can become.

As I fall asleep tonight, it will be as a new man.

No longer the old Lachlan Mount, but not Luca Giordano yet either.

I'm somewhere in between, in the unknown. I have no idea who or what I am becoming, but I have never been more grateful to be alive so that I can find out.

CHAPTER THIRTY-FIVE

LACHLAN

Sunlight filters into my awareness, bringing me out of the depths of sleep. My body, exhausted when I lay down, feels lighter and restored as I yawn and stretch.

I can't remember the last time I slept so soundly or woke feeling so rested. Another yawn and stretch clear the remaining fog of sleep, and my mind switches on. My first thoughts, as usual upon waking, are of Keira and Aurora.

My chin jerks to one side and then the other before I realize that I'm alone on the white sheets in the antique wooden four-poster bed. Levering up to a seated position, I scan the room. There's no sign of either of them within these cream-plastered walls, decorated with garden scenes painted on canvas.

I swing my legs around, and my feet hit the floor as I see the note on the heavy wooden nightstand.

We're at breakfast. We love you.

—K

As if my senses are coming online one by one, the scent of food and the sound of clinking plates and silverware enter my awareness.

Breakfast.

I slept all night. Impressive. I must have needed the sleep.

Normally, I get by on a few hours. I've never been one to feel at ease while in the blackness of oblivion. As a child on the streets, I learned to rest while maintaining awareness of all my surroundings at the same time. It's not exactly a skill they teach Boy Scouts, but it kept me alive through more than one close call. But right now, I can't remember a damn thing after I kissed Keira and my head hit the pillow. I was *out*.

Perhaps my body knew that it was finally safe to let go completely, and it took the opportunity to recharge at deeper levels than it would normally be able to access.

I squeeze the note between my thumb and index finger and lift it to my lips. *My family is safe. They're having breakfast. I got a solid night of sleep. All is well.*

So far, I have to say that this trip to Italy has been the best decision I've ever made.

Feeling more alive and revived than I have in years, I spot the empty duffel bags on the luggage stand and stride over to the closet to dress.

It takes no time at all to toss on a white collared shirt and a pair of slacks so I can find my wife and daughter. *And my brother, mother, and father,* I remind myself, still shocked that those thoughts are in my mind. It's a first.

Now, onto breakfast with my family.

I can't help but release a short laugh. *Who would have ever guessed?* I have a family.

I wonder immediately if my father is still here or if he has returned to Milan already. Given that his son rose from the dead after more than forty years, I'm willing to bet that he's still on the island. If it were me, I wouldn't leave.

With bare feet registering the chill of the marble floor, I make my way out of the bedroom and take a right turn. I haven't seen the entire house, so I haven't had a chance to memorize the layout in detail, but I would never forget the route that got me to this room. Years of milling around in my own maze-like domain help me quickly lock routes into my mind and body so I don't have to think about where and when to turn in the event of an emergency.

But you weren't there during the emergency when V really needed you.

The thought is unwelcome, but true. I allow the guilt and grief to hit me like a punch to the gut, but right now, it's the last thing I want to focus on. Instead, I let it wash over me and pass through.

"I'm sorry, brother. I'll lay your ashes to rest somewhere beautiful, I swear it," I whisper to V's spirit as I continue toward the sounds of life coming from the lower level of the stunning Italian villa.

My focus on life as opposed to guilt, grief, and death allows the emotions to dissipate into the ether before I reach the bottom of the curved marble staircase.

A right and then another left lead me to the warmth and light of the large dining room—where I find my entire family. It's surreal. They're all here. My mother, father, brother, wife, and daughter. Gratitude replaces grief, and it grips my entire being.

This is an experience I never knew I could have, and

I'm so damn lucky I get to have it, regardless of whether it feels real or not.

But what does feel real is my stomach grumbling as I breathe in the delicious scents coming from a sideboard and table loaded with enough food to feed an army.

I haven't been this hungry in weeks. Maybe months.

"Lachlan! Finally! You're awake!" Keira half rises from her seat with Aurora on her lap.

I raise a hand. "No need to get up," I reply as I walk directly toward her and press a kiss to her lips. "Thank you for the note."

When I lift my head, I take in my brother, mother, and father, all staring at me.

"My apologies for oversleeping. Thank you for letting me rest. I must have needed it."

"You were sleeping like the dead," Keira replies with one hand reaching up to graze a thumb across my jaw. "A whole night and day, plus another night. It was my decision to let you sleep. I don't think you've ever been out like that, not since I've known you. I think you needed to recharge more than anything."

A whole night and day, plus another night. Stunned, I blink several times. "I slept that long? I missed an entire day?"

Such a thing has never happened in my entire life. I've never missed a day. Not even when I was doped up on narcotics and recovering from a gunshot wound.

"It's okay. Nothing happened. We're all safe and sound. It's beautiful here. Rory loves it."

My wife and daughter look as carefree as I've ever seen them. Aurora is dressed in a yellow sundress with a smear of what appears to be strawberry jam across her lips, and Keira looks radiant in a white linen tank top and vibrant green skirt.

"I don't even know what to say," I reply, meeting the gaze of my mother next.

"The body knows what it needs. You have no need to be concerned. We have kept ourselves perfectly occupied, getting to know our beautiful granddaughter. She is a delightful ray of sunshine."

I have to agree with her, especially as my baby girl reaches for me with sticky fingers. I press a kiss to her precious curls as my attention moves to my father, who nods in agreement.

"You are lucky we are on a small island or else Francesca would have a stable of ponies for her by now. When we all go to the family estate in the country, she will have her choice of several."

The family estate. Ponies. All completely surreal.

"I have no doubt she'd love that. Thank you," I say to my father.

His expression is soft and gentle, which seems unlike the man my mother and brother described. But if I can sleep for two nights and an entire day for the first time in my life, apparently anything can happen on this magical island away from the world.

Like I woke up in a dream, I turn to my brother, and it's like I'm seeing myself at breakfast with my family. Except, in his open-collared, short-sleeved shirt, I see the artistry of his intricate tattoos on display—heavy black lines with cherry blossoms on branches and tapestry-like patterns in a distinctly Japanese style.

"This is unreal," I say, unable to help myself.

Marco smiles in response. "It has been wonderful,

although I can't imagine what this morning must be like for you, but all is well. Mother is right; you needed the rest. When is the last time you had a full night's sleep anyway?"

Keira laughs quietly. "Full night's sleep? Lachlan? Never. At least not as long as I have known him." She grins with eyes shining. "I'm so glad you were able to sleep. That, in itself, was a miracle."

"Lachlan. That name is hard for me to say it fits you," my father says, seemingly taking in every detail of me as I stand beside my wife and daughter. "But it is not far from Luca, I suppose. If you want to keep it."

"Alesso," my mother says with a warning note in her tone. "He has had nearly as much shock as you. Let the boy have whatever name he wishes. The name doesn't matter. The fact that he is home does."

"I know; I know. It does not matter, but I have only thought of him as Luca. Marco and Luca, our boys."

"It's been a long time since anyone has called me a boy or since I have thought of myself as one," I say.

"But you shall always be our boy. Our beautiful baby boy. We are so glad you are here," my mother says, her hands coming together, as if in prayer, for a beat. "You must eat though. You must be starving since it has been so long since you were fed. Your plate is there beside your wife. We did not know if you would awaken for breakfast, but I had everything prepared anyway, just in case. There are American options as well since we did not know if you would adjust quickly to Italian fare."

"I don't care what I eat at this point. Anything will do."

"Rory recommends the homemade raspberry jam. I'm pretty sure she would smear it all over her body if I let her," Keira says with the brightest smile I've seen on her face maybe ever.

Coming here was the right choice.

I lean down and use my thumb to wipe the smear of red from the silken skin of my daughter's precious face before pressing a kiss to her cheek. *Ah, raspberry, not strawberry.* "Always so sweet."

"And those sticky fingers of hers are about to get you."

I pull back just before Aurora can smear the raspberries on my face in return. "If that is the price I must pay, then so be it. But you're still not as quick as Daddy." I lean in and steal another kiss before straightening.

After loading my plate with a wider variety of options than I would normally eat in a week, I take the seat beside my wife and daughter, across from my brother. My father sits at the head and my mother at the foot of the table, which must be at least ten feet long.

"I still can't believe I slept so long," I say with another yawn before reaching for the linen napkin.

It's truly mind-blowing to me that I could remain unconscious for that long in a house full of people I barely know, on a strange island in the middle of a lake, in a foreign country. But as my mother said, my body knew what it needed.

"You did not miss much," Marco replies as he spreads preserves on a small piece of bread. "Just the tour of the island and villa. Mother will happily give the tour again and again."

"I also learned about some of your family history. Very impressive." Keira wipes Aurora's hands with a napkin as she smiles.

"We can trace our lineage back over a thousand years," my father adds.

"And you did not need to return to Milan for business?" I ask him before taking my first bite of poached egg.

My brother laughs and slaps a hand on the tabletop. "His she-devil of a secretary forbade him to return for at least a month when he told her why he left so abruptly with me."

"She says she can run the entire company without me, if need be," my father says with a soft smile.

"Undoubtedly, it is true," my mother chimes in. "After all, she has been working side by side with you for nearly fifty years. If she can't run the company by now, I would question whether she'd learned anything at all in that time, and we all know she never forgets a *thing*."

My father nods in assent at my mother before looking to me. "Now that you're rested, we can show you your heritage. The islands are only one part. There is the country estate in Tuscany, the chateau in the Dolomites, a building in Milan, the flat and yacht in Cinque Terre, as well as a villa in Palermo. We have a rich history in this country and much to show you. How many months will you stay? Or perhaps you will just stay indefinitely. From what I understand from Marco, things are not ideal in America for you right now."

I glance at Marco and wonder how much he's told our father about me, my business, and my past. He gives me a small shake of his head, and I believe that means he hasn't told the secrets that are mine to tell.

I reach over to squeeze Keira's hand and reply to my father, "I don't know what our exact plans are right now.

We left behind a complicated situation that required space to determine how best to respond. But most importantly, we came because this was an opportunity I could not pass up for the world."

"Complicated situation?" my father asks, hooking into the vagueness of my statement.

I have an option right here, right now, to tell him the truth. It would be just as easy to gloss over it, but something inside me says that my father is not going to tell me to leave now, no matter what I share with him.

"I haven't exactly made my living on the right side of the law. It wasn't wholly by choice, but it is a situation I created, and therefore, I am the one who will have to handle it and deal with the consequences, for better or for worse."

"You are a criminal?" my father asks, although I register no judgment in his tone.

"Yes," I reply honestly.

"What kind of criminal?"

"The kingpin of an empire," Keira supplies, saving me from coming up with an appropriate description of my role in New Orleans.

My father's laugh surprises me more than anything. He sits back in his chair and crosses his arms over his chest. "Of course you are. A Giordano always rises to the top."

His easy acceptance shocks me.

Then, my mother chimes in, "But you do not wish to be this anymore, correct? You have a beautiful daughter. A wonderful wife. Such a life cannot be safe for them."

"No, not anymore. It's time to pull the pin on the grenade that is my empire and let the whole thing go up in flames."

"That sounds dangerous too, my son," my mother replies with a gentle smile.

It's not really the breakfast conversation I anticipated or even wanted to be having, but I can't hide who I am from my family. Through divine timing, my brother and mother arrived just when I needed them most. All I can do is be honest about my intent to change and extricate myself and my family from the hell I created.

"It's necessary," I reply.

"Do you have a plan?" my father asks.

I nod twice. "Yes. I have a dead man's switch in place that has to be activated. To the extent it's possible, it will undo some of what I've done and set many things right. It will also end my association with anything criminal and everything related to New Orleans."

My father's chin lifts, as if in approval. "I like this plan. You should activate your switch so you can live free as a Giordano and enjoy the rest of your life here, in Italy, with your family. There is no need for you to return to America ever."

I feel Keira tense beside me, and I know the idea of never returning to America, where her family lives, is not her idea of happily ever after.

I'm so sorry, Hellion. I'll do my best to make sure that we can return ... eventually. I squeeze her hand with my silent promise, and she squeezes mine back.

"Except I must return to activate my plan. My fail-safe was ... eliminated ... not long ago."

A quiet hush descends over the table, and my mother is the first to break it. "You will stay for at least a week before you return. That is my request. This time with family is both priceless and precious. Anything can wait for a week. Please, give me that, if you can."

Keira's grip tightens on my hand, and I swallow the lump forming in my throat. I know my wife wants to speak for us—to agree that we will *absolutely* stay for at least a week—and staring into my mother's beautiful brown eyes, I can't possibly say no.

"Of course. If that is your wish, a week it is."

"And after that?" my father asks.

"We shall see," I reply. "We shall see."

"Thank you, my son. We shall take this week as the blessing that it is and enjoy every moment," my mother says with a smile. "Now, we dine as a family. Eat, eat."

CHAPTER THIRTY-SIX

LACHLAN

As we're rising from breakfast, Marco catches my attention. "Can I speak with you for a moment, brother?"

I glance at Keira and Aurora.

"I need to clean up Miss Sticky Face and Fingers. Go right ahead."

I lean down to press a kiss to my wife's rosy lips. "Thank you."

"Take your time. There's no hurry," she says to both of us as she lifts Aurora from her antique-looking high chair.

"Come. We can speak in the library," Marco says before nodding to our parents. "We shall return shortly."

"Do not worry about us. We have much to speak about ourselves," our father replies with a lift of his espresso-filled demitasse cup.

I follow Marco out of the dining room and down a hallway to the end. A large arched doorway leads into a stunning library that rises two stories tall. It puts mine in New Orleans to shame.

I take a deep breath, inhaling the scent of old books. "Incredible."

"My favorite room in the house," Marco replies with a grin.

"Another thing we have in common. I've always loved a good library."

He smiles for a beat before drawing his phone from his pocket. "I have something I must show you. It is not ideal news."

"How *not ideal*?" I ask, keeping my tone conversational.

Marco releases a long breath as he brings up something on the screen. "For others, probably devastating. For you, perhaps more mundane."

After years of receiving bad news, this doesn't draw any reaction from my body. "Go ahead. I'm ready."

"I will let you read it for yourself."

He hands his phone to me, and I read the headline of the article.

LACHLAN MOUNT WANTED FOR EXECUTION-STYLE MURDER

I scan the article, including the part about the Feds being called in as part of an organized crime crackdown, and read the quote from DuFort.

> *"New Orleans will not be safe until this man is brought to justice. In cooperation with the New Orleans Police Department, the Federal Bureau of*

Investigation will not stop until he and his entire criminal empire have been smashed to a million pieces and everyone connected has been put behind bars. For too many years, he has gotten away with literal murder in this city, and his days of freedom are numbered."

The irony is not lost on me. DuFort and his entire family regularly torture and murder children in ritual sacrifices to gain power from satanic gods, *but I'm the one who makes the city unsafe.*

Still, I can't argue. I pulled that trigger. I killed that man in broad daylight, in the middle of the street, with a bullet to the brain, and I don't regret it. Any normal person would agree that I should be locked up and the key thrown away. However, I'm not about to let DuFort bring me down without taking him and his entire family out in the process. *Not a chance.* Justice will be served, but not in the way he thinks.

I look up to meet my brother's concerned gaze. "Thank you for sharing that. Has it made national news? Or is it simply in the local papers?"

From the rising eyebrows on Marco's face, my question is not the response he expected.

"I've only seen it on the local New Orleans papers' websites and the local news channels. Nothing national yet."

"Excellent. At least that's one upside to being from a city and country where murder is still so common that it barely raises an eyebrow. People like to think America is so civilized these days, but that's just as much of a fantasy as the stories Keira reads to Rory."

"This doesn't worry you?" Marco asks as I hand him back the phone.

"Worry doesn't do me any good. That's something I learned long ago. It is what it is. I can like it or not, but it won't change the reality of the situation. It's something I did, and therefore, the consequences are also mine. I'll take care of it. I just don't want it to spill over to the national news, as that could potentially reach the international stage, and the last thing I want is for Lachlan Mount's picture to be broadcast worldwide and affect the Giordano family."

"It is us you are concerned about? Not yourself?" Marco asks incredulously.

I nod. "I would turn myself into the Feds before I let this touch your family."

"*Our family,* brother."

"Either way, my response is the same. I won't let this touch you, our family, or my wife and daughter. They stay here. You keep them safe. I created this beast by my own actions and decisions, and it's up to me to deal with it. It touches no one else. This is on me and me alone."

"You're not going back to America alone," Marco says with unyielding emotion threading through his words. "Not a chance. I just got my brother back. I won't let you sacrifice yourself before I even get to know you."

"You might not have a choice."

"You have your choices, and I have mine. When you go back to slay this beast, I go with you. We put this to rest together, and then we both return as Giordanos. Promise me you will not leave without me."

I inhale slowly through my nose and release a long breath the same way before replying, "It might not be pretty. In fact, it could get downright ugly. There are no guarantees that we both return. I can promise you that I will not leave without you, but I can't promise how this is going to end."

"God will take care of that. You have your plans, and I have my faith. But no matter what, we go together."

He holds out a hand, and I take it and shake it, sealing our bargain.

"Then, God have mercy on both of us, because we're damn sure going to need it."

CHAPTER THIRTY-SEVEN

LACHLAN

The last week has passed in a whirlwind of surreal family experiences. My mother showed us her entire island with some of what must be the most exquisite terraced gardens in the entire world. The other two islands that make up the family holdings on *Lago* Maggiore were also stunning beyond belief. I understood how my mother could be a recluse here, in one of the most beautiful places on earth, especially after she showed us her conservatory, where she paints.

It felt familiar somehow, even though I'd never been there before. But it wasn't until she showed us her paintings that I was truly astounded.

I've seen this place before. In one of her paintings. That hangs in my home.

Astonishment filled me when I realized that the conservatory I was standing in was straight out of a painting that hung in the dressing room in the French Quarter that Keira and I shared.

I own one of my mother's paintings.

How could this even be possible? I wondered, staring, open-mouthed, at her work on their easels and the yellow signature in the corner of each canvas.

I'd purchased the painting from Leo. He'd fenced it, as it'd been stolen from someone, somewhere, sometime. Something about it called to me, and I had to have it. It was one of those purchases I didn't question at all. I simply followed my heart and acquired it and then put it somewhere I'd see it every single day. For some reason though, I'd wanted to keep it away from prying eyes. It was special to me. Something I didn't want to share with anyone, except for Keira once she came into my life.

The quirks of life would never cease to amaze me. It seemed fated.

I was so shocked at the realization, and when I told her, we both cried.

"I have been with you for years," she said. "Just as I was meant to be."

It was a moment I would never forget.

The family estate in Tuscany was another revelation. Its gentle, rolling hills produced organic durum wheat for pasta and organic tomatoes that I learned were made into sauce prized by chefs worldwide. The Giordano Brand was sold in supermarkets across five continents and helped feed the world.

"When you are done with your business in America, we have much business here for you to attend. I am getting old. I would happily turn it all over to you and Marco to carry forward the family name and safeguard your daughter's inheritance until she is ready to take the reins herself." My father beamed at my daughter, as if all the work he'd put into his own empire was simply to pass it along to her. His words and attitude were humbling, to say the least.

Everywhere we went, the staff was gracious and welcoming. They cried and wept over the miracle of my return, like I was their very own son. Marco asked everyone to keep the family news private for now so that we could enjoy each other's company without intrusion. Everyone agreed easily, and hugs were exchanged by the dozens. I'd never hugged so many people in my life as I did in the space of a week.

Cinque Terre was an exquisite visual delight and something purely Italy. The yacht was Aurora's favorite though, as she seemed to love being at sea, near the splashing water.

"She is a Giordano through and through," my father said. "We thrive near water. It is our second home. She will be a mermaid by age six. Mark my words."

We finished our weeklong family excursion back on the islands, opting to save the chateau in the Dolomites and the villa in Palermo for when I returned.

It'd sped by much too fast. A week could never be enough time to spend with my family. My mother was by my side nearly every moment, and her love enfolded me in a way I'd never before experienced. My father slapped my back and hugged me as he explained all that would be Aurora's one day. It was the most idyllic week of my life.

The unconditional love of a family was incredible.

Even knowing some of what I'd done and who I'd become, they didn't hold anything back. Nothing mattered but the moments we shared and the joy that was ever present between us.

When the week ends with us back in my mother's

conservatory on *Lago* Maggiore, I know that no matter what happens next, I've been given the greatest gift anyone could ever receive. I've been loved beyond belief and without condition. My family welcomed us with open arms and showered us with hospitality and love unlike anything we've ever experienced before. Without a doubt, I know that my wife is safe and that my daughter's future is more than secure. It's bulletproof. Aurora and Keira will want for nothing—ever.

As a father and a husband, that is the fulfillment of my greatest wish and the abolition of every one of my deepest fears. They will be protected, cherished, and loved. There is nothing more I could want or need.

With the hours ticking down on my last evening in Italy, I know that I can die happy. Come what may, the consequences of my decisions and actions will not affect those I love most. I might be called to Judgment Day, but my blood and my love will live on forever in Italy.

"I do not want you to go," my mother says, her tone hushed, as she holds my hands between hers. "But I know you must. I pray for forgiveness and mercy to be showered upon you, for the life you have lived was not of your choosing. You survived to come home to us. You have given me the greatest joy of all my years this past week. I am complete. I am whole. I am no longer a mother with a lost son. I am a mother of two strong, noble men. I have a husband who has been restored to me. I have the daughter for whom I have always wished. And now, I am a grandmother to a beautiful angel who will no doubt light up the world in her own way. If you could see my heart, you would watch it overflow with joy, for even though it feels ten sizes too big, it is still not big enough to contain all the love pouring through me right now. And that is all because of your presence here with your family."

I don't care about appearing strong. I let tears pour down my face as I bow my head and kiss my mother's hands. It could be the last time I ever see her. I know that. She knows that. We are both in silent agreement that we are going to soak up every moment we have together.

"Thank you for never giving up on me. Thank you for never giving up hope that you would find me. Thank you for praying for me. I love you more than I knew it was possible to love. I thought Keira and Rory had taught me all there was to know on the subject, but I was wrong. I was wrong." My shoulders shake as my chest lifts and falls with my words and tears.

An arm wraps around my shoulders as my father hugs us both.

"Francesca is right. We are complete. This is the greatest gift. For all of us."

I lift my head to see Keira and Marco both crying. I release my mother's hands and hold out my arm to them and Aurora. We all come together, arms turning into lifelines, locking us in the unbreakable bonds of the family I never knew I'd get to have.

This is what I have waited my entire life for—this moment. Right here. Right now.

Thank you, God. Thank you. Thank you. Thank you.

CHAPTER THIRTY-EIGHT

KEIRA

I'm really, really glad I didn't kill Marco.

The thought has floated through my mind a million times this past week. I had no idea that family could be this way. I was raised with love and wanted for nothing as a child, but it wasn't the same as the overwhelming love that has been poured over us for the entire time we've been in Italy. The Giordanos have treated us like we are a precious gift every single second we've been here. Quite frankly, I don't ever want to leave. I want my daughter to grow up here, surrounded by beauty and love and peace. I already know she won't be spoiled, because I will make sure she understands how lucky she is to be the daughter of Lachlan Mount and the granddaughter of Alessandro and Francesca Giordano.

These are things I know.

These are things that give me peace and hope for the future.

It's everything else that I'm trying not to focus on that could destroy that future.

All week, I've been radically present in every moment, soaking up the joy, fun, excitement, and reactions of my husband, our daughter, his brother, his mother, and his father. It was the only way I could enjoy all of it while knowing what is coming after.

Lachlan told me what is waiting for him in New Orleans. A manhunt designed to take him from me forever.

Others might judge me for marrying the kingpin of a criminal empire, but I couldn't help falling in love with him. I saw through the exterior he showed to everyone else, and I saw his truth—buried beneath the surface of Lachlan Mount, the ruthless king of New Orleans, I saw how honorable, thoughtful, protective, and lovable he was. And now, with only hours before he leaves me here with his family, I know that I might never see him again.

How do you face knowing that you might lose the person who has brought you the most happiness in your life and taught you to love at depths you didn't even know were possible?

That's the part I haven't yet figured out.

How do I not cling to him and beg him not to go? The words are on my tongue at every instant.

I don't want you to go. Please stay. Don't leave us. Your daughter needs a father, and I need my husband.

I want to scream them. I want to drop to my knees and plead with him. But I haven't. And I won't. Because I'm stronger than that.

I know the piper must be paid. I know the actions he's taken have consequences. But still, I don't want him to have to face any of it. I want him safe and happy and *free*.

And yet I understand why he must go. If what he knows about DuFort is truly correct, then there's a chance the man will never stop searching for us. And now, after this week, I know that there is absolutely no possibility that Lachlan will allow his past to taint his daughter's future.

He might have committed many crimes according to the laws of men, but he is more honorable than the man with the badge who hunts him.

He will not sacrifice this fresh start to save himself. There's no way Lachlan will ever risk his family's heritage and reputation being entangled with his own dark legacy.

I can't help but love him even more for that, which makes the goodbye that I know is coming even more heartbreaking to contemplate. This is why I've pushed it out of my mind for seven days straight. This is why I've soaked up every moment. Because I might never see my husband again.

He hasn't said it, but I know that I'm not allowed to come after him. I'm not allowed to try to save him if something goes wrong. I can't. My job is to safeguard our daughter's life and her future. That's what matters most to my husband—along with my own safety—and I understand and agree.

When we brought this innocent life into this world, my entire existence and purpose changed. Life was no longer about *me*. It became about *her*.

But still, there's a part of me that wants to scream and cry and rail at the thought of giving up the beauty we've just been given. I want *this life*. I want *this happiness*.

We've just found it, and I want to keep it forever. But that decision is out of my hands.

Tomorrow morning, at daybreak, my husband is leaving, and I might never see him again. He watched me all through dinner, pushing food around my plate, unable to swallow many bites. I know I'm not the only one.

Marco, Alessandro, Francesca, and Lachlan have kept the conversation lively and light, but I have been lost in my thoughts and participated very little.

I think they all understand. We all know what's coming next—the most difficult goodbyes of our collective lives. I surrender to the inevitability, knowing that there's nothing I can do to change anything that's coming. It's in God's hands and not mine.

Please protect him. Please bring him back to me safely. Please. Please. Please.

"Does anyone want dessert?" Francesca asks, a sweet smile on her face as she looks around the table.

"Life is short. Let's appreciate every taste of it while we can," Alessandro replies with a grin.

How they've handled this week—getting their son back and knowing they could lose him just as quickly—has been absolutely valiant. I don't know how they've done it, but I've tried to emulate their attitude. It has made it easier, but I know tonight won't be.

How do you say goodbye to the love of your life?

"Lachlan Mount has to die," is what he told me when I asked what his plan was. "It's the only way to protect the family and Rory's future. And when he dies, I'm taking every corrupt official down with him."

I know he has a dead man's switch. I don't really know what that means though. But tonight, I'm getting all my answers. It might be my very last chance.

Dessert passes quickly, and the light sponge cake, loaded with berries, looks divine, but my taste buds register nothing.

Stop this, Keira. Stop it. He's right here. He hasn't left. Don't let this moment slip away because you're so afraid of what could happen when he leaves. Don't do that to yourself or to him. Don't let this moment be darkened by the fear of grief. It's not worth it. Don't give yourself anything else to regret.

As if by some miracle, the berries in my mouth burst with flavor, and their sweetness floods my senses.

There you go. Come back to life. Be here now.

It takes all the strength that I have to shift my focus and be with what's happening rather than staying lost in my thoughts. *I could have an entire lifetime for that.* The reminder makes it easier to shake off the pall of gray that has colored my evening.

As if noticing the change in me instantly, Lachlan reaches over and squeezes my hand.

"It's going to be okay," he says quietly over Aurora's head. "Don't give up on me yet, Hellion."

Emotion rushes through me, and I can't stop the tears that form in my eyes.

"I'm so grateful we had this week," I say loud enough for everyone at the table to hear me. "It's been absolutely and truly incredible. I love you all. Thank you for being so wonderful to us."

"The joy and the gift have been shared by all," Alessandro says. "We could not have imagined a more perfect homecoming."

"And the second homecoming will be even more beautiful," Francesca adds with a sage expression. "I know we are all thinking the same thing—that this could be it. But I do not believe it. God has blessed us so magnanimously that I cannot imagine it will not continue.

Do not lose hope, Keira. Do not let your faith waver. We are not done."

"Marco will go with you, my son," Alessandro says as a decree.

"Of course I am. Do you think he could stop me from coming?" Marco asks with a grin. "He's my brother, and I've already seen a glimpse of his world. He needs me. He doesn't even know why he needs me, but he does."

"Only if you're truly prepared for the potential consequences of that decision."

Alessandro lifts his chin even higher than his younger son's. "Marco's life has prepared him perfectly for this, even those choices of which I did not approve. I taught him to shoot and shoot accurately. We are both deadly at short and long range. This was simply a hobby, but in your world, it could mean the difference between returning home and not."

"But—"

"No buts," Francesca says, stopping Lachlan from adding any counterarguments. "If there is a chance that Marco accompanying you will bring you home safely to all of us, then how could he not go with you?"

I know Lachlan and Marco have already discussed Marco going with him, and I agree with the decision, even if my agreement feels a bit selfish. But now, it seems like my husband is having second thoughts. He looks around the table, his gaze stopping on me.

"Keira, how do I make them understand that this isn't a game? That maybe Marco should stay back with the family?"

All eyes turn to me. I take a deep breath and reach out to squeeze his hand.

Lachlan's right. They have to know what Marco could be walking into, and the only way I can do that is to lay everything out as simply and as truthfully as possible.

"Your son is the king of the criminal underworld in New Orleans. He's feared, and he's loved. He has greased more palms and broken more laws than anyone I've ever met. I don't know why this Federal Agent DuFort has it out for him, but taking down Lachlan Mount is probably the quickest way to make his career in law enforcement. Whoever could achieve such a feat will likely get all sorts of medals and commendations and awards for doing it. We all know there's a chance he might not come back, and while I don't want to focus on the negative, if Marco goes with him, there's a chance he might not come back either. If he goes, there's a chance you could lose both your sons. Is that a chance you're willing to take?"

Stating it bluntly makes me realize exactly why we all want Marco to go. Without Marco, Lachlan might not have a chance.

And I know what they're going to say before they say it.

"I'm going."

"He's going."

"They both go."

"You're all insane," my husband says, releasing my hand and bringing both his palms to his face. "How could you—"

"For love. For hope. For a chance that you both return. Sometimes, you have to lay it all on the line and trust in the power that has protected you this far," Francesca starts, her tone inviting no further arguments. "You would never have believed the faith that I have kept all these years. And by your return, that faith has become a knowingness deep in my soul that God did not spare you, only to take you both from us. You both go. You both return. Then, we shall celebrate like we have never celebrated before. You cannot change this, my son. You both go. You both return. Of that, I have no doubt."

Where Lachlan's mother gets her faith and soul-deep knowingness, I have no idea, but I definitely want to get some for myself. I suppose after over forty years of praying when nearly everyone else gave up hope, you learn things that others don't understand.

"As long as you're all aware of the risks," Lachlan says as he capitulates.

"I am more than aware of the risk I am taking. I've already lived in your life, as brief a time as it was, brother. Without me, you are walking into a lion's den alone. That is not something I will ever let happen as long as there is breath in this body." He gives me a nod. "We leave at dawn. We're taking a different plane. Different tail numbers. Nothing to alert anyone to the fact that you're returning. This must all be done precisely in order to ensure our safe return."

Lachlan stares across the table at his brother, as if stunned by his statements. "How can you possibly be ready for this?"

Marco shrugs. "I have been preparing my whole life for this moment. Whether I knew it or not, that is the truth. Every single experience I've had has made me the perfect man to have at your back as we free you from your past so that you can live your future. This is the moment I was made for, and I wouldn't miss it for the world."

CHAPTER THIRTY-NINE

LACHLAN

"My family's insane. Nuts. They don't get it. They don't understand what I'm dealing with. They don't understand the risks," I say to Keira after we're alone in our room with Aurora playing on the bed.

Earlier, I saw the advantages to having Marco come with me. He'd been extremely helpful to have as backup before. But now that I've spent time with my family, I can't bear the thought of my parents losing both sons. It seems wrong to allow him to come with me on what might very well be a suicide mission.

"Oh, I think they definitely understand the risks, but they're willing to bet on you and Marco rather than on failure."

"Insanity."

"Or they have trust in life that you don't."

I stare at my wife incredulously. "You agree with them? You really think he should come with me?"

"I would send an entire army with you if I could," she says. "Whatever it takes for you to come home to me."

"It feels selfish to let him come. What if neither of us —" I cut off the words as Keira reaches out a palm to stop me from speaking.

"That's not something you're allowed to focus on right now."

She's right. I have to remove that thought from my mind permanently. I can't focus on the possibility of failure—but I do have to admit that it's a possibility. I can't go into this naive. I know what I have to do, and I know the dangers that could accompany it.

Lachlan Mount has to die.

DuFort won't be satisfied with anything less. He says he wants me locked up, but I know the truth. I'd be murdered inside as soon as he could arrange the hit. I'm well aware of his plans. I've been following the news all week. The manhunt is ongoing. They're watching the French Quarter. They've questioned my known associates. With each public statement DuFort has made, his frustration has been evident. It has taken everything I have in me not to think about what has been happening in New Orleans and instead enjoy this precious time with my family. It's like I'm two different men—one trapped in the past and one tasting the sweetness of a new future.

Even if DuFort didn't want me dead, I know I can't continue living this way.

Lachlan Mount has to die.

I can't be him anymore.

I can't live the life I used to live.

I see now that there is so much more available to me in this world than violence, darkness, and death. Before, I didn't know exactly what would become of us when we walked away from my empire. Yes, I'd made provisions, but I'd be living the rest of my life looking over my shoulder. That was the one factor I couldn't figure out how to eliminate. And now, I see the solution. I can be Luca Giordano. I can be a cherished son, surrounded by the love of his family.

I can give my family a life that I didn't even know existed.

But first, I have to face my past. I have to do what's right. I have to pull the pin and let it all explode and pray I'm able to walk away, unscathed.

DuFort also has to go down.

That's not in question.

He can't be allowed to make this a vendetta that lasts a lifetime. I won't let that happen. I won't let the tentacles of that federally sanctioned criminal family reach this beautiful world I've been shown. *It can't be allowed to happen.*

My dead man's switch is lethal. It will eviscerate many. The city of New Orleans will *never* be the same.

But that all begins tomorrow.

The unexpected guilt for drawing my brother into my mess could drown me tonight, but I won't let it. They've all made their choices. Tonight, I make mine.

"I just want to hold you and Rory all night and forget the rest of the world exists."

Keira comes toward me, slipping into my arms like she was born to fill that space.

"And that's what you shall have, my love. We're yours. Always. No matter what. I would wait thousands of lifetimes if that's what it took for us to be together again. Know that. Feel that."

My arms lock around her, and I cradle her tightly

against me, breathing in her scent, remembering how, in my ignorance, I thought I could own her. Now, I thank everything that's holy that she gave her love to me of her own volition.

"I still don't deserve you, but I am beyond grateful that you're mine."

Her arms tighten around me, and for a few seconds, the world fades away, and nothing exists but our hearts beating against one another.

"Ma-ma," Aurora says, and we both turn instantly. Our hands reach out in tandem as she crawls close to the edge of the bed.

"Baby girl," I whisper, sweeping her up in one arm to cuddle against us.

This is what I'm going back to preserve. This is what I'm fighting for. This is what I'm willing to die to protect. This. Right here.

"Daddy loves you, princess. I won't be gone long. I'll be back as soon as I can," I say, meeting Keira's gaze as it shines with tears.

"Damn right you will be," she whispers back to me. "As fast as humanly possible. We've got a new life to live, and it's amazing."

Neither Keira nor I sleep all night. In the past, we would've spent these hours with our bodies locked together in passion, but not this night. We whisper in the dark, stroking our daughter's hair, talking about what life will be like when I return.

My heart breaks and reforms a dozen times over until

the light of the dawn streaks in through the tall arched windows.

"I love you," Keira whispers for the thousandth time since the sun went down.

"I love you more than I knew it was possible to love," I tell her.

We both know what's coming next.

"I have to go."

She nods ever so slightly. "I know."

"You're safe here. No matter what, they will keep you both safe."

"I know that too."

"I'll come back as soon as I can."

"I know," she whispers once more.

I take a deep breath and release it, staring into the eyes of the woman I love as our child rests her head on the pillow between us.

"Take care of our daughter."

"With my life."

I lean down to press a kiss to Aurora's forehead.

"I love you, baby girl. Daddy will be home soon."

A light tap comes on the door. "The boat is ready."

A tear slips down Keira's cheek. "Go be the boogeyman and then let him die. Leave it all behind and come back to us."

"I will."

After one final kiss to my wife's lips, I rise from the bed, still fully clothed from last night.

"One more thing."

"What?" she asks with a tear tipping over her lower lid.

"I need your ring."

Like the warrior queen she is, Keira doesn't question. She slips it off her finger and hands it to me. "End this, for all of us."

"I will," I reply, closing my hand around the metal and stone. At least this way, I'm taking a piece of her with me —a piece that will help set us free. "Sleep well, my love. I'll be back as soon as I can. I love you."

And with that, I grab the bag I packed yesterday and head for the door.

It's time for Lachlan Mount to die.

CHAPTER FORTY

LACHLAN

"Are you ready?" Marco asks as I slip out of the bedroom and close the door quietly behind me.

"Yes," I reply without hesitation. "The sooner this is done, the sooner we'll be back."

"Exactly," Marco says. "Mother and Father are waiting downstairs to say goodbye."

Mother and Father. The words still shock me when I think about them in reference to myself. *I have parents.* I don't know how long it will take for that fact to feel normal, but it doesn't matter. I'm simply grateful for it—for more reasons than I could possibly list.

"Let's go."

Beneath the vaulted ceilings of the expansive foyer, my mother and father wait, blocking the door, as if to prevent me from leaving without going through them.

It's a new experience, having protective and loving parents, and one that I cherish.

"My son," my mother says, holding out her hands to grasp mine.

"I love you," I tell her before she can continue. "I need you to know that."

Her expression softens, and her eyes fill with tears. "I know you do. You are a good boy. A good man. I am proud to be your mother. I am so grateful you gave me this week. It has been the most wonderful gift of a lifetime."

I lean in to press a kiss to her cheek. "I'm the lucky one. I can't possibly thank you enough for all that you are and all that you've done for us, but still, *thank you*. Thank you for loving my wife and daughter and keeping them safe. Thank you for showing me what it's like to have a mother. You're a dream come true."

She releases my hands, and her thin arms wrap around my shoulders. I lean down, and her grip tightens, like she never wants to let me go. Her entire body shakes with the tears that I know must be pouring down her face, but I don't pull away. For long moments, she just holds on like she might never see me again, and I know that's a distinct possibility.

Come what may, I will always be grateful for this week.

The unwanted little boy I used to be is no more. I'm a man with a family who loves me and is praying for me to return safely. My life and my future have been irrevocably altered by this woman and her love.

"Thank you for coming, and thank you, God, for answering my prayers," she says as she releases me.

My father moves closer to her, wrapping his arm around her side as I wipe the tears from her cheeks with my thumbs.

"I'll be back soon," I tell her, hoping that I'm speaking the truth.

"Yes, you will be," my father replies, slapping a hand

on my shoulder and yanking me in for a hug. "You will be back, my son. We have much to learn about one another and many more happy memories to share."

As his other arm wraps around me, I hug him back —*hard.*

"You are strong," he whispers in my ear. "You are a Giordano through and through. Your brother will keep you safe. You shall both be victorious in all that you do, and you will both come home to us. We will be waiting."

I swallow the giant lump in my throat and barely manage to keep my own tears in check. Never before have I felt this much emotion roiling through me.

"Yes, Father," is all I can manage to get out.

He pulls back and presses a kiss on each of my cheeks. He looks from me to Marco.

"My sons. My beautiful boys, who have become their own men. You both go, and you both return. Understand?"

"Yes, Father," Marco repeats. "You have my word."

Our father's expression is as serious as I've seen it all week as he nods. "Good. Now, go. The boat is waiting. The jet is ready. The Giordano family will be together again soon."

After a final round of hugs, Marco and I slip out the front door, and I follow him through the fairyland of terraced gardens down to the waiting boat.

We don't speak until he tosses off the lines.

"Are you ready?"

"Almost."

He cocks his head to one side as the orange and pink of a brilliant sunrise blazes across the sky and reflects off the calm surface of the lake, like it was painted by the hand of a master—like it was painted by our mother. "What remains to be done?"

I unzip my duffel bag and remove a silver canister. "I need to spread the ashes of my best friend. The only brother I knew before you. V might never have come here, but this is the most beautiful place I've ever seen, and it only seems right to lay him to rest in beauty and peace."

I leave off that I might not have another chance to do it, because Marco knows that already.

His lips curl into a rueful smile. "Of course. It is only fitting. The middle of the lake perhaps?"

I nod, and he takes his position at the helm and backs the boat away from the dock before sending us throttling outward across the water.

As the rising sun creates a moment of heart-stopping beauty, he slows until we're barely moving, and I uncap the urn.

"Rest in peace, Alexander Victorious. May God bless your soul and keep you safe in the hereafter. I love you, brother."

As his ashes hit the water, the tears I held back all morning slide down my cheeks, unchecked.

"You left this world a hero, just like you wanted. Be at peace, my old friend. You deserve it."

CHAPTER FORTY-ONE

LACHLAN

Marco and I don't speak much until we reach cruising altitude aboard a different jet than the one that brought us to Italy. The manhunt is on, and I have absolutely no intention of being swept up in it. DuFort has his game, and I have mine. We have two completely different outcomes in mind, but my will is stronger than his. My power is greater than his. There is nothing—and I mean, *nothing*—that will keep me from returning to Italy to my wife and daughter, short of death itself. I've made peace with my own mortality. I don't get to decide or know when this life of mine is going to end. That's not up to me. I only get to choose what I do with each day I'm given.

And right now, that choice is to ensure that I don't leave a single trace that would give anyone any reason to look for me, my wife, or my daughter ever again. We will disappear forever after I'm done. We will no longer exist.

Which means that, *finally*, we will have peace and a chance at a future untainted by the darkness of my past.

I knew when I drew Keira into the shadows of my life, nothing would ever be the same. I had no right to interfere in her life, but I couldn't stop myself. I was drawn to her like an iron filing to a magnet. I couldn't stay away from her. I couldn't resist, no matter how hard I tried.

I knew she would become my greatest vulnerability, but I had no idea that she would become my greatest strength. If not for her and Aurora, I would have no motivation to leave the past behind. Those moments on my library floor are still all too vivid in my mind. The pain of realizing what I had become and seeing firsthand how it hurt those I love … nothing else could have brought me to my knees. Nothing else could have made me want to change.

In the silence of my own introspection, I can see why I couldn't resist Keira. It all makes sense now. She was brought into my world for this very reason—to be the catalyst that led to this moment. A moment that has been a long time coming, even if I didn't realize it.

I know what I have to do. My empire might have begun crumbling with Aurora's kidnapping, but it was only because it was time. Now, I must demolish it once and for all.

My future has always been waiting for me, but I had no idea that I even *had* a future waiting. In the darkness, I couldn't see beyond my own pain and protecting those I loved. But with one revelation, the world I thought I knew gave way to a grander experience I'd had no idea I could access.

The worst moments in my life led me to the greatest opportunity I've ever been given. If that isn't enough to make someone believe in a higher power, I don't know what is. All I can do now is hope that higher power is going to help me pull off the biggest job of my life—making the world believe I don't exist.

I can do it. I know I can.

With my determination locked in, my motivation stronger than ever, and faith I've never had before, I lean back into the plush cushions of the seat and let out a yawn. My entire body relaxes, as if knowing that this is the calm before the storm. I meet Marco's gaze, grateful that he has left me to my thoughts until this moment.

"Thank you for coming."

His lips quirk with a smile. "You couldn't have stopped me. Literally. We have multiple jets."

I burst out laughing. "I didn't know I could love having a brother."

"I did." Marco's smile is genuine and easy.

It's hard to imagine that any of this feels normal or even okay to someone like him, but here he is. Whether it's out of duty, loyalty, or love, or a combination of all three, I don't really know. Either way, I'm grateful he wants to make sure that I make it back in one piece. I already know that Marco will make it back safely, or I will die in my attempts to make it so.

I refuse to cause pain to another person—ever again—as a consequence of the choices and decisions *I made*. If anyone is to suffer as a result of what I became, then it must be me alone. I alone am responsible for Lachlan Mount. I made those decisions. I made those choices. They might have been out of survival and necessity, but I still made them. Never again will I create such a hell.

Instantly, as if out of nowhere, the truth appears in my

mind. *This is why I avoided love. I always knew it would bring me face-to-face with the truth of what I'd become.*

No one wants to admit that they've created the hell of their own world, and yet I know it's true. I was the only one there for each moment and each decision.

Love forced me to face the truth, and now, love is going to help me write a brand-new story with a completely different ending.

"You do have a plan, do you not?" Marco asks with a casual tone, as if he were discussing our tee time for a round of golf.

"I do have a plan," I reply with a dip of my chin.

"And you're going to share this plan with me?"

I steeple my fingers against my lips. "Yes."

"Soon?"

"As soon as I figure out how not to make it sound absolutely insane."

To his credit, Marco doesn't look concerned. "Excellent. So, by the end of the flight, we'll both know what we're doing next?"

I can't help but smile. "Yes. And despite how crazy it sounds, it's going to work. I know it."

CHAPTER FORTY-TWO

MARCO

The last thing I expect upon returning to America is to find myself outfitted as a fire and rescue worker, sitting in the back seat of a fire truck, beside my brother, who is sporting the same attire.

He was right. The plan he laid out on the jet did sound insane. But there's one thing I've learned over my many years of strange and unexpected situations: we never know how things are going to turn out. All we can do is hope for the best, pray to God to protect us, and walk forward through the smoke until all becomes clear.

"Don't worry; she never fails." This comes from the driver of the fire truck, a man who was introduced to me as Joy.

"I can't believe you still let your mother take part in jobs," my brother replies with a shake of his head.

"Like I could stop Ma from having fun. Are you kidding? She loves this stuff. She calls it her dress-up playtime. I'm pretty sure it's what keeps her young and feisty."

This is what we are waiting on—a septuagenarian, dressed as a courier, whose sole job is to pull the fire alarm somewhere inside the old estate just up the road.

If I had thought we were coming back just so my brother could kill a man, I would have been mistaken. First, we're springing a mental patient from an expensive private mental hospital a few hours from New Orleans. It's undoubtedly a first for me.

"God bless your mother," my brother whispers, but I can feel the tension in the air.

I hope he knows what he's doing, because I definitely don't.

Joy's phone chimes. "And we are in *business*. Starting the countdown."

My brother taps a timer on the screen of his phone as well. "And we're positive the local fire department takes—"

Joy interrupts him. "Nine minutes on average to respond to a call way out here. When we pull up in two and get out in under six, we'll be driving away before they roll in."

The bulky man swings his neck around to look at us in the back seat. "You good on where to go out the back for your pickup?"

My brother nods. "Yes."

"Good deal. I'll be waiting on the other side of those live oaks, and we'll coast off into the sunset with no one the wiser. They won't notice she's gone until the evenin' meds." Joy grins widely, showing off his missing canine. "All right, you ready? Because it's time to rock."

Luca looks to me. "You sure you want to do this? Last chance to back out."

I think of what our father said the night before we left. Even without his words, there's no way I would let my brother do this alone. Other than God, I don't trust anyone else with his life at this point.

"Let's not be late for our date. Time to go."

"Thank you," he says, tone hushed, before giving a nod to Joy. "Let's go."

CHAPTER FORTY-THREE

MOUNT

The estate is a madhouse when we pull up. Workers are hustling patients outside from seemingly all exits. As one might expect with a mental facility, it's not a tidy process. One patient already looks like he's trying to make a break for it, and multiple employees are chasing him down one side of the horseshoe-shaped driveway—where Joy's mother's courier van is driving away.

Someone waves us forward, and Joy drives up under the porte cochere before throwing the truck into park.

"Visors down," I remind Marco before grasping the handle and shoving open the door.

"Thank goodness! That was so quick! Please, we don't know where the fire is, but people smelled smoke. Please, help," a brunette in a white apron says as she wrings her hands. She looks like she's about to fall apart.

"That's our job, ma'am. Don't worry. We've got this."

With a quick glance to confirm that Marco is behind me, I jog into the large historic home. My attention is on high alert, and I check every face that passes me.

Where are you, J? I know you're here somewhere. Make this easy for us.

She wasn't one of the patients out front, which means she's still inside.

I don't know how much she's changed since she's been a resident, receiving treatment, but every instinct I have says that my former right-hand woman and foster sister—also known as Destiny Jones—is exactly who I need to help me pull this off. *If I can find her.*

We check the dining hall—empty.

The back porch—empty.

Three bathrooms and the kitchen—empty.

"Upstairs. Let's go upstairs."

Come on, J. Where are you?

As we jog up the stairs, a woman comes rushing down, slamming right into me. I check her face—*not J.*

"Is anyone still upstairs?" I ask her.

She shrieks and runs past us.

So helpful. I take the stairs two at a time and finally reach the level where the patient rooms are.

"You take the right side; I'll take the left," I call to Marco.

"On it."

First three rooms on the left—all empty.

Fuck. Did I miscalculate? Did she already make her escape, like the guy running down the driveway?

Fourth room—empty.

"Anything?" I call out, hoping Marco will answer affirmatively.

I shove my arm out to open the door to the fifth room, and the wood bounces off the plaster as a reply in a familiar voice greets me.

"Please tell me this is what I think it is. Because I've been waiting."

And there she is. *Destiny Jones—the infamous J.* Her hair is longer, but other than that, she looks exactly the same as the day she left my house for the care of this institution ... after trying to murder my wife and almost succeeding with Magnolia.

I flip up the visor on my helmet. As soon as she sees my face, her entire countenance shifts into a grin. For a split second, she looks like the little girl I once knew. The one who hadn't killed anyone.

"You ready?"

"I always knew you'd come for me, boss. Let's go."

She hops out of the rocker where she's been waiting. From under the blanket that was on her lap, she pulls out a baseball cap. Wrapping her hair into a knot, she puts it on and tosses the blanket aside.

She was ready to go. For some reason, the fact comforts me and makes me think my insane plan might just actually work.

"We have to ditch our gear."

"We?" J asks.

"Where can we leave it that no one will find it?"

Like the genius she is, J calculates quickly. "Go out through the kitchen. There's an incinerator, where the gear can go, and a couple of aprons and chef's hats you can put on. The cameras miss a section, so no one will see you change."

I want to laugh because it doesn't surprise me at all that J knows exactly how to escape this place. She's attempted it many times, resulting in increased security. Hence the need for the diversion.

"Do you need me to start a fire while you change?" she asks.

Of course she would.

"No. Let's go. Lead the way." I hold out an arm, and she hustles in front of me.

Like she's imagined this a million times, J jogs down the back set of stairs, which leads directly to the kitchen.

"Aprons and chef's hats are in here. Change quickly," she says, waving us into a storage room. "The incinerator is by the back door. Hurry. The real fire department will be here soon. They take way longer than you guys did."

"I don't even need to ask you why you know that," I say as I yank off the helmet and toss it on the floor.

"What in the fuck?" J's shocked exclamation grabs my attention as I unhook the jacket.

Whipping my head around, I see her staring at Marco.

"There's two of you," she whispers. Her head jerks back and forth between us as we both strip off the firemen's gear.

"I can explain. Later."

J's eyes are wide and wild. "Am I really fucking crazy?"

I snap my fingers at her, and she looks at me. "Twins. Long story. I'll tell you as soon as we're out of here."

With shock and confusion throwing off her equilibrium, J blinks over and over, looking from one of us to the other.

"Aprons. Chef's hats. Incinerator. Focus, J. I need you."

My words are all it takes to knock her back into a state of semi-normalcy.

"Got it, boss." She swings around and yanks chef's

coats from a tall metal locker and tosses them to us. The hats come next.

Outfitted in completely different attire, I nod to J.

"You lead us out. Point to the incinerator, and we'll shove the gear in. We're heading through the back garden—"

"Down the embankment, through the live oaks, and out to the road," J finishes for me. "It's exactly the way I'd go if there was a car picking me up. Quickest way to disappear. You can head straight for the highway."

"Good. Then, you know exactly where we're going. Hurry."

She nods repeatedly, glancing once more at Marco, and then shoots forward out of the utility closet.

It's only a few steps to the incinerator chute and the back door. Within sixty seconds, we're already through the back garden and down the embankment. As the wail of the real sirens close in, we've reached the live oaks—just in time to see Joy pull up in the fire truck.

I yank open the door, and the three of us climb into the back, slam the door, and cruise toward the highway.

Mission accomplished.

CHAPTER FORTY-FOUR

MOUNT

Once again, I find myself driving a vehicle with someone blindfolded in the back.

Soon, I tell myself, *this will be a thing of the past.*

But today, it can't be helped.

Joy drove the fire truck into a nondescript warehouse on the outskirts of town, where Marco, J, and I hopped out. J laughed when I tossed her the hood and opened the rear door of a sedan for her.

"If this is what it takes, then so be it. I'm just happy to see you, boss," she said with a genuine gleam in her eyes and a grateful expression that reminded me of the little girl I'd once known.

Maybe my plan isn't quite as crazy as I thought. Breaking out a mental patient—who had tried to kill my wife—from the institution where *I paid* to have her kept seemed insane, but so far, so good.

The drive to the safe house was long and circuitous, as always, but this time, it was done in silence, as Marco and

I agreed before we set off to liberate J. Thankfully, there wasn't a single tail. No one knew I paid for J's care at the estate—it was all done through various entities and fake names. However, it will be interesting when the message finally comes through that she's gone. I wonder how long it will take for them to notice her absence and then to notify me. Either way, the countdown to that eventuality is on.

With the garage door of the safe house closing behind us, I shut off the ignition, and a sense of peace settles over me.

Step one: done.

Step two: figure out what the hell I've unleashed with step one.

I honestly wasn't sure what condition we'd find J in, but so far, strangely enough, she seems pretty normal. Then again, I'd had no idea she was homicidal while working for me, so … maybe I'm not the best judge when it comes to her. Soon, we'll all know the truth for certain.

Marco glances at me as he reaches for the door handle, and I nod.

"All good. Let's head inside."

I climb out my door as he exits the vehicle.

Now, for the wild card.

I open the back door and remove the moving blanket covering J. She pops up into a sitting position and immediately yanks the hood from her head.

"I can't even complain about the hood. It feels so damn good to be *free!*"

Her smile is pure and innocent, but it only lasts until her gaze flicks to the man who looks exactly like me. Her lower lip wobbles as her mouth hangs open. Her eyes widen, like she's having a religious experience.

J's lips make shapes, like she's attempting to speak, but no sound comes out.

Before she loses it, I start explaining. "This is my brother. He's my identical twin. You can call him Mr. Mount."

"Two Mounts," she whispers as she looks back to me. "Are you sure? Because I didn't really know if I was crazy before … but now … two of you? Like, how is that even possible?"

"An unexpected twist of fate. One that turned out to be lucky for all of us."

"An identical twin." She breathes the words almost reverently. "Two of you. It's unreal."

"I thought so too," I reply with a quick smile. "Let's go inside. We've got a lot to talk about in a short period of time."

Instantly, J perks up. "It's time to take out DuFort, isn't it? He's all over the news. He's become a problem, requiring a solution."

Even with her homicidal tendencies, I can't help but feel a wash of familiarity and nostalgia at her words. J could always practically read my mind. Like V, much of our communication was wordless, but incredibly effective.

"Yes. It's time to take out DuFort … and Lachlan and Keira Mount."

J's eyes widen once more for a split second, and then she smiles with glee. "It's time to go full-on dead man's switch? I've been waiting for this day *forever*." She hops out of the car and claps her hands. "Come on, boys. Let's do this. I was born ready to pull the pin on this grenade."

"Good," I tell her as I open the door to the house. "Because we're going fishing and we're going to need bait."

CHAPTER FORTY-FIVE

MARCO

Two days back in America, and I find myself in yet another vehicle. This time, I sit in an alley in the French Quarter, waiting for my brother's former foster sister—who we broke out of a mental institution—to execute the next step in the plan to free him and his family forever.

It's a job I never expected to have, but one I'm honestly honored to call mine. It's certainly better than not having a brother at all and definitely more interesting.

I dropped J off on a corner off Bourbon Street a few blocks away, and by now, she should have made her way into my brother's hidden home and hopefully already removed our mother's painting. Mother would paint him a new one, but I can't judge or argue about wanting to bring it with him into his new life. But that's not the only thing J is in the house to retrieve. My brother has another magic duffel bag inside with his dead man's switch. As I understand it, it's a bag full of hard drives. Lachlan Mount's equivalent of his little black book with enough incriminating information on enough people to send the entire city into a panicked frenzy.

However, our mission carries more than one objective. My attention is locked on the gray garage doors that blend into the wall lining the alley. Behind me, closer to the corner, is a black delivery van that Joy informed us is being used by law enforcement to keep tabs on one of the only known entrances or exits to my brother's hidden domain. They don't know where he is, so they're hoping, eventually, someone will arrive or leave that they can either apprehend or follow.

According to Joy, they've been waiting there since the morning after we made our first trip to Italy. Now, J is going to give them quite a thrill, dressed as Keira Mount.

This morning, J walked out of the safe house, wearing both my brother's wife's clothes and her wedding ring. Even I was surprised at how similar they looked when J added an Hermès scarf over her hair à la Grace Kelly. Hopefully, it was similar enough to fool the authorities as well. After over a week of no action, my brother believed they'd bite on just about anything, and Joy agreed with him completely.

I check the clock on the dash again. J is already five minutes behind our projected schedule.

What is taking you so long, woman?

None of us had any real idea what she'd find inside after Luca's weeklong absence, but now, I'm starting to question the wisdom of using a legitimately crazy woman as part of the plan.

Did she go rogue?

Thankfully, the cops in the van ahead of me have no idea she's inside, so the time frame isn't jeopardizing her exit. My brother believes J can and will do exactly what he needs her to, and I pray that his faith and trust in her isn't misplaced.

Three more minutes tick by, and my fingers itch to text my brother that there might be a problem. Before I can reach for my phone, the bottom of the garage door rises from the pavement.

Thank you, God.

My attention instantly splits between the door ahead of me and the van in my rearview mirror.

Come on, J. Let's do this.

We're nearly ten minutes behind schedule, but everything can still go perfectly. I reach for my phone to text my brother.

> Door is rising. Almost on the move.

His response is short.

> 10-4. In position.

As soon as the door has risen halfway, an engine revs inside, and the sound bounces down the alley.

I hope she picked something fast.

Obviously, it's not something I needed to worry about because as soon as a car can clear the door, a black BMW rockets out of the garage and into the alley. Tires squeal as it shoots forward, dodging a dumpster as it flies down the uneven pavement.

I can't imagine the chaos in the police van at this moment, but as the BMW bolts out from the alley and into the street, the van jerks into motion before I have a chance to touch my gearshift. The surveillance van nearly scrapes the side of my Camry as it thunders out of the alley, in hot pursuit of J in the BMW.

Excellent. The chase is on.

I shift into drive and follow the van, hoping that whoever is inside has DuFort on the phone already. To be a fly on the wall of that conversation would be useful ... which is why, in my brother's words, *we're going fishing*.

The van careens around corners, nearly sideswiping other moving vehicles in pursuit of the BMW. Evidently, the van wasn't meant for high-speed chases because the thing looks like it might tip over. I drive sedately several car lengths back, out of the pandemonium, because unlike the van, I know exactly where J's going. But this whole operation will only go perfectly if DuFort takes the bait.

After a few minutes, it's obvious the van is struggling to keep up with J's evasive driving. It runs another red light, nearly colliding with a city bus.

Wow, she's good at this.

Clearly, my brother knew what she was capable of doing. I certainly wouldn't have expected her driving to be so skilled.

Just when I think the van is going to lose her, a silver Mercedes roars past me at the light, cutting off an SUV and the police van. It gains on the BMW with a take-no-prisoners approach to police pursuit.

It has to be DuFort. *It has to be.*

My brother swore that no matter where he was in the city, DuFort would take the bait. He couldn't help it. His arrogance wouldn't let him miss this chance.

J's driving becomes even more skilled as she cuts across lanes, neatly shooting gaps in traffic and totally avoiding collisions. To the untrained viewer, it looks like a mess, but to me, it looks perfect.

Only a few more minutes to the pier. You're so close, girl. Get there, get out, and run.

The van, still struggling to keep up with the cars, nearly takes out a pedestrian and then slams to a halt as a tour bus stops ahead of it with no warning.

I cruise past it and smile when I hear the tires of the silver Mercedes squeal as it tears around a corner to keep up with J.

Almost there. Almost there.

As soon as the pier is in sight, I see a miracle taking place.

J is already out of the black BMW, a duffel bag over each shoulder, racing toward the boat awaiting her at the end of the pier. The silver Mercedes jumps a curb and drives over the grass and nearly rams the parked BMW as it jerks to a stop.

The door flings open, and a middle-aged man in a suit leaps out and sprints toward the pier as my brother pulls J aboard the boat.

The water around the nondescript white charter fishing boat churns as whoever is at the helm buries the twin throttles. The boat roars away with both J and my brother standing on the back deck.

Gun in hand, the man from the Mercedes fires his pistol toward the boat as he runs to the end of the pier.

I park, hop out, and duck down as I jog toward the open door of what I assume is DuFort's Mercedes. It has to be him.

It takes me less than ten seconds to slip the magnetic

tracker and bug under the seat, where it locks onto the metal.

I can't believe this is so easy.

With a final glance at the boat as it disappears from my view, I jog back to the Camry and shift it into drive and roll away.

Through my open window, I can hear the man's impotent rage as he bellows at the boat from the pier.

"I'm going to kill you, bitch! Wait until I get my hands on your little girl!"

Yep, that's him.

The rest of his tirade cuts off as I exit the parking lot, but I know Leo will pick up every single thing he says next.

We got you, DuFort. We got you.

CHAPTER FORTY-SIX

MOUNT

As J runs toward the boat with the duffel bags over her arms, I've never been happier that Keira is thousands of miles away, with our daughter, safe and sound. There's no way I would have let her take part in any of this. Not a chance in hell. Not for all the love or money in the world. My wife will *never* be part of a life like this again. *Ever.*

"Come on! Let's go!" I hold out my hand and yank J aboard as a silver Mercedes nearly collides with the black BMW M5 V loved to drive.

A man emerges from the car, and I know it's DuFort without even seeing his face. The first thing he does is draw down.

Fool. He'll never hit us at this range.

With J safely aboard, I yell to the captain, "She's aboard! Go! Go!"

I grab the fiberglass arch and J to secure us as the twin diesel engines snarl with their full force and the boat jerks forward in the water.

But DuFort has always been a fool. He unloads in our direction, and I watch him with a smile as the span of churning water increases between us and the pier.

You'll always be one step behind, DuFort. That's the price of your arrogance.

And as I watch Marco slip behind the door to the Mercedes, I know that I couldn't have pulled this off without him. *Thank you, brother.*

DuFort's face is red as he yells at the boat as we pull farther and farther away from where he stands on the end of the pier, powerless to do anything to stop us.

It's a beautiful sight.

I salute DuFort, simply to give Marco more time to do his part and slip away.

J swings around to face DuFort too. Her arm comes up, and with her fingers, she forms a gun and pulls the trigger. DuFort's enraged shrieks fade into the roar of the engines and the sound of the water as we make our perfect getaway.

The stage is set.

Now, you're playing my game, DuFort. I hope you enjoy the grand finale.

Less than ten minutes later, J and I climb off the boat onto a low platform attached to a much larger ship. The captain and first mate salute us, and the captain points the vessel upriver toward the marina that is his final destination for the day. The charter boat is no longer solid white either. The first mate peeled back white stickers as soon as we were out of DuFort's view, revealing the boat to be *Roy's*

Rockin' Reels. If the Feds are looking for an all-white fishing boat, they'll never find it. The vessel is now red, white, and blue, and the switch took less than sixty seconds.

Absolutely brilliant, Leo.

I'll thank him in person shortly, as he's the man J and I are now being led to see. We pass through the metal porthole-style door of a rusted cargo ship and enter a completely different world. The inside of Leo's cargo ship looks nothing like the outside. Leather and mahogany cover the interior walls, and brass ship sconces light the way. The twenty-something-year-old man leading us to Leo pauses at another porthole door, this one finished with tufted leather and brass rivets.

It reminds me that I've always enjoyed Leo's taste for the finer things in life.

The man knocks on the door. "They've arrived, *monsieur*."

"Enter." I hear Leo call from inside.

The younger man turns the brass wheel that opens the door and steps aside with an arm out, gesturing for us to enter.

Shifting the duffel bags on my shoulders that I took from J, I stride into the interior cabin.

My shoes sink into the layered oriental rugs that carpet the stunning library. Leo's love of art is on full display here. A Monet hangs on the wall between what I know are shelves of rare first-edition books. A Degas sculpture stands on a pillar in the corner of the room.

Leo stands behind a Louis XV desk, a smile stretching his tanned face.

"He is good and mad, *mon ami*. Spilling vitriol and filth nonstop from his classless American mouth."

"Anything we need to know? And thank you, by the way."

Leo shrugs. "It's my pleasure. And aside from the fact that he wants to do unspeakable things to you, your wife, and your daughter … he has said some things of interest. He contacted a dirty judge for a warrant. I'm sorry to inform you that they are going to ransack your home."

"Expected," I say, feeling nothing about the loss of my possessions. They're only things.

"It must have been," Leo says with a tilt of his head as he hands me one of the receivers for the bug and tracker. "Because Remy says that the pickup at the bar was much larger than expected. I thought you said you were only retrieving one painting?"

My attention cuts to J beside me. "What did you do?"

When she smiles, she looks exactly like the mischievous little girl I once knew. "I figured for five grand, the bar manager didn't care what she was watching … so I robbed the place. Clean."

I look down at J's wrist and see something I didn't notice before.

"You're wearing my watch."

Her grin grows even wider. "I always liked this one. I didn't want that pig DuFort to have it. I didn't want him to have *any of it*."

"What did you take?"

"From what Remy said, we have a Monet, two Picassos, a Van Gogh, the Comesetti, various other impressionist works, plus a dozen heavy, assorted duffel bags of unknown contents." Leo gives J a lift of his chin.

"Clearly, you're an accomplished thief as well. If you're in the market for a new career, I know a guy …"

I cut Leo off with a question posed to J. "How?"

Her smile and shrug remind me of all the times she went above and beyond in my service without my asking her to do so.

She drops her shoulders and bites her lip before speaking. "You know that game people play—what would you get out of your house if it were on fire?"

I nod for her to continue.

"Well, I've thought that through a million times. I never knew when something would go down and we'd have to clear your place out. It took me eight extra minutes, but the Feds aren't getting anything good."

"My personal safe?"

"Empty, boss. You never changed the code after you had me locked up."

"Why would you do that?" I ask her, unable to discern her motive from her features.

"Because you deserve good things, Mikey. It was time for the universe to do you a favor. So, I did it."

An emotion I didn't expect to feel today expands in my chest and fills me with gratitude—and not simply because of her use of the nickname she'd called me as a child. "Thank you," I tell her, swallowing an equally unexpected lump in my throat.

"Excellent," Leo says. "Do you want me to arrange all the cargo for shipment or simply the Comesetti painting, as previously discussed?"

"Sell everything but the Comesetti—that gets delivered to the airport. You already have the account number for the deposit."

"Perfect. Is there anything else I can do to assist you in your final exit from the stage that is New Orleans?"

"Yes," I reply, knowing he would ask. I lower one duffel bag onto the desk between us. "I need you to do me a favor. Several favors actually. You'll be well compensated for it, I promise."

Leo eyes the bag. "You've always made sure I was well compensated, Mount. I don't doubt you now. But I have to admit, I'm curious. What's inside?"

I unzip the heavy zipper and pull the edges open so he can see inside.

"Keys?"

I nod and remove a sheaf of papers from an inside pocket. "And a list for their distribution." I spot the gold key on top, hanging from a square gold tab. I grab it and offer it to Leo. "This one is for you."

"What does it open?"

With a smile, I tell him, "You'll have to find out for yourself."

J chimes in with an explanation. "Each key opens something—a safe deposit box, bus station locker, gym locker, amusement park locker. You name it, and boss has stashed something there."

Leo looks from J to me. "Are you serious? There must be a hundred keys in here."

I hand him the folded papers. "The recipient of each key is listed, along with what the key opens and where to go to open it. On the first sheet, you'll see the list that needs to be delivered today. Take an extra hundred grand commission off the art sales to get it done, but it must be done today."

Leo takes the papers from me. "Coroner, fire inspector,

fire investigator, police detective ..." He looks up as he trails off. "Your exit strategy, I presume?"

"No." I shake my head. "That's simply to take care of any potential questions."

"But you have an exit strategy, correct?"

I hold up the other duffel bag. "Indeed."

"You don't need to share any further, my friend. I trust that you've got everything worked out perfectly."

I can't help but smile, because I feel like he's right. It's all going perfectly.

"Starting tomorrow at nine a.m., the city of New Orleans will never be the same again." My phone buzzes in my pocket, and I pull it out. "Our ride is here. Thank you for your assistance, Leo. I will always be grateful for your help."

"And I'll always be grateful you didn't kill my nephew. *Bon chance, mon ami.* Working with you has been a pleasure."

He holds out his hand, and I shake it.

"The pleasure is mutual. Have a good life, Leo."

With a grin, Leo replies, "I shall. That is certain."

CHAPTER FORTY-SEVEN

MOUNT

The following morning at nine a.m.

"No, I'm in traffic. I haven't made it to the office. What's going on?" DuFort's voice comes through the receiver that we've had on high volume since we left Leo's and made our way back to the safe house.

My New Orleans home was searched from top to bottom, and DuFort was furious that it had already been hit before he and his thugs could pick the crown jewels for themselves. That's the least of his worries, although he's just about to find that out.

"No, I haven't posted anything on social media. Do you really think I have time for that shit?" DuFort says to whoever is on the other end of his phone call.

"What do you mean, I need to check it and see? Hold on." There's some crackling, and then he speaks again. "It says I'm logged out. I can't see anything. Let me put you on speaker. What the hell is going on?"

Another voice comes through the receiver. "There are

pictures posted all over your accounts, on multiple platforms. Sir … I don't know what to think."

"What the fuck pictures are you talking about? I didn't post any fucking pictures. Did my wife post something stupid? She loves that social media shit."

"Uhhh … yeah, there are some pictures of your wife. But, sir … there are kids in the pictures. And your father … and …" The voice on the other end of DuFort's call sounds equal parts afraid, confused, and disgusted.

"What do you mean, pictures of my wife and my father and kids in them? What the fuck are you talking about? What kind of pictures?"

DuFort's tone is changing fast. Irritation and annoyance have given way to a thread of fear.

Good. Be afraid. That's fair, considering what you've done to so many.

"It's not just you, sir. It's … fuck. I don't know what to think. There's shit all over the internet. The judge with the warrant last night, the mayor, the police chief, my buddies, shit … every third name, you know you're finding out shit you never expected to see. I don't know what to do, sir. The whole office is freaking out."

A few beats of silence pass before DuFort erupts.

"Fuck! Fuck! Fuck! That fucking bastard! That fucking bastard! I'm going to fucking kill his wife in front of him while he bleeds to death. FUCK!" Banging intersperses the words, and I can picture DuFort beating his steering wheel as he realizes what I've done.

I pulled the trump card. *And now, everyone's going down.*

"You're saying this is real, sir? Oh my God. Those pictures—I think I'm going to be sick."

A program J wrote over five years ago unleashed nearly twenty hard drives' worth of compromising information and thousands of photographs that I've spent *decades* collecting. She hasn't slept all night, as it took nearly twelve hours to finish the final technical steps to flip the dead man's switch.

Every single instance of a dirty official taking bribes, committing crimes that I knew about, or breaching the public trust in any way has now been shared on their own social media, as well as on the websites and social media accounts of every major media organization in the city, along with the city's own site and every single branch of law enforcement that operates within it.

Basically, today, the internet has been papered over with the dirty laundry of every single corrupt and crooked official in New Orleans and beyond.

I might have lived in the darkness and the shadows, but today, every shred of truth that I've known all these years has been brought to light for the entire world to see.

There's no hiding anymore, DuFort. Your entire family is disgraced.

DuFort is losing his mind over the receiver. Clearly, he hung up his call. But it doesn't take long for him to make another.

"General. General, have you heard?"

His father. John Pierre DuFort is one of the joint chiefs of staff and an avowed Satanist who drinks the blood of tortured children in rituals to gain power. They do shit I've always wished weren't real. He's a nasty piece of work, who I've long wanted to wipe off this planet.

"Have I heard? Are you serious? We're fucked. Absolutely *fucked*."

"I need backup. You gotta send me people. We have to take Mount out."

"Did you hear me, son? *We're fucked.* There's nothing we can do. He went scorched earth. There's nothing left. Every person I could call is living their own personal hell today because of that son of a bitch. I knew I should've taken him out years ago. That motherfucker."

"That's it?" DuFort replies, disbelief dripping from his words. "You're just … giving up? We have to do something. We have to—"

"Do what? Suicides are already on the rise. Three of my friends ate bullets this morning. That's what he wanted. And he's getting it. They're all taking themselves out. That bastard knew exactly how to cause the most chaos and destruction. Even Kostegov has already bailed. Fucking hell."

"Then, eat a bullet if you want, old man. I'm going to fucking kill him and everyone he loves. And I'm going to start with burning that fucking distillery to the ground."

Something thuds in the car, and my imagination tells me it's DuFort's phone landing against the door.

I rise, looking at Marco and J, who are still seated around the coffee table of the safe house, staring at the receiver.

"Time to end this. Let's go."

CHAPTER FORTY-EIGHT

MOUNT

The fire alarm is already blaring when we reach Seven Sinners, and several people are on cell phones in the parking lot.

Wearing a hat and dark glasses, Marco throws the Camry into park, and I jump out, rushing for the entrance.

"Is anyone hurt?" I yell as I run toward the shattered double glass doors.

"Mr. Mount, thank God you're here. Where is Keira? We need her!"

"She's on her way," I lie to them. "Get everyone out of the building. Call the fire department and the police!"

Bullet holes riddle the wall above the whiskey-barrel reception counter that stands opposite the front entrance.

He shot his way in. Excellent. All I can hope is that DuFort hasn't killed anyone yet. Only a handful of employees should be here right now.

I take the shortest route to the stairs, shove open the side emergency door, and use the wooden chock to keep it open for Marco and J to enter out of sight of the employees.

Now, to find DuFort. If he's going to burn the place down, he'll start with the still room.

It takes me less than a minute to push open the correct door. Quietly, I step out onto to the polished concrete floor. Over the intermittent fire alarm, I hear a woman shrieking.

Fuck.

"Where is she? Where is that redheaded bitch?"

DuFort has a gun to the head of one of Keira's employees. It's the woman who started apprenticing as a taster only a few months ago.

"I don't know! She's not here! I don't know."

I waste no time. "Let her go, DuFort. She doesn't know anything. You wanted me? You got me. Leave my wife and her distillery out of this."

DuFort throws the woman to the floor as he spins to find my voice. As soon as he sees me, he unloads his magazine.

"Run," I yell to the woman as I dive behind a still as bullets ping and sink into the copper.

Steam spews out from one of the giant stills, and an alarm honks in warning.

"It's going to blow, DuFort. Better get out and save yourself."

I peek out from behind the still. DuFort drops his mag and jams another one into his pistol. He takes aim at me again.

"No!" J, wearing a scarf over her hair again, runs through the same door I used. "Get down!"

DuFort unloads again, spraying bullets in our direction. J screams.

"I got you, bitch! You're both gonna die!"

I scramble for J and see blood pouring from her arm. *Fuck.* This wasn't part of the plan.

"Come on. We gotta get you out of here."

As I pull her toward safety, DuFort appears around the side of the still.

He slaps the bottom of the magazine into the pistol, and I can only assume he has reloaded once more.

"You're not going anywhere. Either of you. You're both gonna die right here. And then I'm gonna find that little girl of yours—and I will fucking find her—and you're gonna wish she were already dead."

He stands above us, taking aim at J's head as I shelter her in my arms, hoping the vests we're wearing will save us both.

"Pitiful. The ruthless king of New Orleans, cowering with his wife, at the end of the barrel of my gun. You piece of shit. Do you even know what you did today? You signed the death warrant of everyone you love, and I'm gonna fucking kill them all myself."

J wiggles against me, but I stay focused on DuFort, making sure not to look at Marco as he slips into the room in my periphery.

"I think it's everyone you love who's pulling triggers today, DuFort. Your dad still alive? Or couldn't the General handle the shame of the nightmare he created being brought to light? People thought I was the criminal … but it's you fucks in suits with badges who take the cake."

"Shut the fuck up!" He lunges toward us as J flings her hand in his direction and throws herself over me.

A blade embeds itself in DuFort's throat as the honking

alarm grows in speed and volume. Flashing red lights give him a demonic glow.

A still is going to blow. We have to move.

DuFort doesn't even reach for the knife. He pulls the trigger instead, and gunshots explode as he empties his pistol.

"No!" Marco yells as he throws his entire body at DuFort. But not before I take two rounds to the chest like sucker punches.

With a thud, DuFort's body hits the concrete floor with Marco on top of him.

Blood is everywhere. Red steam fills the room. J's body feels like dead weight.

"J, are you ok—" My words cut off as I realize she's missing part of her head so she won't be answering me ever again.

Fuck. Fuck. Fuck. I'm so sorry, Desi. This wasn't part of the plan. I had another body lined up. It wasn't supposed to be you ...

But something inside me knows that she wouldn't change a thing. Not J. She'd do it all over again—twice—just to save me.

Equal parts grief and gratitude slam into me as Marco climbs off DuFort and turns over his body.

We both take in his glassy eyes and the gaping hole in his throat. Marco looks at me as I slide out from beneath J's remains.

"We have to get out of here," Marco says. "This whole place is going to go up. DuFort started a fire, and it's spreading fast."

I grab DuFort's hand, thankful he kept himself in good

condition and that his height is close enough to mine. I slide my wedding ring onto it.

I squat down next to my foster sister and say a quick prayer. "Thank you for your loyalty and help, Destiny. I never wanted it to end like this, but I couldn't have done it without you. May God bless you and keep you. Rest in peace, my friend. Rest in peace."

Marco grabs me by the arm, and together, we charge out of the still room. When we reach the exit, an explosion rocks the building. Marco shoves me into the bushes, covering my body with his.

"Fuck, you're heavy, big brother."

Marco rolls off me. "And we're both alive to tell about it."

I look behind us, where the beautiful distillery building my wife loved more than anything but me and our daughter burns with licking flames.

She'll forgive me for this.

Fire trucks roll into the parking lot with sirens blaring, and I know it's the last time I'll ever see this place.

Marco shoots to his feet and holds out a hand. "Let's go home, brother."

I take it and rise. "Yes, let's go home."

CHAPTER FORTY-NINE

KEIRA

If I hadn't seen them both leave the building on the security cameras, I'd be losing my mind right now.

I nearly lost it when I saw the man with a gun standing over my husband and that woman. In that moment, I wouldn't have thought twice. I would have killed that man myself.

Who was she? Who was the woman who looked like me and lost her life?

It's a question only my husband can answer, and I thank God my intuition told me to check the cloud for Seven Sinners' security feed after I put Aurora down for a nap. I only caught the tail end of the disaster, but it was enough. Enough to know that my family's distillery is likely a total loss, but my husband's life—and his brother's —were preserved.

That's when it hits me. I know who she was. Destiny Jones. The woman who tried to kill me. She took a bullet meant for my husband.

The gratitude I feel for her sacrifice drowns out the pain of losing something I worked so hard to save.

It's just a building. Just a company. Just whiskey. My parents and sisters will understand completely when I explain it all to them—*soon.*

All that is *nothing* compared to the value of life.

Knowing what I have to do next, I click the button that Lachlan built into my system by his own security expert. *BURN SYSTEM—ERASE ALL CLOUD FILES PERMANENTLY.*

And with a single click of my finger, all of the evidence of everything that happened today and every day at Seven Sinners is gone. Forever. Just like our past.

I don't know what wakes me, but instantly, sleep fades from my mind, and I sit up in bed. *He's here.*

I look around the room, and there he sits, in an armchair, facing the bed, watching me and Aurora sleep.

Carefully so as not to disturb our daughter, I slide out from beneath the covers and bolt across the room.

Lachlan rises and catches me as I fly at him. His strong arms wrap around me and clutch me to his body.

Tears pour from my eyes. "You're safe. You're safe, and you're here, and you're never leaving me again."

"Never, Hellion. Never again. It's over. It's all over," he whispers into my hair. "We're free. It's all over now. We're free."

I pull my face away from where my tears are soaking his fresh, tailored shirt. "Truly?"

Lachlan nods slowly. "It's over. Lachlan and Keira

Mount are dead. So are DuFort and his father. Their family home in the Garden District burned to the ground, and both bodies will be found inside. No one will ever ask questions. It's truly over. We're free."

I squeeze him tighter, overwhelmed by the riot of emotions coursing through me. *Our daughter is safe —forever.*

"Thank you," I whisper as I cry on his shoulder. "Thank you."

"I love you, Keira. Now, no more tears. It's time for the best years of our lives. And they start right now."

CHAPTER FIFTY

KEIRA

The next morning

NEW ORLEANS IN TURMOIL

Following the release of sensitive personal information relating to government and law enforcement officials on the local, state, and federal levels, the city of New Orleans is in a state of chaos and disorder today. Social media platforms have attempted to censor much of the content, but once seen, the alarming and disturbing photographs cannot be forgotten. Careers have been ended, and suicides have been rampant among those affected. Most notably, John Pierre DuFort—one of the joint chiefs of staff, a New Orleans native, and a trusted advisor and friend for many years to the current president of the United States—is said to have ended his life and intentionally burned his Garden District home to the ground after evidence allegedly tying him to years of satanic ritual child abuse became public knowledge. The body of his son, an agent with the Federal Bureau of Investigation, was also found among the ruins.

Our prayers are with the families of all affected by this spread of information, for which no organization, terrorist, or vigilante group has yet to claim responsibility. Others, however, are rejoicing that the truth has been set free and decades of corruption and its perpetrators have been exposed.

Where does this leave the great city of New Orleans, other than without a mayor, three-quarters of the city council, the police chief, countless judges, law enforcement, and government officials? At this time, we are not certain, but one thing is for sure: this moment will never be forgotten, and New Orleans will forever be altered by what has been brought to light.

In other potentially related news, the manhunt for Lachlan Mount, the city's most infamous resident, has been called off with the discovery of his remains, along with his wife's, in the aftermath of the destruction of Seven Sinners Distillery ...

I didn't know what my husband's dead man's switch entailed, but as I read article after article, I can't help but smile. Not because of the chaos or the nightmares come to life for many people, but because I should have known. *I should have known.*

Lachlan Mount is a man like no other. He lives according to his own set of rules, and he always has.

That's one thing that has been consistent every moment that I've known him. They might not be the rules that society deems proper and acceptable, but they're rules that guided his actions and behaviors in a world that society could never possibly understand. When you're the ruthless king of New Orleans, you can do anything. But Lachlan didn't use his power the way many would have. From the slew of articles, I know that Lachlan has been collecting and keeping this information for *years*. Many would've used it for blackmail, but he used it for freedom.

Only those who were already guilty by their own actions were exposed. Who knew that the boogeyman could be used by the hand of justice to see so many wrongs made right?

"Have you finished catching up on the news?" the most beloved voice in the world asks me as I close my laptop.

I turn to look at him on the bed, where our daughter uses him as a jungle gym. With his hair askew and the shine of drool from Aurora's kisses on his cheek, an overwhelming wave of love washes through me.

"I didn't know I could love anyone as much as I love you," I tell him. "You're a genius. A brilliant, unpredictable genius."

"Love is a crazy thing, isn't it?" he replies with the easiest and most carefree smile I've ever seen on his face. "It's the most powerful force in the world, hands down. It's been the driving motive behind the most important things I've ever done."

I think for a moment of all that I've done out of love, and I know he's speaking the absolute truth.

"So, now what?"

A grin flashes across his face, and it's a gift to see it there.

Things have truly changed. This is a new day. A new chapter in our life. An ending that became a beautiful new beginning.

"This little girl is ready for breakfast, if the nibbling on my fingers is any indication."

I laugh with a smile. "Definitely time for breakfast."

"And," Lachlan adds, "I have a surprise for my mother. Do you think she's awake?"

I glance out the window at the light pouring over the island. "She loves to paint in the morning light. I would be willing to bet she's in the conservatory."

"Excellent," he says, scooping Aurora up and rising to his feet. He holds out a hand, and I take it to stand. "Let's go. This will be fun."

I squeeze his hand and press a kiss to Aurora's chubby cheek. "And then breakfast for you, little princess."

We make our way downstairs and find Marco munching on a piece of biscotti with his coffee. His smile lights up his face when he sees us.

"Brother, lovely Keira, and the luckiest little girl in the entire world. I have never been happier to welcome you all to a new day in the most beautiful place in the world. I hope you slept some."

Lachlan releases my hand to place his free one on his brother's shoulder. "We did. And you?"

"Like a baby. Never better."

Lachlan squeezes his shoulder and then asks, "Do you think Mother would enjoy her surprise at this hour?"

"Mother would enjoy a surprise at any hour. Especially

one from you. The crate is in the hallway. Let us take it to her."

My curiosity is off the charts, but I know it'll be satisfied soon enough. "I'll take Rory," I say, reaching for our baby girl. With her snuggled against my shoulder, I follow the twins—something that will still take me time to get used to—as they grab a large rectangular crate and lead the way into the conservatory.

Not only do we find Francesca there, but also Alessandro. He's been near her side every moment I've seen them since their sons left for America. Clearly, he's making up for lost time, and I, for one, think it's wonderful.

"Mother, Father. Good morning," Marco says as we enter the room.

Francesca's brush hovers midair as she takes in her tall, dark, and handsome sons.

The joy that sweeps over her is tangible in its effect. Her entire being becomes lighter and brighter as she sees them together.

She drops her brush into the water and rises, rushing toward them.

"We have been waiting for you to awaken. I could not breathe easily until I saw you both together, standing in front of me." She throws her open arms around her sons, disregarding the wooden crate they carry between them.

After a few long moments, she pulls back and looks from one face to the other. "You're both even handsomer than when you left."

"And we come bearing a gift, Mama," Marco says, lifting his end of the crate.

"No gifts are necessary. I have everything I could ever want. What more could I possibly need?"

"Do you remember when I told you about the painting from my dressing room?" Lachlan asks her.

Francesca gasps and presses a hand to her heart. "You have brought it home? One of my babies?"

Alessandro gestures to a glass-topped table. "Put it here. Let us see."

Marco and Lachlan lower the crate to the table, and Marco pulls a screwdriver from his pocket. In moments, the crate cracks open, and Marco moves aside the padding to reveal a cloth-wrapped canvas.

He glances at Lachlan. "Would you like to do the honors?"

With a smile that I hope becomes a permanent fixture on my husband's face, Lachlan lifts the painting from its nest and carefully unwraps it. I can't stop myself from gasping, along with Alessandro and Francesca. Although I saw the painting daily for years, I'm stunned to see it again here.

Francesca bursts out laughing.

"My beautiful conservatory. Right there in paint and right here in reality. I was here in this room, all these years, painting, and you had a painting of me painting, in this room, in your home. How wonderful are the twists and turns of life?" she asks with tears tracking down her cheeks.

Alessandro points at the painting. "I bid on that over twenty years ago. I lost to a bidder in London, who was robbed shortly after. I never heard the painting was recovered." He looks at his son with a question in his gaze. "Did you steal it?"

My husband chuckles. "No, but it made its way to my fence, and when I saw it, I had to have it."

Alessandro nods in approval. "Clearly, it found its way to its rightful home."

"Just like our family," Francesca adds, reaching for my hand to draw me and Aurora into the family circle. "We are all home—finally. Once and for all. The Giordanos are complete, and our happily ever after begins right now."

EPILOGUE

LEO

I didn't know what to expect from the key that Mount left me, but as I open the safe deposit box in this little private room, I'm glad I'm sitting down.

I remove the letter and read it first.

> LEO,
>
> IF YOU'RE READING THIS, THEN LACHLAN MOUNT IS DEAD, AND EVERYTHING IS AS IT SHOULD BE. I'VE ALWAYS APPRECIATED YOUR HONESTY AND INTEGRITY IN A BUSINESS WHERE THAT CAN EASILY BE LACKING. THANK YOU FOR HELPING ME EVERY SINGLE TIME I ASKED. KNOWING I COULD COUNT ON YOU GAVE ME PEACE OF MIND, AND THAT WAS PRICELESS. I PICKED THESE THINGS UP FOR YOU OVER THE YEARS AS A WAY OF SAYING THANK YOU WHEN I DIDN'T KNOW HOW. THANK YOU FOR EVERYTHING, MON AMI. REMEMBER TO GET OUT OF THE GAME

BEFORE THE GAME TAKES YOU OUT. LIVE
WELL, LEO.
     MOUNT

Enclosed with the letter are two deeds. A quick scan of the contents has me laughing out loud. Twelve acres of prime Mississippi River frontage, located on either side of Marchand Marine and Salvage. Property that my father and I have been trying to buy for *years*, but could never get a response from the owner.

That tricky bastard. He had it all along.

I can't help but shake my head as I fold the letter and deeds and set them on the table beside the safe deposit box. The remaining space is taken up by a leather box and a soft cloth bag. I reach for the box first. Flipping it open reveals an antique French pocket watch. Something I definitely would have picked for myself.

You have excellent taste, my friend.

Next comes the bag. The small drawstrings are nearly too thin to support its weight. From the clinking of the contents, I have a sneaking suspicion of what it is. Tugging the gathered mouth apart, a flash of gold tells me I'm exactly correct. Judging by the weight of the doubloons, Mount was much too generous.

You think you know a person, but you truly have no idea who they are until they show you through their actions.

If each box and locker he left a key to contains treasure of this magnitude ... I can't even imagine the amount of good Lachlan Mount is having me help him carry out.

It's an honor, my friend.

Lachlan Mount might have been a ruthless bastard, but he is a better man than the ones he took out with his stunt that left the city reeling. There's a power vacuum in play, and I know the city will never be the same. But one thing is for certain: no one will ever be able to fill Lachlan Mount's shoes.

"Bravo, *mon ami*. Bravo."

For the last three weeks, we delivered key after key. Mount's employees, his tailor, his favorite club manager, an old woman who gave tarot card readings in Jackson Square, a heavyset man named Joy and his mother, and countless other people we had to track down. Street musicians. Bartenders. Homeless. Waitresses. Nuns. Priests. Taxi drivers. Tour guides. Souvenir shop owners. Shelter workers. Foster parents. Cemetery keepers. Trash truck drivers. City workers. You name a forgotten person in the city of New Orleans, and Lachlan Mount remembered them. *Generously.*

The treasure of his sinful empire was distributed one deserving soul at a time. Lives were changed irrevocably, and the city wept for the passing of a man no one had understood—only feared.

The fear, I've learned, was his greatest illusion. You only had something to fear from Lachlan Mount if you had bad intentions or hurt those he considered to be innocent. He saw clearly into people's minds and hearts, and he didn't discriminate in his gifts or his justice.

At the end of my monumental task, I have only one thing to say:

Long live the ruthless king of New Orleans. You will be missed, my friend.

What began as an ending has become a new beginning.
The Mount Saga will continue in *Resurrection.*

Are you a true Meghan March super fan?

Do you want to read every new Meghan March romance before it releases to the public and for FREE? If you're nodding your head or yelling F YEAH, then *this is for YOU*! Now, you can become an official Meghan March SuperFan inside Rebels + Runaways, Meghan + Jake's new online community! SuperFans get a *free* **EARLY release ebook copy of every new Meghan March romance**, plus a behind the scenes look at Meghan's writing process, an exclusive window into Meghan and Jake's amazing and unique life, tons of insider videos, along with early announcements, giveaways you won't find anywhere else, and special content you won't ever see on social media. Get the full, authentic Meghan March experience by becoming a SuperFan today!

Visit www.meghanmarch.com/community to join Rebels+ Runaways and then sign up to be a SuperFan or scan this QR code and become a SuperFan NOW:

Also, if you haven't already, make sure you subscribe to Meghan's newsletter to receive the awesome content she creates for her subscribers, including the fan favorites— Meg's Musings and Meg's Awesome Finds.

Visit http://meghanmarch.com/subscribe to sign up or scan this QR code:

Looking for your next awesome Meghan March read? Meg is so happy to be back in the writing cave and new books will be coming! SuperFans get to keep up with Meg via behind the scenes videos as she writes every new book. But first, keep flipping pages for the first Meghan March book you can read with your kids!

ACKNOWLEDGMENTS

Thank you to God for this talent with which I've been blessed, the stories that come to life through me, and the most wonderful people in the world with whom I get to share them. All glory belongs to you, Lord. I could never do this by myself.

I also could not have written this book without my incredible husband, Jacob Wilson, whose ideas and fingerprints are all over it. I have been blessed with the greatest teammate in the entire world and the most incredible support system.

It takes a village to bring these creations to life, and my village deserves all the credit in the world. I couldn't do this without you. I love you all more than you'll ever know.

HAVE YOU MET BEATRICE?

Did you know there's now a Meghan March book you can share with your kids? There really is! Meet Beatrice, a hairless cat who thinks weird is a code word for awesome. Check out the gorgeous artwork from Josh Woods, a world famous tattoo artist who you might have seen on Ink Master Season One!

www.beatricebooks.com

ABOUT THE AUTHOR

Making the jump from corporate lawyer to author was a leap of faith that *New York Times*, #1 *Wall Street Journal*, and *USA Today* bestselling author Meghan March will never regret. With over forty titles published, she has sold millions of books in over a dozen languages to fellow readers around the world. She's a creative artist, a divine adventurer, a force of nature, a race car driver, a visionary, and a philosopher. She loves to inspire people around the world to believe in themselves and chase their dreams. A nomad at heart, she can be found on the edge of a canyon in the forgotten wilds of the Northwest, living happily ever after with her real-life hero and soulmate.

Meghan loves to connect with her readers and fans in Rebels + Runaways, her 100% positive and uplifting community and digital home.

ALSO BY MEGHAN MARCH

FICTION

THE ANTI-HEROES COLLECTION

MOUNT TRILOGY

Ruthless King

Defiant Queen

Sinful Empire

SAVAGE TRILOGY

Savage Prince

Iron Princess

Rogue Royalty

MAGNOLIA DUET

Creole Kingpin

Madam Temptress

THE MOUNT SAGA

Redemption

Resurrection (Coming Next)

BENEATH SERIES

Beneath This Mask

Beneath This Ink

Beneath These Chains

Beneath These Scars

Made in United States
North Haven, CT
17 October 2023

42878277R10195